THE REPLACED

Also by Kimberly Derting

THE BODY FINDER

DESIRES OF THE DEAD

THE LAST ECHO

DEAD SILENCE

THE TAKING

KIMBERLY DERTING

THE REPLACED

An Imprint of HarperCollinsPublishers

HarperTeen is an imprint of HarperCollins Publishers.

The Replaced
 For information address HarperCollins Children's Books, a division of HarperCollins Publishers, 195 Broadway, New York, NY 10007.
www.epicreads.com

Library of Congress Control Number: 2014952541
ISBN 978-0-06-229363-3 (trade bdg.)

Typography by Andrea Vandergrift
15 16 17 18 19 PC/RRDH 10 9 8 7 6 5 4 3 2 1
❖
First Edition

To Hudson James

You make the world a brighter place!

PART ONE

"Will you walk into my parlour?" said the Spider to the Fly,
"'Tis the prettiest little parlour that ever you did spy."
—Mary Howitt, *The Spider and the Fly*

CHAPTER ONE

Day Twenty-Five

Silent Creek Camp

DEAD.

Or rather, like I was dying.

That's the way I felt, watching the screen go all black like that. Like my lungs had gone from two functioning things that were pink and plump and filled with life, to shriveled-up hunks of useless meat that could no more pump air from them than I could sprout wings from my back and fly.

It had been seventeen days since I'd watched the guy I love be plucked from the ground by aliens and then vanish in a blaze of light. The same night I'd lost my dad in that very desert. And now the first actual hints of the two of them being out there had just flashed across the screen, right before the computer shut down.

That was the worst part of all this, that I still had no idea where my dad or Tyler were. That was the thing that was driving me utterly-madly-*insanely* crazy.

For the past seventeen days I'd been consumed by thoughts of them, convinced I might never see either of them alive, all while I've been trapped here, in the mountains of nowhere, Oregon, in a camp for the Returned—others like me, who'd once had normal-ordinary-*regular* lives, but who'd had the rug pulled out from under them the same way I had when I'd been taken. Abducted and experimented on by aliens. All because I'd had the dumb luck to be in the wrong place at the wrong time.

Like them, I'd come back different. *Changed.*

And now people around me got hurt. Even my own mother had said as much—I was a danger to others.

I'd spent the past seventeen days living with the proof of just how deadly I'd become. I mean, how many normal girls had poisoned their own boyfriends simply by accidentally cutting themselves?

None. That's how many.

I get how crazy it sounds, the whole idea of alien experiments, and I wouldn't have believed it either if I hadn't seen the proof with my own eyes—including the part where Tyler had almost died right in front of me.

If only I'd been one of those normal girls when I'd sliced my hand with that box cutter, then I'd never have needed to take Tyler to Devil's Hole that night, hoping those same aliens who'd made my blood toxic to him in the first place would whisk him away, too, and undo the damage I'd done to him.

Maybe then Tyler would still be alive and safe, and my dad wouldn't have gone missing the way he had, before I'd even had the chance—*a real chance*—to tell him how sorry I was for doubting him and his "crazy" abduction theories, and to tell him how much I'd missed him. *Him*, the dad he'd always been . . . always, even when I'd been missing for five years and he'd never, ever, not for a second, given up on me. Not even when everyone else had, including my boyfriend, Austin, my best friend, Cat, and my mom—whose betrayal hurt most of all because mothers shouldn't ever stop believing their children are out there, somewhere, wanting to come back to them.

But my mom did. She gave up on both of us, me and my dad. She left us behind and started a new life, with a new husband and a new son—her new family. And I tried to forgive her, to understand her motivations, but I wasn't sure I could, not entirely.

But none of that meant I didn't love her, or that I didn't miss her or even my new "brother" in the same way I sat here missing my dad.

They might not spend every minute of every day thinking about me, but that didn't change the way *I* felt about each and every one of them.

Especially after seeing the message that had popped up

on Jett's screen . . . seventeen days after Tyler and Agent Truman . . . and my dad had just . . .

Poof!

"Does someone want to explain what the hell just happened?" I was surprised I'd even been able to force the words from my mouth at all, considering those messed-up lungs of mine. I whipped around to face Jett, who was already leaning over my shoulder and punching frantically at the keyboard in front of me. He tried his best to boot the computer back up, but I could already tell there was no point. Everything we'd been looking at a moment earlier was just . . . gone, and now we were left staring at a big empty field of nothing.

He shook his head. "Someone shut us down," he muttered, but he wasn't talking to me now—his comment was directed at Simon. He lifted the computer from my lap and dropped it onto his own as he hunched over it, his fingers gliding in a way that made it look effortless while he got lost in a series of commands and functions I'd never understand. Jett handled a keyboard the way I handled a softball, like it was second nature. "They knew we were in their system and they locked us out." He unconsciously rubbed his arm and I recognized the gesture. It was Jett's tic whenever he mentioned the No-Suchers, as he called the NSA. Even though they hadn't directly been responsible for branding him back in the day, when the government had begun covertly hunting for the Returned, and even though he'd healed from the firefly image they'd scalded into his skin—the way we all healed from our injuries—his hand instinctively stroked the spot.

"They," I repeated. Of course it was them. We'd intercepted one of their classified emails right before that cryptic message had popped up, and somehow they'd caught on to us.

That dying sensation was back, rendering my lungs utterly ineffective, and even though I wanted to talk, the words were stuck so far down in my windpipe I practically had to cough them out. "But . . . he . . . he was right there," I sputtered, and even that came out sounding like someone had just punched me in the throat. I pointed at the deceased computer Jett was furiously trying to revive.

Even though it had only been a single word, that message from my dad had flipped my entire world upside down. For a split second I'd actually allowed myself to believe this seventeen-day nightmare had finally come to an end. Now, with Jett's computer struggling to come back to life, I had no idea if, or when, I'd ever see my dad again.

"Kyra," Simon tried. "We're not even sure it was him. It might have been *them* all along."

"Yeah. Coulda been a trap," Jett paused to interject.

I glanced down at the gibberish-looking commands that filled the screen, and felt a flare of hope when I saw that he at least had the thing rebooting. I held my breath, hoping against hope that the pop-up message we'd seen right before the whole computer had shut down might somehow—yes, miraculously, I get that—still be there after Jett was done working his magic.

But I knew better. It was gone for sure.

"Shut up," I insisted to both of them. Then I sighed

because I knew they'd never help me if I didn't at least *try* to be nicer about it.

I hadn't been all that nice to Simon since he and I had had to leave Devil's Hole all by ourselves, without either Tyler or my dad. I'd avoided him whenever possible, even though I wasn't sure if it was because I was ashamed of what I'd done by poisoning Tyler with my blood, or because I was mad Simon hadn't warned me in time to stop it all from happening in the first place. The only thing that was clear was that I hadn't wanted to talk to him about any of it. And even though I didn't particularly want to be nice now, it wouldn't do any good to alienate them when they were only trying to help. "You're wrong, both of you. It had to be him." I exhaled, scowling now because they'd seen the same thing I had, my nickname—*Supernova*—clear as day in that message. "Who else would call me that?"

Simon's black brows met over the bridge of his narrow nose, and he was so close I could make out the golden-y flecks that seemed to float in his copper-colored eyes. "You know that was your dad's online handle the entire five years you were missing." It wasn't a question, and he wasn't wrong.

Supernova16. It had been plastered all over my dad's crazy internet message boards for years. Anyone who wanted to could have sleuthed that mystery out on their own.

He held my gaze, and for a minute I thought he was waiting for me to back down, to admit there was at least a possibility I might be wrong, because there was always a possibility, wasn't there? And when I didn't—not so much as a blink, since there was no way I thought I was mistaken, not this time—his gaze dropped to the screen and he studied Jett's impressive recovery of the laptop with just a little too much interest.

But it was too late because I'd already recognized the look in his eyes.

Pity.

Simon hadn't for one second believed it had been my dad who'd sent me that message. And now, because he knew I did, he felt sorry for me.

I stormed away from Simon and Jett, leaving them alone with their stupid computer . . . and all their stupid unwanted pity. I wasn't sure why I was so pissed that neither of them came running after me, especially since I hadn't really expected them to, but I still totally was. And since I was the heroine in this melodrama in my head, I could be as pissy as I wanted.

But even if they'd tried to stop me, I'd have been pissed about that too, so they couldn't win for losing.

I was surprised to find Thom, the leader of the Silent Creek camp, waiting outside the temporary communication base, looking like he had something to say. But carrying on an actual conversation was the last thing I wanted to do, so I lowered my gaze and bulldozed past him, feeling only the slightest stab of guilt.

Mostly I was aware of how loudly I'd been muttering beneath my breath, and even as I kept moving, determined to make a quick getaway, I uncrossed my arms and tried to look a little less crazy, hoping that, at the very least, he hadn't heard the foul things I'd been saying about Simon and Jett.

In Silent Creek, we didn't have girl residences and boy residences. We had the Silent Creek campers' residences—entire houses where Thom's Returned dwelled, sometimes *with* roommates and sometimes being assigned the entire homes to themselves—and the two small rooms we'd been allotted when Simon had ushered us here after his camp had been disbanded. After the No-Suchers had discovered his hidden fortress at the abandoned Hanford site back in Washington.

But two rooms were all we needed. It's not like we slept or anything, not really. It was just nice to have a place we could call our own, even if we had to bunk with our fellow Returned. Willow's bed was directly across from mine, and even though I knew she didn't like anyone touching her things, I nudged her storage container—one of those plastic bins—with the toe of my shoe, pushing it back beneath her bed.

Apparently, having a few minutes to myself didn't just make me calmer, it made me bolder.

Unfortunately, I wasn't alone for long.

When Simon finally found me, I was still sitting there, staring sullenly at the floor. I glanced at the bedside clock, and an uneasy jolt rippled through me as I realized that over an hour had passed—sixty-six whole minutes, to be exact—while I'd been sitting there, brooding over Simon and the lost message and all the reasons we were stuck here in the mountains of central Oregon in the first place.

"Kyra?" Simon stepped inside the doorway, and I felt my stomach drop when I heard the way he said my name, all patronizing, like I was too soft and needed coddling. As if he *pitied* me, and the very idea made me want to hit him all over again.

This whole situation was so hard to wrap my head around. Just twenty-five short days ago, my life had been so boringly normal. I was an ordinary small-town girl who wanted nothing more than to sneak behind the bleachers so I could make out with my boyfriend.

But the whole twenty-five-days thing was a lie—just smoke and mirrors used to disguise the fact that I'd been missing for five entire years. The truth was, that normal life of mine had vanished the instant I'd climbed out of my dad's car in the middle of Chuckanut Drive and had been carried away on a flash of light.

It was the stuff bad sci-fi was made of: a girl, a flash of light, and a missing chunk of time. Yet it was all true. Ridiculously-appallingly-*crazy* but true.

And I'd seen it happen again with my own two eyes—one of those "takings"—the night Simon and I had dragged Tyler up to Devil's Hole, hoping, because it was his very last chance in the world, that whoever they were would take him the way they had me.

And they had.

The fireflies had come, the way Jett had told me they would, as a precursor to the light. Except he'd made it sound like we'd see a small cloud of them, twinkling in the night sky to let us know we'd found the right place.

Instead, those fireflies had engulfed us, nearly choking me. And when they'd gone, it wasn't just Tyler who was missing, it was my dad and Agent Truman too.

"I don't wanna hear it wasn't him," I countered before Simon even had the chance to start in on me. "Who else would know my nickname?" It was the same argument I'd used before, and I hazarded a sideways glance when Simon sat down on the twin-sized bed right next to me, the mattress dipping heavily beneath him.

He sighed and sagged forward, balancing his elbows on his knees. His broad shoulder brushed against mine, and it was impossible *not* to notice the way he restrained himself for my benefit, like he wanted to tell me all the reasons I'd been wrong about the message being from my dad, reasons I knew, really, if I'd just stop being too stubborn to admit it.

Instead of saying any of those things, he scrubbed his hand over his dark, closely sheared hair and said, "Maybe you're right. Maybe it was your dad. But I'm not here to talk about that. If it was him, he'll have to wait. At least for now. I want to talk about the other message. The NSA email." He sighed again. "If it really means that much to you, I think we should go there, to the Tacoma facility. I think we should find out if it's really Tyler they're holding." He faced me, his unusual eyes capturing my attention.

"I thought you said that's the kind of place the Returned should avoid." My voice was pinched and tight, but my chest—my lungs—filled fully for the first time as my heart crash-crash-*crashed*, making those crappy old windbags vibrate like crumbled parchment.

"True enough. But if it's important to you . . . ," he added, a smile slipping over his lips as he shrugged. "I just need to think. Come up with a plan . . ."

"You'd really do that for Tyler?" I bit my lip and lifted my eyes to his. "For me?"

"I know you don't believe this, but I want you to be happy, Kyra."

Regret over the way I'd behaved pricked me, and I had to stop myself from leaning into his arm, which was so much bigger than mine.

Then I grinned, because to borrow one of my dad's expressions, even though I shouldn't look a gift horse in the mouth . . . come on. "And what else? I mean, besides getting Tyler back, what are you hoping to gain, exactly? I know you, Simon. You must think you can get something out of going there, or you wouldn't risk it."

I expected him to give me some cock-and-bull story about bringing me into his fold, or about teamwork, or . . . I don't know, how it's *us* against *them*—the Returned versus the No-Suchers. Instead, he answered candidly, "If we're lucky, we're hoping we can scrounge up some classified documents, maybe get our hands on some alien technology they're hiding in there. Mostly, I wanna know more about these guys. What makes them tick. Figure out the chinks in their armor."

"What if they don't have any?" I asked.

Simon's smile turned up full blast. "Everyone has 'em."

In the end, it didn't matter to me what his reasons were. I tried to tell myself not to get my hopes up, but it was almost impossible because I'd seen the email too. It might not have been *from* Tyler, but I'd already committed every word of the classified email to memory, and I was convinced it was *about* him:

> "Washington State Patrol reported an unidentified male between the ages of 16 and 20 years old at a rest stop just south of Olympia, Washington. . . . Subject was carrying no identification and refused to reveal his name to officials. Subject is currently being held at the Tacoma facility for my inspection."

But it wasn't the content of the email, it was the signature line—from NSA Agent Truman, the very same agent who'd ambushed us that night at Devil's Hole and then had disappeared himself—that had me convinced: the boy in question *had* to be Tyler.

We'd all been looking at that email right before my dad's message had popped up, and to say that I'd hoped it was Tyler the NSA email referred to didn't even begin to describe what I felt.

Because here's the thing: if I could dream, it would be of him.

Tyler.

But dreaming was one of those things only afforded to those who could sleep. And since I no longer needed much—sleep, that is—it meant dreaming was pretty much a thing of the past. Like the horse and buggy, or phone booths, or floppy disks.

But I missed dreaming so, so, *so* much. I missed the way you could dream about something you'd seen on TV or overheard during that day, even if you barely remembered noticing it. Or the way dreams could be completely-utterly-*totally* random and have nothing to do with anything at all. Like this one time when I dreamed I was dragged onstage during a Wiggles concert, and it was so embarrassing because *what was I even doing at a Wiggles concert in the first place*?

And just like all those million fireflies that had been there that night at Devil's Hole—appearing right before the flash of light, their sticky feet clinging to my skin and their wings tangling in my hair as they forced their way up my nose and invaded my ears and my mouth—that ache for Tyler crawled over me, making me itch and burn and want to scream for some sort of relief. Even seventeen days later, it was maddening. Exhausting. Every time the sun came up, I got this sharp ache in my gut like I was one day closer to something.

One day closer to missing him more maybe. Or to finding him possibly. Or to never seeing him again . . .

I didn't know what it was, but it was like a knife twisting my insides each and every morning, and each morning it was worse. As if each passing day the knife turned a notch, tangling into my viscera, becoming so enmeshed it was almost a part of me, and if I couldn't relieve it soon, it would eventually rip me apart.

All I could do was pray that finding Tyler would be the cure.

I was desperate to see him one more time. To touch him or taste the mint on his breath. Each night I prayed for sleep . . . just so maybe I could dream of him.

But even without the dreams, I still saw his face every time I closed my eyes, with every blink . . . blink . . . *blink*. It was like my own personal hell, torturing myself with what-ifs and what-could-have-beens. My dreams had been replaced by pacing and journaling and drawing, anything to find some way to extinguish my guilt.

I was haunted by what I'd done, and by all the unanswered questions: What really happened to Tyler the night he vanished? Where had he gone?

Had he even survived?

Except the thing was, if the NSA really did have Tyler, the way their email said that they did, then they'd had him for weeks, because Jett had given me the numbers—the Returned always came back within forty-eight hours.

Well, everyone but me, of course. I had to go and be all different.

March to the beat of your own drummer, my dad always said.

Simon reached over and gripped my knee. "I need you to do one thing for me." He leaned closer so I could smell the peppermint on *his* breath. "I'll do everything I can to help you with this, but I need you to keep quiet about it for now. At least until I can talk to Jett and Willow and figure this thing out."

I nodded once, and he stood abruptly to go.

"Simon," I said, stopping him. His hand was on the door-jamb as he raised a dark eyebrow and looked down at me. I suddenly wished I hadn't been so hard on him all this time. "Thanks." It didn't seem like enough to say to someone who was about to risk so much for me and for Tyler, who he'd barely known at all, but it was all I had to offer him.

"If Tyler's really there, we're gonna find him, Kyra. I swear we'll get him back."

CHAPTER TWO

NATTY WAS THE EXACT POLAR OPPOSITE OF CAT, who used to swoop into a room and take up every spare iota of space with her energy until you sometimes felt it would suffocate you because there'd be no air left to breathe. Except, there always was, because Cat just had this way of making room for you.

Natty, on the other hand, moved like a shadow, to the point that you sometimes missed her if you weren't paying attention. It probably should have freaked me out, the way she'd just out-of-the-blue clear her throat, letting you know she'd been there all along waiting for someone to notice her.

This time, Natty made a point of being noticed as she knocked at my door.

"Oh, hey," I said, which had become kind of our standard greeting. Like, *Hey, I almost didn't see you.* Or *Hey, you're just sitting there, watching me . . . that's not weird or anything.*

Except, the thing was, it kinda wasn't, not with Natty. It was just her way. Her quiet, reserved Natty way.

"Hey. You left this." She held out the journal I'd had with me in the old church-house dining hall when Jett busted in all bright-eyed, telling me I had to come with him when he'd first intercepted the NSA email about Tyler. Natty had been with me then, doing her Natty thing: making sure I actually ate something. She was like that, the mother hen type. She seemed to know what I needed, when I needed it. Ever since we'd arrived at Silent Creek, Natty had taken me under her wing. She understood me in ways no one else seemed to—knowing to stay quiet when I didn't want to talk, or talking to fill the space when she somehow sensed the silence had grown unbearable.

We hadn't known each other long, and we didn't finish each other's sentences or anything, but she didn't have any expectations of me, and right now Natty was the closest thing I had to a friend.

"Thanks," I said, taking the journal from her outstretched hands. I ran my finger along the already worn cover, where I'd written: "I'll remember you always." It was the same phrase Tyler had written in bold sidewalk chalk outside my house, right after I'd been returned, when he'd first told me he once had a crush on me.

While I hadn't aged a day in the five years I'd been gone, Austin's kid brother, Tyler, had grown up during that time, and while everything else in my life had changed beyond recognition, the change in Tyler had been . . . steadying. I'd finally seen him for who he was.

Now his words filled my head, reminding me I could never forget Tyler, not as long as I lived . . . even if I never laid eyes on him again.

Natty watched curiously. I'd never told her what it meant, the saying, or why I'd spent hour upon hour drawing the fireflies, although that part was no great mystery. I'm sure she knew their link to the abductions, the same as any of the Returned. The way they seemed to swarm right before the aliens came.

She ducked her head, her dark blond hair falling around her flushed cheeks. She glanced up through the wispy curtain and I saw her eyes—sharp the way they were—studying me.

Natty had explained about the eyes, something I hadn't realized at first, and still didn't always recognize.

On Simon, it was obvious: the shocking copper with the gold flecks. I thought they were just unusual at first, but Natty told me his eyes weren't just strange, they were unnatural.

Natty had them too, maybe the only thing on her that was striking at all, her eyes. They were hazel, which sounded ordinary enough to say: hazel. A color that could never decide whether it was green or brown or gold or even blue. On some people, it was almost muddy-looking.

On Natty, that mixed-up blend somehow managed to be arresting.

It happened sometimes, she'd told me, to the Returned. Our eye colors were . . . enhanced. The same, but brighter. Bolder.

Unnatural.

Like Jett's, which almost looked like stained glass pieced together, or a kaleidoscope.

I didn't see it on Willow or Thom. Their eyes just seemed ordinary, but maybe that was only me. Maybe if I'd known them before, I'd notice it now. Maybe their eyes were more vibrant now than before either of them had been taken. When they'd both been . . . *normal.*

It took a while, but I could see it in the mirror once I knew what I was looking for. I almost couldn't believe my parents hadn't noticed it too. Or if they had, that they hadn't said anything.

Five years, I had to remind myself. It was a long time. Maybe they'd just wanted me to be the same so badly that they'd been willing to overlook anything that made me different from the way I'd been before.

"Thom says you got a message," Natty said hopefully. I'd forgotten how quickly news traveled in a camp of fewer than a hundred people.

But because there was still this strange divide between Simon's people, which I was considered part of, and *their* camp, the Silent Creekers, which Natty belonged to, I wondered how much she'd actually heard through this strange grapevine of gossip. Sometimes I wondered if it was like that game Telephone we played as kids, where someone started a rumor, but by the time it reached the last person, it had been repeated so many times the meaning had been jumbled and it was something else entirely.

I thought of the way Simon had asked me not to say anything about our plans just yet. "I—uh . . . yeah." *Way to be subtle,* I thought. I glanced at the clock and my heartbeat settled. It always calmed me to know the time.

At first, back when I'd realized I had a problem, I'd tried to convince myself that my preoccupation with the time was just idle curiosity, a way of grounding myself in the present. But I couldn't lie, at least not to myself, anymore. This thing, whatever it was, had gone way past idle curiosity. It consumed huge chunks of my day. I went out of my way to find clocks and cell phones and microwaves—anything that had the time—so I could set my mind at ease.

My fixation was teetering on the brink of neurosis.

It was as if each second that passed meant one more second of my life lost . . . one more second without Tyler or my dad.

Or maybe . . . maybe I was just delusional.

When I felt like I could look at Natty with a decent poker face, I cleared my throat and nodded, trying my best to look earnest. Simon never said I couldn't mention the message. "We did."

"So? You think the message was from him. That he's alive?" Natty's poker face sucked, and instead of trying to hide her eagerness the way I had, she plopped down next to me, searching my face.

She didn't mean my dad, she meant Tyler, because even though I hadn't told her everything, I'd told her that much at least, that I was waiting for word he'd survived. That he'd been returned the way the rest of us had.

"Maybe," I answered hesitantly, evasively.

But this was Natty. It was ridiculous to pretend I didn't care, or that there wasn't anything to be hopeful about.

I reached for her hands. "God, I hope so, Nat. I want it to be him so badly. Simon says it could be a trap, and that I shouldn't get my hopes up. But how can I not? What if it *is* him? What if he's back and we can rescue him?" I squeezed, probably too hard. Definitely too hard.

"Are you? Gonna try?"

Simon's words echoed in my head: *Don't tell anyone.*

I held back my automatic yes, and instead bit my lip. "I don't know yet."

But Natty wasn't so easily dissuaded, and her eyes shone, reminding me that she, no matter which camp I belonged to, was on my side. "I'll do anything I can to help."

"I know you will." And even knowing she was telling the truth, I still didn't mention the other message—the one that maybe, hopefully, was from my dad. I just couldn't bring myself to share everything.

★ ★ ★

After Natty had gone, Thom was waiting for me when I finally came down the front steps of the tiny house we'd been set up in. I thought about ditching him again, if only to avoid talking about the message or any possible plans Simon might be working on to try to breach the Tacoma facility, but it seemed pointless since he was blocking my way, and there was no one else around.

"Wanna talk?" His simple two-word question cut right to the chase, and encompassed more than just concern for my well-being. It was Thom's economical way of letting me know he didn't miss anything inside the perimeter of his camp. He was like that, always using his words sparingly, like they could be banked for a rainy day.

It was only one of the million differences between him and Simon, the two camp leaders—that spare use of words of his.

"I'd rather not," I answered. But I kinda liked that he'd come here to check on me. And I especially liked that there wasn't the slightest trace of pity in *Thom's* eyes—only concern. And there was a huge difference between the two.

Pity meant I was someone to feel sorry for.

Concern meant I mattered . . . that I was important.

"Fair enough. If you change your mind . . ."

I blinked against the unwanted sting of tears. I damn sure wasn't about to cry just because Thom made me feel like I mattered.

Full-on crying in front of people was a definite *don't* in

my book. It always seemed so staged. Like those pageant girls who theatrically fanned their faces when they won, even though you knew they'd rehearsed their tears in front of the mirror a thousand times before.

I didn't cry the pretty kind of tears that came from practice, either. When I cried, it was ugly crying, with snot and swollen eyes and blotchy cheeks. If Thom did that to me—made me cry—I would have to be pissed at him too.

I reminded myself that all he'd done was be nice.

"You don't have to go with them," Thom told me. And in case I wasn't certain what he was referring to, he added, "When they leave—Simon and the others. You're welcome to stay at Silent Creek, Kyra."

A knot formed between my shoulder blades. "Why? What have you heard?"

He shook his head. "Nothing. At least not yet. I just want you to know you have a place here, with us, if they decide to move on. Make camp somewhere else."

I relaxed. He didn't know about our plans to go after Tyler. But his invitation to stay at Silent Creek wasn't entirely unexpected. Natty had been hinting at it for the past two weeks. She'd made her feelings about me jumping ship from Simon's camp more than clear.

Still, I wasn't sure how *I* felt about it.

I didn't even think I belonged with Simon's camp, at least not officially, despite the fact that everyone else seemed to believe I did. Whatever claim Simon had on me was like this weird Finders-Keepers kind of claim—like I was some toy he'd found on the playground, and since no one else had seen me first, I belonged with his camp.

The thing was, today was the first day I'd really even talked to Simon since the day we'd arrived here at Silent Creek, which meant I hadn't had the chance to explain I wasn't playing in his sandbox, and that I'd make my own rules, *thankyouverymuch.*

Then again, hadn't Simon just offered to help me find Tyler? I couldn't exactly deny I might be at least somewhat important to him if he were willing to take such a risk.

But until we had that conversation, about which camp, if any, I was going to set my roots down with, I planned to keep my options open.

My uncertainty over Thom's offer must've been written all over my face, because he let me off the hook with a relaxed smile. "You don't have to decide now," he told me. "There's no rush. But consider this," he added, his expression growing decidedly more somber. "Sometimes those close to Simon get hurt."

There was some definite history between the two camp leaders, and I still hadn't figured out what it was exactly. It made me wonder why Simon picked this camp, when he'd once explained there were others out there—places like Silent Creek and the camp we'd fled, where the Returned banded together to stay safe from the reach of the No-Suchers and anyone else who sought us out. Because this feud, or whatever it was between them, made them both so obviously uncomfortable.

All I knew for sure was that whenever they accidentally bumped into each other, everyone around them got all quiet, like they were waiting for something to happen. It was as if a timer had just been set on a bomb, but instead of running away, they all just stood around, waiting for it to detonate.

It always ended the same, though, with Thom and Simon taking off in opposite directions. As if being near each other was physically painful.

We did this science experiment in junior high, where we learned that some magnets attract other magnets, while others repel each other. Simon and Thom were the repelling kinds.

I understood, because that's how I'd been with Simon too, ever since the incident up at Devil's Hole.

And now here was Thom, warning me against Simon. *Awesome.*

Whatever it was that had happened between them, my dad had been wrong: time *doesn't* heal all wounds.

I tried to look contrite. "Look, I get you don't like him, and I appreciate the warning. Really, I do. But I think I'll just keep my options open for now. No offense."

Thom smiled a knowing kind of smile, his brown eyes warming. "None taken." And then he pushed his hands into the pockets of his neatly pressed slacks, yet another difference between him and Simon. Simon wouldn't be caught dead wearing slacks. I noticed the way Thom's hair, black and shiny, slipped sideways across his forehead, refusing to stay in place, defying his tidy exterior. "I just want you to know, I'm here." He shrugged. "If you need me."

CHAPTER THREE

Day Twenty-Six

"EVERYTHING ALL SET?" SIMON ASKED WHILE WE were throwing the last of the equipment in the back of the SUV. Most of the stuff we were taking was either electronic gear that looked useless to me, medical equipment in case Tyler was injured and couldn't heal on his own the way the rest of us could, or explosives I was warned to stay clear of—as if I had to be told twice.

"Locked and loaded," Jett answered, jerking to attention to salute Simon as he passed.

Simon hesitated midstep, giving Jett a skeptical once-over. "Did you just say 'locked and loaded'?"

Jett grinned, biting back a smile as he lowered his hand and shrugged. "Couldn't help myself. I've just always wanted to say that."

Simon lifted an eyebrow, giving me a this-is-what-I-have-to-put-up-with look, and then shoved Jett playfully before continuing on.

"Hey," Jett complained, rubbing the spot on his chest where Simon's hand had just been. "What happened to respecting your elders?"

Simon raised his hand in what definitely was *not* a salute and just kept walking, leaving Jett and me to finish loading the vehicle.

Sometimes it was hard to remember that, despite their still-teenage appearances, Jett was an old man compared to Simon, and that both of them were practically geriatric compared to me. As the most recently Returned, I was by far the baby of the group.

I shot a cursory glance at Willow's toned and tattooed arms as she hefted a duffel bag into the back of the SUV.

"Need a hand?" I asked.

Her response was a terse glare, pretty much the only kind of look she gave me, right before she slammed the back hatch closed and stomped away, putting an end to yet another attempt to make nice with her.

Jett nudged me in the ribs. "Someone's making *progress . . .*" He said it singsongy, like a deranged cheerleader.

"Why, because she didn't growl at me this time?" I watched as Willow trudged toward Simon.

Jett chuckled, while Willow spit in the dirt and then rubbed it in with the toe of her scuffed leather boot. It wasn't hard to guess the topic of their discussion. Willow didn't second-guess Simon or his orders, but she had a hard time keeping her opinions to herself. And her opinion today was that we should definitely-absolutely-*for sure* not be going to the Tacoma facility.

Least of all on some jacked-up mission that would get us all "sliced-and-diced." Her words, not mine.

Thankfully, Simon disagreed.

"What do you think?" I asked Jett.

"About you, or about the Tacoma facility?"

I considered that and then sighed. "Are they really all that different?"

His gaze slid sideways. Without realizing it, he did that rubbing-his-arm thing as he contemplated both me and my question. "I think neither of you is as impenetrable as you'd like to seem." He dropped his hand, and a slow grin eased over his features. "Besides, I think Simon's right. There's a reason the No-Suchers keep that place under such tight security. They're hiding something. If we can just get in there . . ."

I didn't really care what else they were keeping there—if they had Tyler, that was all that counted. I watched as Willow crossed her arms while Simon said his piece, probably something along the lines of what Jett had just told me, and then he walked away, leaving her there. She didn't look too happy about whatever he'd said, and almost immediately she turned her attention back to me. This time, even from all the way over here, I *felt* her growl.

"See?" Jett said, nudging me again. "If that's not a smile, I don't know what is."

Groaning, I turned away from Willow's glare and glanced down at Jett's wrist. His old-school digital watch made it easy to catch the time because its backlit face was ginormous.

It was 11:38—only twenty-two minutes 'til we'd be leaving camp. I was anxious about the possibility of finding Tyler. But it was more than that, because there was another possibility as well: the very real chance I might run into Agent Truman again.

In almost every comic book I'd ever read, or every cartoon or movie or TV show I'd ever watched, there was a bad guy. A nemesis for every hero. A villain.

For Superman, that enemy was Lex Luthor. For Luke Skywalker, it was his very own father, Darth Vader. For Cinderella, there were three of them out to get her: her evil stepmother and her two ugly stepsisters.

For me, it was Agent Truman. I'm definitely not saying I'm a hero or anything. I was just trying to get by, to survive this craptastic situation I'd been dropped into. But that didn't make me hate Agent Truman any less. Ever since I'd been back, he'd done everything in his power to ruin my life, which was pretty much my definition of "nemesis," and why I'd been blindsided when I'd seen his name on that NSA email about Tyler.

So why, then, had Agent Truman referred to Tyler as an "unidentified male" in his email? Assuming they actually had Tyler at all, why had he gone out of his way *not* to name him? The only thing that even kinda-sorta made sense was that he was worried that if he leaked Tyler's name that we—those of us looking for Tyler—would somehow find out he'd been returned. That the NSA had gotten to him before we had.

He wasn't wrong. We had discovered the email, after all.

Still, it wasn't just Agent Truman and the other No-Suchers I was worried about—I mean, yeah, I was worried about the whole breaking-Tyler-out thing and all. Anything that had Simon packing the SUV full of explosives must be pretty risky.

But as crazy as it sounded, I was almost as worried we *would* find Tyler as I was that we wouldn't. Not because I didn't want to save him or anything—it's just that I worried about what his return would even look like. And I didn't mean that in the shallow I-won't-still-love-him-if-he-has-scars kind of way, because I swear nothing could change my feelings for him, even if he was a complete mess on the outside.

That wasn't it at all. It was more about what all of this—this being infected by me, and then taken and experimented on—might have done to him on the inside I was worried about.

Being one of the Returned had done a serious number on my head. I'd lost my friends, my family, my home, and even who I was in a sense, since I was now a danger to those I used to care about. Case in point: look at what I'd done to Tyler.

Jett dragged me back to the present when he asked, "What d'ya think that's all about?"

I glanced up in time to see Natty—my *quiet-as-a-mouse* Natty—charging like a determined bull toward the SUV we'd just loaded. She was dressed in head-to-toe black—fitted black T, black fatigues, black boots—and her hair was pulled back in a supertight ponytail that made the attack-mode expression on her face seem all the more serious. Hot on her heels was Thom, and he looked as pissed as she did adamant.

When he caught her, he grabbed her arm and yanked her to a stop. Fire flared in Natty's eyes as she whirled to face him. Almost as quickly as he'd touched her arm, she yanked it away from him.

The argument, and it was most definitely an argument, went on for several seconds, and when *she* folded her arms across her chest, much the way Willow had when she'd been talking to Simon just moments earlier, I was pretty sure she was letting Thom know that whatever she was saying, whatever decision she'd made, was final. Unlike Simon, Thom looked defeated by her refusal to back down, and he just shook his head. And then he did the last thing I expected.

He reached out and brushed an invisible strand of hair

from her cheek, tucking it neatly back into place behind her ear.

She didn't flinch, or even react, but the gesture was so intimate that I nearly did. I'd spent almost three weeks here, holed up with these people, confiding in Natty about Tyler, and somehow I'd missed this . . . whatever it was, if it was anything at all.

But it *was* something, I was sure of it.

I glanced at Jett and his eyes widened back at me, an I-didn't-know-either look, before I let myself spy on them once more, feeling more than a little voyeuristic now. And just when I thought the show was over, Thom's nearly black eyes shifted away from Natty and slid all the way to where Jett and I stood—scratch that, to where *I* stood.

I wanted to turn away or to blink or anything to stop him from looking at me the way he was, but I couldn't. The blame I felt coming from him had triggered my defiant streak—it was the same thing that had kept me from speaking to Simon for days on end, the same thing that had caused me to get out of my car after my championship game back on Chuckanut Drive the night I'd been taken in the first place. That condemning gaze rubbed me all kinds of wrong and I knew why, even without being told. *I knew* that Thom thought whatever Natty was up to was all my fault.

It was Natty who broke up our little staring contest, when she swiveled on her heel and shoved past Thom on her way to where Jett and I stood next to the vehicle.

"Check it out," I said beneath my breath, trying my best not to crack a smile. "I think Natty's planning to come with us."

Jett leaned back on his heels and let out a low, almost inaudible whistle. "Didn't see that coming."

"Nope," I added.

"Man, Simon is *not* gonna like this," he stated, like that wasn't the most obvious thing ever, and then he shut his mouth as soon as Natty was within earshot.

Natty didn't say a word to either Jett or me, but she didn't need to. She just climbed into the backseat and waited the remaining—I looked down at Jett's watch—nineteen minutes.

And for once, even Simon managed to keep his mouth shut.

So Simon never really got the chance to say if he hated having Natty with us or not, because Thom seemed to have made his own decision the second Natty climbed in the SUV.

As if it were nothing, as if he weren't abandoning his entire camp by doing so, Thom marched right up to Simon, getting closer than I'd ever seen the two of them get to each other, and announced, "I'm coming too."

It wasn't what Simon wanted to hear.

They faced off for a long tense minute, neither looking like they were going to blink first—not Thom, who intended to go wherever Natty went, and not Simon, who didn't want Thom anywhere near his mission. The air was so thick with guy hormones it was hard to breathe. I was convinced someone was getting punched, and as I anticipated who it would be, my insides felt like someone had set a weed whacker to them.

And I guess that's when I had the answer to my whole where-do-I-belong? thing, because I knew exactly who I was rooting for, no question.

Simon.

It was weird how quickly it came to me, especially considering how close I'd grown to Natty, and even to Thom and some of the other Silent Creek Returned. But as much as I liked being here, I'd mentally drawn my line in the sand in that instant, when I'd bristled at the idea of Thom hitting Simon.

Not that Willow would've let that happen anyway. I saw her reaction as clearly as I felt my own. She was there, ready to spring into action to defend her leader—any excuse she could get to swing a fist.

But it never came to that. Simon stepped aside, and all at once everything inside of me loosened as I realized there'd be no fight. "We can always use an extra set of hands," Simon said, like it was no big deal that Thom was leaving his camp behind to join us.

Thom ignored Simon's olive branch, if that's even what it was, and shoved past him, making his own statement with his actions: he wasn't doing this for Simon. He climbed all the way in the back, to the third row, where no one else was sitting. He didn't acknowledge anyone, not even Natty, like she wasn't the reason he was there in the first place.

"Can he do that?" I whispered to Jett before we got in too.

Jett just shrugged. "He can do whatever he wants. It's his camp. Besides," Jett said, looking back to where a few members of Thom's camp council had gathered to see us off. "In case you hadn't noticed, this place is like a well-oiled machine. I think they can spare him for a day or two."

True, I thought, sliding in beside Natty and ignoring the tension already mounting inside the vehicle. If it kept up like this, I'd have a raging headache before we made it fifteen miles.

It felt strange leaving Silent Creek. It might not be my home, exactly, but I'd gotten sort of used to the orderliness of it here.

Silent Creek's remote mountain location made it ideal for what Thom needed: hiding an entire camp of eternal teens from civilization. What had once been a thriving logging community had turned into a virtual ghost town when timber laws had changed decades earlier. Most of the locals fled, leaving only a handful of holdouts who'd refused to vacate the outlying areas. The decaying old church in the center of the small settlement had turned out to be the perfect operation center for the Returned.

During my time there, I'd only seen a single car pass through Silent Creek, which Natty said almost never happened, mostly because the place was so far off the beaten path. And since there were no stores or cafés or gas stations, not even a single latte stand, there were zero reasons to stop, even on those rare occasions when someone did stray their way.

And it hadn't escaped my notice that up here, cocooned in the mountains the way we were, it felt somehow safer. I mean sure, Jett had to "jack" his internet connection, which I assume meant he'd illegally hacked into someone's satellite service or something, and the closest groceries were some forty miles away at a convenience store where truckers and RVers stopped to stock up on energy drinks and chips while they filled their tanks, but at least we didn't have the No-Suchers breathing down our necks.

Plus, the stars here were so bright they were practically fake, and yet every night they appeared, they sort-of-totally-*absolutely* took my breath away.

According to my calculations, and trust me, I'd done the calculations, the drive from the central Oregon camp to Tacoma should have taken somewhere along the lines of six hours. If I was being completely honest, I knew *precisely* how long it should've taken—you know, because of the calculations and all—six hours and seventeen minutes. And I'd planned to count down every last second on Jett's watch.

But things didn't go exactly as planned, and instead of

taking just over six hours, we were closing in on eight and a half, none of which was because Willow had decided to take the scenic route. A mere fifteen minutes had been eaten up at a run-down little nothing of a gas station we'd stopped at to refuel. Simon had picked the stop because he doubted they had surveillance cameras the NSA could tap into. He was so certain, in fact, he even let us get out and stretch our legs while we waited. But fifteen minutes was nothing, no big deal.

The other hour-plus was taken up by the tire we'd blown in the middle of the winding two-lane mountain highway. I shouldn't complain—we were lucky. One, Willow had mad driving skills and had somehow managed to keep us from crashing into the guardrail, or worse, from plummeting over the side and ending up in a fiery heap of scrap metal at the bottom of the mountain. And two, and significantly less dramatic, we'd had a spare. So we'd been able to change the flat.

And when I say *we*, I mean Willow and Simon. I was useless, mostly because there was no way Willow would ever have let me help, so I stood there watching, along with Jett, Natty, and Thom—who was still doing everything in his power to avoid everyone. Even Simon wasn't a huge help, mostly just serving as Willow's one-man pit crew, while she was the one who got her hands dirty.

But apparently our "spare" was just that, a temporary fix until we could get a replacement. When we finally made it to the next crappy little station—also presumably without cameras—Simon managed to procure us a not-necessarily-new but definitely-not-flat tire to get us back on the road again.

Every time Simon mentioned security cameras, my shoulders tensed up all over again. I didn't want to admit it, but the closer we got to Tacoma, the more worried I became. But none of these things changed the countdown in my head.

The hours, the minutes, the seconds . . .

All potentially leading me to Tyler.

I might not be able to get back any of the time I'd lost during the five years I'd missed, but at least with Willow, who didn't worry about such insignificant matters as speed limits or laws or anything like that, behind the wheel we might make up some of the time we'd lost on the road.

When we crossed the bridge over the Columbia River, I found my eyes glued to the sign indicating we were entering Washington—the state where I'd been born . . . the state Tyler had vanished from, and where I hoped to find him again.

As I glanced over my shoulder, I saw that Thom was still staring resentfully out the window, pretending there was some invisible barricade between him and us.

Super. Mature.

I turned back around to Natty, deciding enough was enough. "I don't care what anyone thinks." I made sure I was loud enough to be heard in both the front *and* the back seats. "I'm glad you decided to join us."

Natty's surprising hazel eyes got all huge and her cheeks flushed pink. "Um, thanks . . . ?" She hedged over her words, like even acknowledging my approval might keep her in the doghouse with Thom.

I twisted around again, this time to Thom. "You too," I added, and now I was probably the one in trouble. I could practically feel Simon's disapproval drilling into the back of my head. "Everyone's acting so calm, like this is no big deal, but I'm freaking out. It makes me feel better you guys are here."

Thom stopped staring out the window and faced me, and even though he didn't actually answer me, his expression softened just the slightest bit and his nod said what he couldn't. We were cool.

Jett was the first one to use real words. "I'm glad you're here too," he said, from the other side of Natty.

From the driver's seat, Willow followed Thom's lead and jerked her head in an almost nod while her eyes strayed briefly from the road to the rearview mirror. It was the closest to an acknowledgment that she didn't at least hate me that I'd gotten from Willow.

Simon kept his mouth shut, but the second I caught him glancing my way, I made a face at him, letting him know what I thought of his ridiculous pigheadedness.

"Fine." He let out a long, dramatic sigh. "Me too." And then he gave me an are-you-happy? look, to which I smiled, because I *so* was happy.

If we were really doing this—going into an NSA stronghold, a place no Returned had ever gone into on purpose—I'd rather we not do it wearing our angry eyebrows. If I could have convinced everyone to hold hands and sing a chorus of "We Are the World" or "Kumbaya" or some other can't-we-all-just-get-along song, I probably would have. But for now, I was satisfied we weren't at one another's throats.

I'd take my victories where I could get them.

CHAPTER FOUR

ONE TIME, WHEN I WAS MAYBE THREE YEARS old, my dad took me to this mall where they had this giant stuffed polar bear—a real one that was posed so it was standing upright on its hind legs. Its front paws were outstretched with its claws fully extended so it was in a perpetual state of attack mode. People stood in line to get their picture taken with it, smiling and posing and petting its patchy fur.

What I remembered most were its teeth, which were long and yellowed from age, but still pointy and sharp.

I don't think I knew at the time *why* we were standing in line, at least not until it was our turn and my dad pushed me out in front of the bear, all twelve feet of it—I know it was twelve feet because, years later, I looked it up on ask.com, and that's the answer I got: *twelve feet*. But at that moment, when my dad made the decision to shove his innocent three-year-old daughter with her scraggly little blond ponytail toward that twelve-foot bear with all those razor-sharp teeth, she totally lost her shit. That was when the screaming started.

I don't really remember screaming, but my dad used to tell me about it. He said they were gut-wrenching, blood-curdling screams—the kind of screams that aren't supposed to come from little girls. The kind you hear in horror movies. He said people in the mall shot him dirty looks, trying to decide exactly what he'd done wrong to make me scream like that, while he did his best to ignore them, and their judge-y stares, as he carried me—still screaming, mind you—all the way through the mall, and then the parking lot, to our car.

He said the screaming didn't end until way, *way* later, when I'd finally fallen asleep during the drive home. I hadn't even stopped screaming when he'd offered me ice cream in an attempt to bribe me into silence.

At least that's the way he'd always told the story. All I remembered were those teeth.

That was maybe the last time I'd felt like something deserved the word *daunting* until this very instant. And even though this wasn't at all like the "polar bear incident," my feelings were precisely the same. I wanted to scream and run away.

The building didn't look all that special, just a regular

building that was huddled among a bunch of other regular-looking buildings—the kind of place where something as ordinary as zippers or lip balm might be manufactured. Not so much the kind of place you'd expect the NSA to be concealing an undercover operation. A place where they kept teens who were newly returned from alien experimentation.

Yet here we were.

And in there . . . who knew. Would we find Tyler? Agent Truman . . . ?

I shuddered as that nemesis feeling gripped me again.

From the moment Agent Truman had landed on my mom's doorstep, he'd given me the creeps. There'd been something off in the way he'd pretended to be all friendly and concerned about me, asking where I'd been during those five years, like he was a regular cop but never telling me who he really was. Yet all along he'd suspected I was one of the Returned.

I might never have discovered in time how shady he was, except my mom had already taken me to the dentist. We'd already learned I hadn't aged—that the comparison of the X-rays I'd had done before I'd been taken and the ones done after I'd come back had proven I hadn't gone from sixteen to twenty-one the way I should have during my absence. Agent Truman had known it too, even though he hadn't said so at first. But when he realized I wasn't going to cooperate, he'd come back, along with a team of NSA agents, all suited up in hazmat gear and brandishing the kind of medical equipment designed for dissecting people like me.

If Simon hadn't come along and saved my ass . . . well, let's just say my head would probably be mounted and stuffed on Agent Truman's office wall as we speak.

So maybe it wasn't the building after all. Maybe it was the idea of facing my nemesis again, if he was in there at all, that made me think of the polar bear incident after all these years.

I was sure I was overreacting. I mean, I'd already proven I was physically stronger than the NSA agent. Heck, his hand was probably still broken from when I'd shattered it with a baseball.

Plus, there was that other thing I could do—that weird thing no one in either camp, other than Simon, knew about . . .

Except I hadn't been able to do it again, not since that night at Devil's Hole, and I was starting to think that whatever it was, it controlled me rather than the other way around. So far, I'd only managed to make it happen twice, and neither time had been entirely on purpose.

The first time had been right after I'd infected Tyler. I'd left him in the motel room where we'd been hiding from Agent Truman and the rest of his hazmat team, while Tyler had been delirious from fever. I'd been desperate to find a way to make him better. So desperate that, without meaning to, I'd moved an entire display of pain relievers across a cashier booth at a gas station, using only my mind . . . all to get my hands on some Tylenol.

If anyone had been there to see it, they wouldn't have

been more shocked than me.

The second time it happened, Simon had witnessed it. We'd been up at Devil's Hole, where Agent Truman had tracked us down and was holding my dad hostage. I'd seen the look in the agent's eyes—he was going to kill my father.

But I hadn't let him, and again, there'd been the familiar throbbing in the back of my head, and before I'd realized what was happening, the gun he'd been holding just a moment—*a second*—earlier, flew, rocketed, from his hand. Disappearing into the depths of Devil's Hole.

It had been me. *My mind* that had done that.

Since then, I'd tried to roll pencils or to make water slosh or to flip on a light switch—just by concentrating. Anything to prove I had control over it, rather than the other way around.

So far, I'd gotten nothing but a headache for my efforts.

Simon hadn't mentioned it again, not after that night. Maybe he would have if I'd given him a chance, but I didn't think so. Without saying so, it had become a secret—*our* secret. And I wanted to keep it that way. I didn't want the Silent Creekers to know. I didn't want *anyone* to know because it made me feel like a freak. A freak among freaks.

But that didn't mean I wouldn't use it again if I needed to. Like now. I'd do anything to save Tyler, even if it meant revealing my secret in front of everyone.

"You guys ready for this?" Simon asked from the passenger seat, his eyes moving around the inside of the vehicle, where we'd parked it across the road from the warehouse-looking building. He stopped at each one of us, including Thom.

"Ready," Thom announced, sitting straighter, and looking like he was prepared to take any order Simon threw at him.

I nodded, trying to convince myself I was ready too. My heart jackhammered in my chest, the way it used to right before the start of a crucial pitch—the kind of pitch that wins or loses games. Except this time the stakes were so, *so* much higher than just a championship trophy.

I remembered what my dad always said about those clutch plays. *It's not the best athlete who wins the game; it's the one who stays cool under pressure.*

Instead of thinking of all the things that could go wrong, and all the things I couldn't do, I forced myself to focus on the things we could control—just like in a big game.

"Let's run over the basics one more time," Simon said. "Just to be sure everyone's got it down. If you have questions, now's the time."

Jett broke out his trusty laptop and opened up a blueprint, and I wondered again where he'd even gotten a blueprint of a secret government installation. It didn't seem like the kind of thing you found on Google.

"What's the 'Daylight Division'?" I'd been so focused on the ins and outs of the plan, I hadn't noticed the watermark running across the top of the schematics before.

Jett gave me a curious glance. "That's the name of their division, the underground branch of the NSA that your

Agent Truman and the other No-Suchers searching for the Returned belong to." He pointed at the screen again. "The NSA is headquartered back east, but this place, the Tacoma facility, is the Daylight Division's main base of operations."

It was a strange name. "Why the Daylight Division? It seems a little . . ." I shrugged, because I wasn't quite sure what it seemed. ". . . *innocent* sounding."

"That's the point," Willow said. "It's always the opposite of what it is with this government shit. Like, if you hear of something called Operation Rainbow, it's probably nuclear fucking winter coming."

Jett nodded in agreement and then got back to the task at hand. "We already agreed to break into two groups," he explained eagerly. "Team One, that's my team—" he started.

"Team One?" Simon interrupted cynically from the front seat, giving Jett a pointed take-it-down-a-notch look.

"Fine," Jett conceded, lowering his enthusiasm a degree or two. He tapped the screen. "So, *Team One* will come around back with me, while *Team Two* waits near the entrance for the all-clear signal. Team One already called dibs on Kyra."

"*Me?* Why me?"

Jett perked up, and Simon flashed him that look again. He withered, putting his business face back on. "Because. It's dark and you can be my eyes. You're like a human flash-light."

I would've argued, or pretended to be embarrassed, but he wasn't so far off. They might not know I'd moved things just by concentrating on them—even if it only had been a couple of times—but there were things they *did* know about. Like that I could see in the dark and hold my breath underwater for what seemed like forever . . . and that I could throw crazy hard. I almost smiled, because that last one was the reason Agent Truman had been wearing a cast the last time I'd seen him.

I might not have liked that I was different from the others, but there were definite advantages.

"So you really think you can disable their security system?" Willow asked.

"Not disable exactly. If we shut it down, then they'll know there's a problem and come looking for it." A sly grin slid over his face. "I was thinking a more subtle approach is in order. Something that makes it so they never see us coming."

Now that we were here, I tried not to freak the hell out. We were a group of perpetual teens about to break into an undisclosed government facility with state-of-the-art security.

When I thought about it like that, the whole idea sounded half-baked. But instead of losing my shit, I forced myself to stay calm, centered, reminding myself we were no ordinary kids. We were different . . . special.

Me most of all.

My concern must've been telegraphed all over my face because Simon's sympathetic look almost did me in. "You can do this, Kyra. Just . . . *breathe*."

I swallowed my doubts as I rubbed my sweaty palms over the tops of my knees, and then nodded again while I kept my eyes trained on his, hoping to soak up some of his confidence.

Jett tapped Simon on the shoulder and handed him a white key card, turning his attention back to the plan, while I thought about what Simon had said about everyone having a weakness. He was right, at least as far as I could tell. We might be able to heal faster than normal people, me more so than the rest of them, but that didn't mean we were invincible. Not by a long shot. Simon had made it more than clear that these "Daylighters" knew ways to kill us.

"Team Two," Jett said, his finger dropping to a place in the center of the plans on his computer screen—a place that looked like a large, open space that could be any kind of room. "Once you're inside, you locate the central lab. That's your best chance of finding Tyler if they've got him."

Lab. I swallowed a golf ball–sized lump that formed in my throat every time they used that word. It conjured gruesome images that made my stomach pitch. I was sure I didn't want to know the answer, but it didn't stop me from asking, "What do you think they're doing to him in there?"

"Nothing good." Jett shot me an apologetic look as he snapped his laptop shut, and then his fingers drifted to the spot on his arm again. "We need to be in and out as fast as possible."

No one said anything more about the lab thing as we piled out of the SUV. We were parked in an ordinary public lot and our vehicle looked like all the rest, blending nicely in a sea of other SUVs, minivans, and sedans. But even so, I hoped there weren't cameras out here, already keeping an electronic eye on us, because if there were, we were screwed.

"Okay. New plan," I said as firmly as I could, and before I had the chance to change my mind. "I'm on Team Two now."

"What? No . . . ," Jett sputtered, getting out the same door I had, right behind Natty.

But Simon put his hand on Jett's shoulder to stop him. "Why?" he asked, his copper eyes probing mine.

As far as I was concerned, there was no question. "Because Team Two is going after Tyler. That puts me on Team Two."

I thought Simon might throw a fit, extolling the dangers of marching into the lion's den or some other such crap, and I braced myself for it while Thom opened the back hatch and started sorting the gear. Instead, after a few seconds of staring at each other like that, like we were in a silent standoff, Simon just . . . shrugged.

And that was it.

"Okay. So, Jett—I mean, Team One—you take Thom and Natty." The two teammates in question exchanged a look, and I tried to decide if I could decipher any hidden meaning there, something to tell whether or not there really was something more than just leader and devoted follower between them.

Simon flashed Jett a wry smile. "Sorry, you'll have to make do with a *regular* flashlight," he added. "Willow and me'll take Kyra. We'll wait out front 'til we get word that the coast is clear." Then his eyes dropped to the key card in his hand. "You sure this thing's gonna work? Those of us on Team Two are counting on you."

Jett practically beamed back at Simon. "I guess we're about to find out."

CHAPTER FIVE

BOOM!

The explosion wasn't so much a sound, the way I'd always imagined an explosion would be, but more like a vibration. Except that wasn't exactly right either. It reminded me more of thunder, that deep booming feeling that seemed to center somewhere in my chest or belly and was trying to rumble its way out, jangling my bones and my teeth, and making my skin scream. My eardrums seared like someone had stabbed them all the way through with just-sharpened icepicks.

The whole thing lasted only milliseconds, even though it seemed like forever, especially since so many things went through my head at once, like: Where had the blast come from? Had Jett caused it, or were they in trouble because they'd walked into some dangerous NSA booby trap? What if we were all walking into traps?

And where was Team One now?

My eyes had gone wide and I was buzzing with excess energy. I knew this was what my science teacher meant when he explained fight-or-flight, which meant I was on high alert for attack. But the weird thing was, I felt numb at the same time, and that confusion was making it hard to focus on any one thing. Just when I thought my head might finally be clearing and I was about to tell Simon we should make a run for it, I saw this plume of black smoke rising from behind the building, and every light inside the facility shut off all at once as it went entirely black.

Behind the glass entrance, sirens blared to life.

"That's our cue!" Simon shouted above the alarms as he pulled out the key card Jett had given him. But instead of using it to access the security panel beside the door, Willow pulled out a long, metal crowbar-looking thing and smashed the glass entrance to smithereens. When I didn't follow right away, Simon asked, "You coming?"

"Wait! *That* was the plan? No one mentioned an explosion!" I knew I was yelling, but I couldn't help myself. From inside my head, my voice sounded like it was coming from underwater.

Simon grinned and lifted his finger to his lips. "Don't

worry. We got this. Jett knows what he's doing," he said, a million times more quietly than I had.

So Jett's part of the plan was to draw them away from the front entrance by blowing up the back one? *Subtle*, I thought, squeezing my eyes shut. The increasing pressure behind my ears made my skull and teeth ache. Whatever did the job, I supposed.

But even as I thought it, I could already feel my body reacting to the assault, curing whatever in my head felt . . . *broken*. Healing me.

I wasn't sure whether "our cue" had been the sirens or the smoke or the brain-jarring blast itself, but I wasn't about to be left behind, so I ducked through the hollowed-out frame. My feet crunched over broken glass as I hurried after Simon and Willow. The siren sound was louder, and there was some sort of generator or emergency lighting system that had kicked on, bathing the entry in a ghostly red pall that made everything seem super creepy.

"Which way?" Simon asked Willow.

Willow grunted and pointed down a deserted hallway. I wondered where all the people were. Scary-cute name or not, the Daylight Division was part of the NSA, after all—the dreaded Tacoma facility—shouldn't there be an army guarding it?

As if my thoughts were being transmitted along the ear-splitting sirens that cut through the air, Simon told us both, "We won't have long before they figure out the detonation was just a diversion. We need to hurry."

Hurrying wasn't a problem. Now that we were in here, I felt trapped. That sledgehammer sensation in my chest was no longer from Jett's distraction, but was exactly what it was supposed to be—my heart trying to crack a rib. Simon hadn't explained in detail what would happen to us if we were caught, but he'd explained enough and my imagination had filled in the rest. In my mind, there was no amount of self-regeneration that could undo the damage Agent Truman and his buddies had in store for us.

We reached a doorway, and again there was an access panel, and again Simon ignored it, choosing not to use the key card he still clutched in his hand. He pulled something from his backpack, and I watched as he affixed a small piece of what looked like Silly Putty—that gooey gray stuff that came in a plastic egg and that my dad and I used to stretch and bounce and roll over the newspaper comics and then stretch some more—to the panel. Yet even without being told it wasn't Silly Putty, because of course it wasn't, I took a few steps back at the same time Simon and Willow did. Simultaneously we all covered our ears and ducked, and my heart continued to punch my chest.

This detonation wasn't nearly as intense as the first one. In fact, I'd hardly heard it above the wail of the sirens, which were still screaming so loud my ears felt like they were bleeding. This explosion didn't come with a rumbling boom or all the smoke, just a satisfying bang, followed by the even more satisfying sight of the heavy, locked door releasing.

That was when things got real, and this ordinary-looking building suddenly became so much less ordinary and so much more frightening.

"This is it, isn't it? The central lab?" I eased past both Simon and Willow, not sure I'd have been able to stop myself even if they would have told me not to go in there.

They didn't even have to answer because it totally was—I would have known the place anywhere. There was nothing else it could have been. If my dad had been there, I probably would have had to wipe the drool from his chin—this place was like crack for any alien conspiracy theorist.

It was like I was standing on a movie set . . . or a lot—an entire frickin' movie lot.

The ceiling shot all the way up—two or three, maybe even four, stories. The floor of this "central lab" was made from these enormous glass tiles that, in this light—the emergency light—seemed like they were tinted red, just like everything else around us. Suspended some ten feet or so above the glass-tiled floor, along one entire wall, was what appeared to be an observation chamber of some sort that was set behind even more glass. Inside, the chamber was pitch-black, but my eyesight was better than anyone else's and I could see past the glass. I knew there was no one in there . . . watching us.

There were too many things to look at all at once: sleek metal tables, like the gurneys that belonged in a morgue. Huge glass cylinders that were so big you could probably fit an entire grown man in them and still have room left over, which made me wonder if that wasn't exactly what they were for: people. They had these giant tubes sticking out of them, some wide and some not, some attached and some not. There were shelves littered with bottles and beakers and rubber hosing, and things I couldn't even make sense of because I'd never even seen anything like them before. Everything in here seemed to be made of steel or glass, and had that hospital-sterile appearance, but smelled . . . *not quite hospital-y.*

I couldn't quite place the smell, but it was off somehow. Like antiseptic, but not.

I shook my head because that so wasn't what mattered right now. This place . . . here . . . Simon had been right about it all along. My gut said we shouldn't be here. None of us. They did things here . . . really, *really* bad things, I just knew it.

If this *was* where they'd brought Tyler . . . my stomach plummeted because we were standing in a place no Returned should ever be.

I spun in a circle, because another thought was crashing down on me. "Where is he?" I needed one of them, Simon or Willow, to tell me we hadn't made a huge mistake coming here, that we hadn't just been tricked by Agent Truman. The alarms and the red light pushed my fears to the surface. "You said he'd be here. You said we'd get him and bring him back with us."

I made a fist, suddenly wishing we were back at camp, and I could change my mind about the outcome of the standoff between Thom and Simon. I wanted Thom to smash Simon in his lying face after all. Maybe then, instead of ending up here, in the middle of this empty freak show of a lab trying to convince myself that I'd known this was a possibility all along, and telling myself to *buck up, soldier*, we could've just stayed back in Silent Creek, where we'd all have been safe. Safe.

Safe!

"Kyra . . ." Simon's voice was slippery. "We haven't looked everywhere—"

"I'll check the computer wing," Willow said, hiking her backpack higher on her shoulder. "Meet me in the research chamber, near the east exit." She took off, leaving me to wonder how we were supposed to know where these places were, but also filling me with renewed hope as the icy grip around my throat eased and I inhaled sharply.

The computer wing and the research chamber—there were still places we could search for Tyler.

Maybe, at long last, I'd get the chance to tell him I was sorry.

Simon had turned his attention to the maze of large glass human-sized canisters, and even though I was desperate to find Tyler, my curiosity compelled me to follow him. That and the fact that I had no idea where the research chamber was.

These canisters were enormous, towering above our heads, and we threaded our way in and around and under the tubing that stuck out from them.

I nearly crashed into Simon's back when he stopped directly in front of the last one—the only one that was covered by some sort of shiny, silver sheet. Beneath the wrap, there was a static-y hum that reminded me of a giant metallic beehive, buzzing with life.

"*What are you doing*?" I whisper-accused when he reached for the thin casing, but already my skin buzzed like the tube, anticipating what might be hidden there.

Just then, there was an abrupt hush. The alarms went suddenly and totally silent. Simon's face, still frozen in shock or horror or . . . revulsion, stayed that way as we looked around us like stupid, startled rabbits.

The absence of sound was a million times more disturbing than the shrill warnings had been. And when the red lights switched off too, and there was that brief moment when there was total blackness—just the blackness and the silence—I knew we were done for.

It took a second, but then one at a time, and row by row, the white fixtures on the ceiling high, high, *high* overhead began switching on. The lights were blazing, so bright I flinched as if I'd just accidentally looked directly into the sun. And while I waited for my eyes to adjust, I found myself studying the floor and I realized that the glass tiles weren't red at all, but were actually an eerie shade of blue.

We heard shouts—a jumble of voices mingled with footsteps that were heavy and hollow—that could have been coming from above or behind, or right in front of us, for all

I could tell. It was like being in a twisted version of a carnival funhouse. One where the end result was being strapped to a metal gurney and being dismembered.

Beside me, I jerked Simon away from the canister or tube or whatever it was, deciding we needed to get the hell outta Dodge at the same time he whispered, "*Run*," as he reached for my hand.

I no longer cared that just seconds ago I'd wished he'd been punched in the face. I was like that, I guess—fickle.

Blood rushed past my ears as he dragged me. I glanced behind my shoulder, and then up to the observation room and all around us, convinced that at any second we were going to be caught. Willow was already gone, and my fingers clung to Simon's.

The exits no longer seemed like viable options—we had no idea which direction they'd be coming from when they finally arrived. Ahead of us, though, there were several vents of some sort, giant grills in the walls. Instead of waiting to find out if Simon had a plan, I let go of him and rushed to one of them. I tried to pry it off myself, but my hands were fumbling and awkward. The voices grew clearer, louder . . . sounding like they were right on top of us.

"Here," Simon said, coming in behind me. His breath was hot against my cheek as he leaned over the top of me, his fingers surer than mine as he removed the grate deftly. "It's okay. Trust me."

I hated the way he said it, like he was my hero, but I didn't have time to complain. Instead, I eased into the dark opening behind the wall, with Simon coming in right behind me. He reached for the cover, and within seconds, he'd managed to secure it back in place. Just as the central lab was swarmed with an army of footsteps.

The only light came in through the vent openings, from the lab beyond. It was bigger back here than I'd expected, more like a hallway than a space behind the walls. I leaned my head against the wall, trying to slow my breaths and waiting . . . waiting to see if we'd been discovered. We stayed like that for an eternity. I was terrified that the slightest sound, the barest scrape of my hair or the rasp of my breath might give us away. And the entire time my heart was ripping a hole in my chest.

"They got away," a man's voice said from inside the lab.

"You!" someone else shouted—an order, "Take a team to sweep the perimeter. Make sure they don't get too far. But suit up, and be careful. These kids are dangerous. I don't want any Code Reds on my watch." My skin crawled with recognition. The voice . . . the man giving the order, I knew it. It was him . . . Agent Truman.

"Sir, there aren't enough bio-suits for everyone," the other man responded.

There was a pause, a heavy, thought-filled pause, and then Agent Truman answered, "So pick your best men and suit them up. We need to shut this down. And fast."

My eyes went wide as a flurry of activity came from inside the lab and then it grew somewhat less frantic.

He was here. Agent Truman was here, right on the other side of that wall. My head swam as I considered just how close he was. How easy it would be for him to find me. To capture me.

Not only that, they knew it was us they were after.

"We have to go!" I half mouthed through the semi-darkness. "There," I said, pointing because Jett hadn't been wrong about that human-flashlight thing. Here, I definitely had the advantage.

Ahead of us, there was a staircase. I had no idea where it led, except down. But since our alternative was to turn ourselves in to those Daylighters in the lab, I figured it was worth a shot.

The moment I started toward it, Simon reached for me, and, feeling somewhat smug to have the upper hand, I repeated the words he'd used on me back in the lab: "It's okay. Trust me."

I half worried Simon would trip since the stairway was so steep and I was practically running down them. When we reached the bottom, I glanced around wishing I'd spent more time studying Jett's blueprints.

It was as if we'd entered a giant hamster maze, those colorful plastic ones you find at pet stores. Except instead of being plastic and colorful, like the hamster tubes, the ducts we were standing in were industrial and metal and supersized. We wouldn't have to crawl on our hands and knees.

It was the sound that made me realize what this was: the

kind of ductwork that circulates air through office buildings, the constant *whoosh-whoosh.* And I was right, there were fans every twenty paces or so all along the corridor behind these enormous screened openings—even bigger than the one we'd crawled through. And when we rushed past them, which we did because the sensation of being sucked at creeped me out, the whooshing sound grew louder and my hair whipped my cheeks.

I leaned close to Simon's ear so he could hear me, and I still had to shout. "What now?"

"Keep going!" Simon yelled back. "And if I give you the word, then whatever happens, *don't breathe*!" He said the last two words super slow, making sure I knew this part was extra important.

Like instructions: *Don't breathe.*

"What's that supposed to mean?" I asked. "What word?"

He just repeated himself. "*The word.*" And before I could ask again, he shoved me. "Go, Kyra. We don't have time for this."

Yes. Right. No time. The throbbing noise of the fans had me rattled, but I didn't need to be reminded why we were running: I was sure that the others—not the good-guy others of our team, but the bad-guy ones—would be right behind us any second, and I hurried to get past the next vent.

The tunnels felt endless, and there were several places where we had to make a decision to go left or right. I was the one who could see, but it was Simon who made the call. I got the sense that he understood this place, and the layout of it, far better than I'd realized. As if he'd not only studied the schematics, but that he'd committed them to memory.

The ceiling never got lower, but the passageways definitely got narrower, and it was the narrow part I wasn't thrilled with. I wasn't crazy about *narrow.* It wasn't that I was claustrophobic per se, at least not in the sense that I was going to have a full-on panic attack or anything, but I definitely wasn't in love with confined spaces.

I guess you could say I was claustrophobic-light.

Just knowing that Simon was already blocking my escape route going back made my heart trip over itself whenever I spent too much time thinking about it. And the farther we went, the more reckless it beat as this awful feeling that these tunnels might never, *ever* end became something heavy and solid and real.

Then something snared me, strong fingers seizing me, pinching the bones of my wrist, and I jolted backward. My breath caught hard in my throat. If Simon hadn't been there, still blocking my exit, I would have fallen over for sure.

"*GO!*" I shouted, trying to shove Simon out of my path, but I was already being dragged toward whoever had ahold of me.

The man appeared then, coming out from where he'd been hiding, waiting for us, I was sure, in an opening in the passageways. I could see him as clearly as if it were daylight, and it was my second polar-bear moment of the day.

"Gotcha," he growled, looking more military than Agent Truman ever had, right down to the black grease paint smeared across his sharp features. He wasn't suited up, which was a scary thought, because if this guy wasn't one of Truman's best, then I definitely didn't want to run into one of the suited-up dudes!

His eyes were a shade of blue so pale they were virtually colorless and downright chilling. I could almost imagine that even his teeth, if he were to show them to me, would be polar-bear sharp. He raised his hand and before I realized what was happening, there was a flashlight shining directly into my face.

He might as well have set off a nuclear blast. I winced, taking several seconds to adjust to the sudden flare, and then I watched as behind that light, he cocked his head to the side, studying me with those frigid eyes of his. "It's you . . . ," he exhaled, forcing me to taste the sour combination of coffee and tobacco on his breath.

"Simon, run!" I kicked at the guy, but the hand clamped around my wrist was strong, and the arm behind it was thick and muscular. The guy jerked me back before I could figure out a way to stop him. I pitched backward, my head slamming against the metal wall as I tried to find something to grip on to. Everywhere around me—the walls, the floor, and the ceiling of the ducts—was sheer and smooth. There was nothing I could grasp.

"Kyra!" Simon called out to me, his voice filtering

through my hysteria. He should be trying to run, I thought, but instead he said calmly, "*The word,*" and somehow, even above all that fan noise, I heard him.

I knew he was saying something vitally-critically-*majorly* important, but for a split second I couldn't quite grasp it. He'd just explained this, hadn't he? "If I say the word . . . ," he'd told me, then . . . *what?*

I was supposed to do something . . . but no . . . I was supposed to *not* do something.

Yes! That was it.

I clamped my mouth closed and stopped breathing altogether, and at the exact same moment, that key card—the very same one Jett had given Simon earlier, the one Simon had made Jett assure him would work—landed with a clank on the metal duct floor right at my feet. It was plain and plastic, and it just sat there, doing what looked like a whole lot of nothing.

I glanced up at the guy, the one with the death grip on my wrist. He looked blankly back at me and then down at the useless-looking key card. Only *he* didn't have the instructions for "the word" and *he* was still breathing.

I didn't even know if anything was happening at first, or *what* was going to happen, but after a few seconds of looking back and forth between the card and the guy, I started to notice something: the guy—this giant behemoth of a man—was getting woozy.

Even if I hadn't been able to hold my breath for as long as I could—which was *way* longer than everyone else—what happened next happened crazy fast. Within seconds, milliseconds even. First there was just a whole lotta blinking, something the poor guy probably wasn't even aware he was doing. And then I felt his hold on my wrist slipping, his fingers sliding.

I didn't react, mostly because I didn't think I needed to. Like I said, it all happened so fast. And it wasn't like in the movies, where you could see the steam or smoke or toxic fumes coming out of the key card—there was nothing to indicate anything had happened at all. Except the blinking and the loosened grip, and then the nodding.

And then, when I thought maybe the guy was just going to fall asleep standing there like that, I reached over and prodded him, with only my index finger.

That was all it took . . . he tumbled over, falling flat onto his back.

The crash echoed up and down the walls of the ductwork like thunder. Simon bent over and took the flashlight, then grabbed my hand. "Let's get outta here. And don't breathe too much just yet." Instead of Simon hauling me backward, away from the guy, we climbed over him, like he was a giant, slumbering mountain.

The back of my head throbbed where I'd smacked it against the metal wall. I reached up to feel it. "What did he mean?" I asked Simon, who was dragging me along now that he had the flashlight and could see where he was going.

"What did who mean?"

"That guy? Back there, when he said 'It's you,' what do

you think he meant by that?"

Simon's delay wasn't necessarily long, but it wasn't short either. "Nothing, probably. Just that he found us, I guess."

He waved the light toward a ladder, its rungs welded to one of the sheer walls. "There, up ahead. See that? We made it."

"Wait. How do you know this is the place?" Simon stopped and pointed at a metal sign that was riveted to the sheer wall. Research Chamber, it read. The exact place Willow had told us to meet her, and I was impressed again. Simon had a serious grasp of the inner workings of this place, since he'd gotten us here through a bunch of tunnels in the near dark.

I tugged at the back of his shirt. "What if they're up there, waiting for us?" I'd only seen Jett give Simon *one* of those toxic key-card thingies.

He didn't seem all that concerned, and he pocketed the flashlight as he started up the ladder. "Only one way to find out." Then he paused. "But if anything does happen, you need to save yourself. Find someplace safe and stay hidden. Someone—Jett or Willow . . . or someone will come back for you." He shot me a pointed look over his shoulder. "I mean it, Kyra. Stay hidden." He paused, waiting for me to agree.

My mom and I spent a girls' night one time watching *Titanic*, the version with Leonardo DiCaprio and Kate Winslet. And the way Simon was looking at me was like the scene where the two of them are floating in the icy waters of the

Atlantic, after the ship has sunk, and Leo's character, Jack, tells Kate's character, Rose, to "never let go" . . . minus the freezing waters and blue lips.

"I will. I'll stay hidden," I finally caved, even if it was just to make him stop giving me that look.

Satisfied with my answer, Simon turned and scaled the rungs two at a time, and I followed right behind, not wanting to be trapped down in this place a second longer. When we reached the top, there was a heavy grille blocking our way. He glanced back at me, grinning over his shoulder as he reached out and scratched his fingertips along its surface, creating an almost imperceptible rasping sound.

I was about to ask if he needed a hand, or maybe a straightjacket, but when there was a matching response that came from the other side, all scratchy and quiet—an acknowledgment—my eyes widened.

"Willow?" I whispered up to him. "How'd she know we'd be down here?"

"She didn't," Simon answered, right before the grate slid open above his head. "That's why I gave her the signal. In case something went wrong. It was our backup plan."

Willow stood above us, peering down into the opening impatiently, as if we'd kept her waiting. "What took you two so long?" she criticized, but she was smiling when she reached out for us.

When I was on my feet again, I checked out the sterile-looking hallway we stood in. The lights here were bright, reflecting off the ultra-white tiles beneath us. The whole thing—the explosion, the gas-releasing key card, and the underground tunnels—was so secret agent–y I couldn't help feeling like some kind of superspy.

"We safe?" I asked Willow, searching for signs we weren't alone.

"Safe-*ish.* Most everyone was sent offsite. They're convinced we got a good five-minute lead on 'em." Willow scoffed. "That Agent Truman's sure a piece'a work. Thinks his shit don't stink, don't he? Wouldn't even put on a haz-suit."

Willow hadn't heard what we had, about them not having enough suits for everyone. Still, it was hard to imagine Agent Truman sacrificing his own safety for that of his men.

"I don't think your boy's here, though," Willow said.

My heart withered.

"Surprised you waited for us." Simon winked at her.

"I planned to give you another sixty seconds, and then you were on your own," she shot back.

"That right?" Simon questioned, his black brow raised challengingly.

Willow glanced at her watch—a black timepiece that looked like it was issued straight from the military and could withstand a nuclear blast. Envy that she knew the time ate me up inside. Her eyebrow ticked up as a small grin parted her lips. "No, actually. You were down to forty-three seconds."

Simon laughed and nodded toward Willow's backpack, which was bulkier than it had been when she'd left the lab, and sagged like it was being weighted down—a telltale sign that she'd been scavenging while we were laying low in the underground tunnels. "Looks like you found some stuff we might need."

Willow's grin just grew. "You know . . . I had some time."

CHAPTER SIX

IT WAS DARK WHEN THE THREE OF US SPILLED out of the east exit door, which dropped us into a dim alleyway behind the building. The only light out here came from a parking lot in the distance. A tall chain-link fence ran along one side of the narrow street, separating this building from the one next door. On the other side of the fence I could see broken glass and litter and pieces of flattened cardboard stacked on pallets. The oily smell made me think they must do something mechanical in that other building, like build engines or tractors, and it made me curious what they thought happened over here, in this place.

Somehow, being out here, in the alley and breathing the fresh-*ish* air, made me feel moderately less . . . claustrophobic.

"Where to now? Any word from the others?" I asked Willow, wondering where Jett and Thom and Natty had gone after the explosion. It freaked me out, not knowing where they were, or if they'd been captured, but it freaked me out even more that we hadn't seen a single No-Sucher since that guy in the ventilation shaft had tried to grab me.

Even if most of them had been sent out to search for us, shouldn't there still be some left to guard the place? I glanced up at a security camera above the door and wondered if someone was on the other end, watching us. A chill ran over my skin.

"It doesn't work." The unmistakable voice gave me a second chill, this one gripping my spine and rendering me immobile as I realized my Spidey senses had severely underestimated the danger we were in. "It's still down. Impressive bug you kids set loose in our system. Kudos."

We weren't alone, and we were never safe. That oily voice belonged to Agent Truman.

I thought I might puke.

When I trusted myself, I finally turned to face him. It was the first time I'd actually set eyes on him since that night we were all at Devil's Hole, and he was no less formidable than I remembered. To sum it up: he was scary as shit.

If it hadn't been for the gun he was clutching, I might've allowed myself to relish a twinge of satisfaction over seeing his other hand still encased in plaster. All because of me and what I'd done with the baseball. As it was, however, all I could concentrate on was that he didn't seem to be holding the gun as awkwardly as he had been the last time I'd seen him, up at Devil's Hole, despite the fact it wasn't his natural shooting hand. Like, maybe he'd had time to practice since then.

It wasn't a comforting thought.

"I knew you wouldn't be able to stay away," he said, and I hated the way his voice turned my knees to rubber.

I barely trusted my own voice, but I had to know for sure. "So you . . . you *don't* have Tyler?"

He had the nerve to shrug—I mean, he actually shrugged, like we were just hanging out, talking about grades or a ballgame, like we were a couple of buddies.

We definitely weren't.

"The boy made for good bait," he remarked, taking a measured step toward us and sounding far too flippant. His eyes squeezed into narrow slits. "It's sweet, the way you came running."

I glanced down at my empty hands, wishing I had something to hurl at him. I desperately wanted to break his other hand.

"You're a prick," Willow sneered from behind me.

"Yeah?" Agent Truman sneered back, raising his gun in her direction. "Well, right now I'm the prick who has you cornered."

Simon shouldered past Willow, pushing her behind him.

"You won't shoot us." He said it boldly, as if it were a fact. And maybe it was, I thought, realizing Agent Truman really didn't have a hazmat suit on, but it still seemed like a bad idea to goad the guy with the gun. "It'd be suicide."

Simon's prediction fell on deaf ears. Agent Truman's weapon stayed exactly where it was, aimed at Simon, who'd taken Willow's place, and just when I was convinced this whole shooting-us thing had to be a bluff, Agent Truman proved me wrong.

He pulled the trigger.

It was one of those moments where everything happens too fast and too slow at the same time. My brain felt scrambled as it tried to make sense of any single thought, even while every detail that unfolded seemed to do so with startling clarity: the look on Simon's face as he tried—*and failed*—to get out of the way in time, the ringing in my ears, which was back because the sound of the gun firing was so much louder than I'd ever imagined, and the smell . . . that odd crisp and chemical smell that I could only assume must be gunpowder.

Watching Simon take the impact of the bullet made my blood turn to ice. He looked like a ragdoll as he slammed backward, his unusual copper eyes brimming with all the disbelief I felt. He hit the ground so much harder than the soldier we'd gassed in the ducts, and I cringed when his head cracked sharply against the pavement behind him.

I shrank back against the wall, even as Willow launched forward, dragging Simon out of the way. Agent Truman fired again, only this time he was a split second too late. Willow tossed Simon aside as her attention turned to the agent.

When she charged Agent Truman, she looked like a bull—nostrils flared, jaw set. She was seriously pissed.

And he may as well have been standing there waving a red bullfighter's cape. He dug in, securing his stance and setting his feet shoulder width apart. And then, just when I thought I'd seen it all, he pulled the trigger one more time.

When the bullet caught Willow square in the chest, I thought my own might collapse as well. Willow gasped, her mouth open for an eternity, like a fish gulping and gulping for air.

And that's when I realized what was wrong. With everything. With this whole scene.

It was the reason Agent Truman hadn't been worried about shooting us.

There was no blood.

He was shooting at us . . . he *had* shot Simon and Willow, but there wasn't a single trace of blood.

I dropped to my knees and lunged for Willow, who was still grappling to catch her lost breath, and I wondered if her ribs had been shattered by whatever Agent Truman had fired at her. I wished she'd hurry up and mend already, but Simon had told me that I healed faster than anyone else, and clearly that included Willow. Her hands clawed at mine as if somehow, some way, I might be able to give her what she needed. But I couldn't.

I scoured the ground around her, trying to find a reasonable explanation for the lack of blood, and when my eyes fell on the lone capsule, I snatched it up and closed my fist around it.

When I looked to Agent Truman, he met my gaze with a vicious sneer.

The exit door crashed open, and two more men came bursting into the alleyway, stopping behind Agent Truman's back. Unlike him, they were in full hazmat gear, but beneath those plastic face masks, I could see what they really were: soldiers. Just like the one we'd left behind in the ducts beneath the lab, their faces smeared in black paint.

They'd come prepared, as if they'd known all along where to find us. My eyes strayed to the security camera as I wondered if Agent Truman had been lying about it, the same way he'd lied about Tyler being here.

Simon was still trying to get to his feet, so I grabbed Willow, meaning to drag her out of the way. But she was dead weight and I couldn't make her budge. Not even an inch.

A tremor rippled through me as I watched, frozen in horror, while one of the men lifted an enormous rifle of some sort. Its barrel was too wide for bullets of any kind, and when he pulled the trigger, I realized why. Netting burst from the end of it, hurtling toward us—toward Willow and me—unfolding and spreading toward us.

It was a net gun, and we were about to be tangled in its web.

Simon's hand closed over mine, and he yanked me out of the way just as the edge of the rope glanced off my cheek.

Willow wasn't so lucky. The heavyweight mesh trapped her, making it impossible for her to move more than a few inches in either direction.

She thrashed beneath it, still not breathing.

Simon's grip tightened as he continued dragging me away, and from behind us, I heard Agent Truman's voice shouting, "Don't let her get away!"

But they were too late because we were already running in the opposite direction, through the darkened alleyway.

Away from them . . .

. . . and away from Willow.

Jett, Thom, and Natty were waiting for us in the SUV not too far from the place we'd left it. They spotted us way before we saw them, and they were flashing the headlights even while they were speeding right toward us. Since they barely slowed, we had to run-jump to make it inside the still-moving vehicle.

Once the doors were closed, Simon panted, "*Go!*" to Jett, but even from the backseat, his devastation was palpable.

"Where's Willow?" Jett demanded to know from behind the wheel.

Natty and Thom turned to stare at me, and for the first time since I'd been returned, I wished I *couldn't* see in the dark. I wanted their expressions to be as veiled from me as mine was from them.

Eighty-four minutes. That's how long it had taken us to cause an explosion, break into a secret NSA lab . . . and to lose one of our own.

Had we really just abandoned Willow at the Daylight Division's headquarters? Did Agent Truman really have her now? How did that make us any less monstrous than the men we'd just handed her off to? What kind of friends were we?

I pressed my forehead against the glass, watching the Tacoma facility recede out of the corner of my eye. Somehow, it looked so peaceful from here. "What are we going to do?" I asked, breaking the silence at last.

When we turned a corner, disappearing behind a row of darkened warehouses, Jett slammed on the brakes. "Someone tell me what happened back there. Where's Willow?" he repeated, while he massaged that memory of a wound on his arm.

I turned to Natty, who was watching me. When she didn't answer, I looked to Thom, but he just shook his head. Maybe Willow didn't matter to him because she wasn't one of his people.

It had only been seconds, but it felt like forever since anyone had spoken.

"Simon?" I reached in front of me to the passenger seat, settling my hand on his shoulder. He flinched, rolling his neck and shoulder, reminding me that Willow wasn't the only one who'd been shot. He was healing—I was sure of it—but slower than I would have. "What are these things?" I dropped the pellet I'd picked up in the alley. It fell with a dull scrape on the center console.

Jett picked it up and rolled it between his fingers. "It's a beanbag." It was smaller than a golf ball and nearly as dense. "Damn," he said, awed. "If this is what you were shot with, no wonder you're hurting. Willow . . ." His voice drifted away. "If they got her with these . . . well, then she must be . . ." He didn't finish. "Shot at a high velocity, this could be lethal to a regular person." My gut recoiled over the way he said "regular person," like I needed to be reminded we weren't normal. "To us"—he looked at Simon sympathetically—"it must suck. Hurts like hell, I bet—maybe even incapacitates us temporarily—but probably won't kill us. Looks like they've come up with the perfect weapon," he added, tossing the thing in the air and catching it. "Because it also won't make us bleed. It's low risk for the No-Suchers."

"How's your shoulder?" I asked.

Simon peeled away the collar of his shirt. Beneath it I could see the bruises—large and deep and dark purple, but they were already visibly retreating. It was fascinating to watch. "It'll be fine."

"Good," I said, inhaling as I made a decision. "Because I can't do this. I can't abandon her."

Simon's brows met over the bridge of his nose. "Kyra, there's nothing we can do for her now. This is no longer a sneak attack. Those guys know we're here and they'll be halfway expecting us to come back for her."

I shook my head, refusing to accept his explanation. "*She* would try if it were one of us." I didn't know if that was true or not, but it sounded like the thing to say.

From the other side of Natty, Thom piped up. "Simon's right. It's too late for her. They'd be waiting for us if we tried to go back again. She knew the risks when we went in. We all did."

I closed my eyes at the word "risks." Nausea choked me, and throwing up became a very real possibility. I'd seen that lab and the equipment they had, and I knew the kind of person Agent Truman was.

Whatever happened to Willow in there was all my fault, because I'd been so desperate to find Tyler. Just like it had been my fault when Tyler got sick because I didn't know my own blood was toxic.

I was a killer, whether I meant to be or not—the kind of person no one, not even other Returned, apparently, should get too close to.

I looked around at the others in the car with me—Thom, Natty, Jett, and Simon—and wondered which of them would be next if I didn't put an end to this.

I had to do something.

"I don't care what you say, or what any of you think might happen," I said. Before Thom could stop me, I grabbed his gun and was out the door when I shouted back to them, "You can come with me or not, but I'm not leaving without Willow."

Natty jumped out behind me, plucking the gun away before I realized what she was doing. "I'm with you. But here, if you're gonna use that thing, let's give you a crash course."

She came up behind me and showed me how to wrap my fingers around the black grip of the gun. "Use both hands for maximum support. This," she instructed, "is the safety. On this gun, you slide it like this . . ." She flicked a small black switch. "Since you haven't done this before, get as close as you can and try to keep the gun in line with your elbow." She moved through the brief lesson effortlessly. "For now," she finished, "keep the safety on, and tuck it back here." She slipped it in the back of my jeans, away from view but still within reach.

Simon was out of the SUV now too, and I knew he'd reluctantly joined our mission. "You sure you can shoot someone?"

Any qualms I might've had evaporated the minute Agent Truman had fired at us. "Let's hope so." I glanced over my shoulder, to where Jett had the driver's side window down. Thom was already out of the vehicle, standing decisively close to Natty. "What about those key-card things? Got any more of those? That thing was sorta awesome."

Jett grinned, but shook his head. "Sorry, that was a prototype. But I'll pass your comments on to R and D."

"R and D?" I repeated uncertainly. Who was Jett even talking about?

Simon just rolled his eyes. "It's Jett. Jett is Research and Development. Now come on, we don't have time for this. The longer we wait, the more likely they are to have their security up and running."

"I got that part covered. I'm still in their system." Jett

pulled out his laptop. “I’ll log in remotely and buy you about three minutes. After that, they’ll override me and have their cameras up and running again. It’s the best I can do, so better get a move on.”

We moved, all right. And three minutes were more than enough to get us back inside. But that wasn’t the hard part. The entrance was easy—the glass door was busted out and most of the personnel were still off searching for us.

The hard part would be facing Agent Truman and his hazmat army.

The hard*er* part would be finding Willow and saving her ass.

The hard*est* part would be getting us all out again in one piece.

The light on the camera above the main entrance was off. As far as I could tell, it was only a matter of seconds before Jett’s hold on their system was up and we’d be surrounded. We stayed in formation, the way Simon told us—me in front, Natty right behind me, and Thom and Simon flanking her. We moved like we meant business and showed no fear, even though my blood was pumping hard and fast and white-hot.

When we reached the central lab door, it was still ajar from Simon’s Silly Putty blast.

“Ready?” I whispered. And then, because it didn’t matter whether we were ready or not, I swallowed hard and shoved the door open, hoping against hope we’d find Willow alone and the lab otherwise deserted.

No such luck. Agent Truman was there, with no fewer than a dozen of his Daylight Division soldiers—only three were suited up in protective gear, and the rest were as exposed as he was.

I felt sick with horror when I saw Willow, fastened to one of those gurneys. She wasn't making it particularly easy on them, though, thrashing beneath the leather straps they'd bound her with. Her head banged against the slick metal, creating a crashing sound that echoed off the glass tiles and walls.

"Her!" Agent Truman crowed triumphantly, pointing at me. "*She*'s the one we want."

When eight of those soldier-y guys descended on us, I held up my hands in surrender.

But Natty made sure every last one of them was paying attention as she jabbed her gun right between my shoulder blades.

It made sense I would be the one who got shot. Not just because it had been my idea to come back for Willow, but because *I* would heal so, *so* much faster than the rest of them. If Natty actually had to pull the trigger, an idea that turned my stomach because it meant exposing those soldiers who weren't suited up to my deadly blood, I could potentially be up and running again by the time we had Willow out of her restraints.

I managed to grin when I said, "Stand back or *the girl* gets it," by which I meant me, of course. I could practically feel Simon rolling his eyes behind me.

Despite my lame attempt to be funny, and my seriously poor timing, the mood in the room shifted as my meaning sank in. Those not in gear collectively rocked backward, as if just easing away might keep them safe.

All except Agent Truman. He shoved his way to the front, casting me a vicious glare. "What do you think this is? A negotiation?" He glanced toward Willow before raising his voice. "We're not offering a trade. *None* of you is getting out of here."

"We're not here to trade," I told him, keeping my arms in the air. I stayed focused, breathing evenly to calm my heart as I evaluated the opposing team. Sure, they looked fierce, but I reminded myself they were just people—regular-ordinary-average men who just so happened to be soldiers.

Big, yes. Trained, no doubt. But still, just normal guys.

We had something they didn't: the ability to heal . . . and that whole toxic-blood thing.

"Don't be stupid," Agent Truman intoned. There was something cagey in the way he moved, and my heart picked up a beat, and then another as I kept my eyes trained on him. It wasn't just that he didn't back away like the others; he was up to something. He put his hands up placatingly, and even his voice became somehow less threatening. "These guys haven't done anything wrong. Leave them out of it."

These guys—it was a strange way for him to phrase it, since I was including him in my threat. But the guys in question looked relieved, like they were glad he was offering them an out.

They didn't want the dreaded Code Red, which was what they called it when someone was infected by our blood, any more than I wanted to take a bullet through my shoulder. I might heal, but it would still hurt like a mother.

A few men backed up another step, but Simon must've sensed the same thing I did, that Agent Truman was up to something, and he called out a warning. "Don't move! Everyone, just stay where you are." When they all did as he ordered, freezing in place, I finally started to believe we might actually pull this thing off. Then he said, "Get her off that thing," and Thom slipped past me, and past the guards, to Willow.

No one stopped Thom. No one so much as lifted a finger when he unfastened the straps, or when Willow jumped up, sending the gurney crashing to the glass tiles beneath us.

"You're making a big mistake." Agent Truman was still inching toward us, his face devoid of fear.

"Seriously. Stop where you are," I said, part of me hoping Natty would go through with it when the time came, but hoping almost as hard that she'd chicken out.

We never got the chance to find out.

Thom tried to warn us, Willow too, with their shouts of "Behind you!" and "Run!" But it was too late for warnings because suddenly Simon was tackled from behind. I recognized the soldier who took him down because I could never forget those eyes—ice blue. The same guy Simon and I had knocked out with Jett's sleeping gas. He grinned down in Simon's face. "Got you now, you little piss."

Natty was slammed from the side, and her gun toppled to the floor, skittering noisily across the tiles and coming to rest against one of the tall glass cylinders. In the sudden chaos, Thom went down too, hurled to the ground, and buried beneath a pile of bodies.

Willow, who'd just gotten to her feet, had this strange faraway look in her eyes, like she was dazed, and I was sure I knew why: they'd drugged her. Just one more reason we had to get her out of here.

I was the only one of our group still standing and able to fight.

Now it was just me and him—Agent Truman.

The back of my head ached. It burned and buzzed, and I tried to place the sensation.

I looked back at Agent Truman . . . and past him, to the central lab. To the glass tubes and the gurneys and the soldiers who could ruin everything.

Dread rippled through me.

Agent Truman started toward me when the explosion happened. It wasn't the ground-shaking explosion of pyrotechnics, but a sudden-unexpected-*out-of-nowhere* burst that sent glass torpedoing in all directions.

I ducked my head instinctively. Shards of glass sprayed across the tile floor. When I glanced up again, I saw that it had been one of the human-sized canisters. It had spontaneously exploded.

No, not spontaneously, I realized, when I caught Agent Truman's incredulous eyes shoot my way.

Me. I'd done that.

My ability.

"My suit!" one of the soldiers shouted. "It's been compromised."

He'd been caught by a piece of flying glass.

Agent Truman crossed the floor, his feet grinding through crushed glass, almost meeting me but not quite. I eyed his cast. I imagined myself on the pitching mound. This was it, my clutch play.

Fast, like the wind-up release of a pitch, I reached behind my back and closed my fingers around the grip of the gun hidden in the waist of my jeans, just beneath my T-shirt. Even before my shoulder had whipped back around, my thumb found that sweet spot, the safety, and released it.

I studied him, waiting to see what his game plan was, because everyone—pitcher, batter, coach, NSA agent—had some sort of plan. I did. Agent Truman did.

But my dad used to tell me, *Whoever blinks first loses*, so I waited for it.

"Shoot me, and your friends here all die."

That was his blink. He was threatening me, letting me know I should give up because he didn't want to die.

I had him. "Who said anything about shooting you?" I pointed the gun at my thigh, and because I couldn't stomach the idea of killing everyone in the room, I said, "This isn't a bluff. This whole place is about to go Code Red in three . . . two . . ."

And that was it. I had them. Not all of them, maybe.

There would be two left, but two in uncompromised hazmat suits were better than a dozen. They knew it and we knew it too.

Soldiers scrambled for exits as if we'd set the place on fire. Thom was released and grabbed for Willow, who wobbled slightly but kept her balance.

I'd planned to say "I told you so" to that SOB Agent Truman when I pulled the trigger, but the last thing I remembered was the sensation of my leg being ripped wide open, and then everything going black.

CHAPTER SEVEN

Day Twenty-Seven

Somewhere Along the I-5 Corridor

THE INCESSANT TAPPING SOUND WOKE ME, BUT there was something else too. Something soothing and warm, like skin, fingertips, grazed my jaw.

Nice, I thought. This is nice.

I was curled on my side in the back of the SUV, and I blinked, trying to determine the sound in the darkness. It didn't take long, though. It was Jett's keyboard, a sound I'd grown more than accustomed to over the past few weeks. He might as well be dating that laptop of his.

"Hey," Simon said from above me, his voice hushed. And when he ran his hand through my hair, I realized those had been his fingers touching my jaw, and it was his lap my head was cradled on. "You're back," he said softly.

I shot up, glancing out the windows into the night. "How long was I out?" I rubbed my head, then my face, doing a quick inventory as I tried to put the pieces together. My memory was still fuzzy. Everything was fuzzy.

When I reached my leg, and my fingers traced the bloody opening where my jeans were shredded, I paused, everything clicking neatly into place. "Crap," I whispered, my fingers diving into the opening to test the skin beneath.

"Yeah," Simon agreed, from right beside me, still using that too-soft voice he'd adopted, like I was in a delicate state. "You had us scared there for a while. You were out a good forty-five minutes."

My eyes flew wide. "Forty-five minutes?" That was forever. More sleep than I'd had since I'd been returned, at least in one stretch. Up 'til now, all I'd managed were half-hour naps, and those had been major victories, considering how few and far between they'd been. "What happened? How'd we get outta there?"

"You definitely didn't make it easy on us. It was bad enough *she* could hardly walk a straight line," Thom explained from the driver's seat, lifting his chin to indicate the *way* back, behind where Simon and I were. I twisted in my seat and Willow was there, sprawled in the third row, arms and legs spread wide as she snored away, sleeping off whatever Agent Truman and his Daylighters had used to sedate her. I envied that—her ability to sleep—even if it was drug-induced. "Good thing you're not heavy," Thom added.

Jett, who was in the passenger seat now, stopped working on his computer. "All I saw was a rush of guys getting the hell outta the building, like it was about to explode or something. And then a few seconds later, Willow came out . . . carrying you."

I frowned, turning a skeptical eye on the snoring beast draped on the seat behind me. "*This* Willow? Bu—I thought you said she couldn't walk a straight line."

From the other side of Simon, Natty leaned forward and shook her head. She wore a huge knowing grin as she, too, surveyed the slumbering giant. "Didn't stop her. She wouldn't let anyone else touch you." Her smile widened. "I think you have a new admirer."

I turned to glance at Willow again. Her spiky brown hair, which had seemed prickly whenever she'd snarled at me, now swayed gently, giving the impression of downy feathers. It was her mouth, which dangled open while the most horrendous sounds poured out of her, that ruined the effect.

It was as if she'd swallowed a bear and it was fighting to get out.

A satisfied smile touched my lips, and I couldn't help the swell of pride over my decision to go back for her.

Still serious, Simon's jaw flexed. "How's your leg?"

I prodded it, running my fingers over the skin, which had already closed around whatever wound had been there. There were sticky bits of debris that didn't belong, and my stomach churned when I realized what they were: pieces of my own flesh that had been blown away in the blast of the gunshot. *Gross.*

But there was no pain. Shocking, considering the way my jeans looked and the patches of blood smeared on my leg. There were flecks of dry skin and flesh that hadn't been incorporated into the healing process. Seriously, I looked like some kind of war refugee.

Except, I'd survived intact.

"Fine," I answered truthfully, because I did feel okay, all things considered. "I must've slept through the healing part."

"It was crazy . . . how fast it was," Jett said. "We knew you could do that, but watching it—seeing it with our own eyes . . ." He looked around, finally landing on Natty. "Am I right?"

"It was," she agreed, "crazy."

I was glad I hadn't been awake to see the looks on their faces, or to hear whatever they might've had to say about the whole thing. I didn't need to be reminded I was the freak of the bunch.

"Do you think anyone got hurt? Like, infected, when I did it?" Maybe I'd be better off not knowing—the whole ignorance-is-bliss thing—but I couldn't stop myself from asking.

"As far as I could tell, you cleared the entire lab with just the threat of the Code Red." Simon reached over and patted my leg.

"Yeah. Even the guy whose suit got ripped when that . . . thing, that glass, broke . . . he took off in time." Natty's face screwed up. "What was that all about anyway? What do you think happened?"

I flashed Simon a pleading look, but he just shrugged. "Who knows. They're just beggin' for trouble with all that techno-crap they have. I doubt they even know what half that stuff is. They're lucky they haven't blown themselves up yet," he told Natty, ignoring me altogether. "But whatever it was, it sure had them scrambling." And then I felt it, the slight squeeze of his fingers on my thigh.

He'd known all along it was me.

"What about Agent Truman?" I asked. The last thing I remembered was his face as he stood in front of me when I pulled the trigger. I'd probably see that face every day for the rest of my life. It was forever branded in my mind.

It was Natty who answered. "Yeah, so that was weird. He was the one person who didn't run when the rest of 'em did. He just stood there, while you were bleeding and"—she frowned—"he just let us get away." She turned to Thom and sighed. "For a minute there, we thought we'd lost Thom too. He was the last one out." Tears welled in her eyes. "He stayed behind to fend off those last two guys in hazmat suits so we could get away."

Thom just smiled at her, his hand crossing back to squeeze hers. "You could never lose me."

My eyes widened, but I couldn't get past what Natty had said about Agent Truman. "So Truman didn't shoot at us?"

Thom answered, "No. It was the weirdest thing. It was like he was frozen or something." He shrugged. "Maybe he was shocked that you really did it. Think about it: the guy just got himself exposed. He was probably freaking out a little."

Freaking out. Hard to imagine Agent Truman would be worried about anything except whatever mission was at hand: namely, getting his hands—or hand, as the case may be—on us.

"At least we don't have to worry about him anymore," Natty said. "Did you see those dead eyes of his? Gave me the creeps."

I wasn't as convinced as Natty. "I don't know about that," I said, hating that I felt even the smallest twinge of guilt over what I'd done to him. I mean, seriously, the guy had pretty much backed me into a corner—he'd strapped Willow to a gurney and was probably going to dissect her—and here I was actually feeling bad that I'd gone to such extreme measures to *rescue* her. I'd warned him. It wasn't my fault he hadn't been smart enough to run.

Guilt sucked.

"I wouldn't count him out just yet," I said with a sigh. "I doubt getting sick is enough to stop him from coming after us. We shouldn't stop worrying about him . . . at least not yet."

"Can I just say I wasn't sure you'd have the balls to go through with it?" This was from Willow now, resurrected from the dead and gripping my shoulder from behind.

I had to smile at that. I couldn't say I blamed her for doubting me; there was a point there where I wasn't sure I could do it either. "Is that your way of saying thank you?"

Another squeeze, just a slight tightening, and then she collapsed backward against her seat. "If that's how you want to take it."

I was relieved. To have Willow back, to be away from that place, and even a small part of me, a secretly terrible part of me I didn't want to admit to, was glad knowing that Agent Truman might not be a problem for much longer. Still, there was something bugging me.

After everything we'd just been through, I should probably banish any lingering concerns to the darkest corner of my brain, but I'd never been the kind of girl who could ignore something once the question was niggling at me. Even when I was little, I'd always wanted to know why the sky was blue or birds flew south for the winter . . . to the point that I'd driven my parents crazy because "I don't know" or "because that's just the way things are" were never good enough answers for me.

"So that lab . . . and all that equipment . . . ," I started on a shaky voice, because maybe, for the first time, these were the kinds of answers I really didn't want. "What exactly are they hoping to gain? From us, I mean. What is it they expect to find . . . from whatever it is they plan to do to us?"

There was a hushed kind of silence. The heavy kind that comes when no one wants to talk and you know it's bad. The worst kind of bad.

It didn't surprise me that Simon spoke up first. "Look, Kyra, I planned to tell you this eventually . . ." The deliberate way he said it caused a sour taste to flood the back of my mouth.

"You're kidding, right? There are *more* secrets? So what now? What is it you thought we couldn't handle?" I turned to the others, thinking we were in this together. But as soon as I saw their faces, I knew: I was the only one out of the loop. "Awesome." How could I possibly have thought it was nice when Simon was stroking my hair, unconscious or not? There wasn't anything *nice* about him. "What was it that you all decided I was *too delicate* to know?"

I braced myself for what was coming.

"The experiments," Simon finally said.

"*Experiments?*" I let my lack of enthusiasm hang there in that one word.

"That's right," Simon acknowledged when I just crossed my arms and waited for him to elaborate. "The experiments I told you about, the ones that were done on you when you were taken."

I hugged myself tighter. "The ones the *aliens* did," I said, emphasizing *aliens* because even though I'd let go of my disbelief, saying it out loud hadn't gotten any easier. "The experiments they did on all of us? What about them?"

He shrugged. "I didn't tell you everything."

I rolled my eyes. "Um, yeah. I kinda got that. So, go ahead. Tell me now."

He gave me an are-you-sure? look, and all of a sudden

we were in some kind of weird argument. But I was so sick of Simon holding back information for my own good. I was a big girl; I was perfectly capable of deciding what was good for me and what wasn't.

"They weren't random, these experiments. There's a reason we can heal and that we don't need much food or sleep." He still hadn't told the others about how I could move things—or shatter glass—with my mind, and all at once this seemed like as good a time as any. Maybe we'd had enough with the secret keeping.

Nevertheless, I wasn't exactly spilling either.

He looked me over. "How come you never asked *why* we can do those things—what it is they did to us that makes us different?"

"You told me. You said it was *because* of the experiments. That they messed with us and we didn't come back the same." I remembered when he'd explained that I'd been gone longer than the other Returned, and that he thought that meant they were perfecting whatever it was they were doing to us.

He'd used the word "special" when he'd told me I could heal faster than the rest of them.

Me, I didn't feel special. I felt weird.

And now what? Was he saying it wasn't tests they'd been doing on us? "So, what is it, then? What's worse than experimenting on us?" I'd already lost five years of my life. I'd already had to give up my family because of what happened. "Did they expose us to radiation? Kryptonite? Am I gonna lose my teeth? Grow an eye in my back?" I tried to laugh, but I was way past amused, and the sound lodged somewhere deep in my throat.

Simon swallowed my name, and I knew he was stalling. "Kyra."

"*Simon*," I shot back acidly. "Say it already."

"It's not like radiation or anything. And they didn't just *mess with* us and our DNA, they introduced *their* DNA to ours."

I faltered. "*They . . . introduced . . . ?*"

He glanced uncertainly at Thom, who gave him a you-do-it-or-I-will look. Simon exhaled noisily. He definitely didn't *want* to do it. "We don't know everything," he went on. "Just that whatever it is, it's some form of genetic splicing. They *replace* some of our DNA with theirs."

"Replace?" I repeated, finding it almost impossible to form even that single word.

Simon nodded, having the decency to look chagrined. "Yes, *replace*." He hesitated, and for the first time in forever the leader in him vanished. He was just a kid when he met my gaze. Like me. "That's what this whole abduction thing seems to be about. Genetic manipulation." He swallowed, his brows lifting.

I shrank back. "Whoa, whoa, *whoa*!" I put my hands up to warn everyone to just . . . *stay back!* even though not one of them had moved so much as an inch. I needed a minute, or maybe a lifetime, to process what he'd just said because it was so *are-you-kidding-me?* When I finally tried to talk, I'd reached that hysterical edge where my voice had shot up about ten octaves. "Let me get this straight. You're saying that *I'm* . . . that you think *I've* got some kind of *alien DNA* in me?" My last few words were laced with so much disbelief there was no doubt what *I* believed. "This isn't for real. You can't be serious."

"The proper term for it is hybrid," Jett offered, like he was being helpful or something.

My face crumpled, and my stomach plummeted. "Dude, no. Not you too."

But Jett just nodded. Clearly, I was the only one who wasn't onboard with this insane theory of theirs. "That's what the offspring of two species are called: hybrids."

"But that's not what we are. We're not"—I used air quotes to show what I thought of it—" 'offspring.' It's not like we were up there doin' it or anything." I knew I sounded like a twelve-year-old, but I was way past caring about my maturity level.

"No," Jett agreed, and the way his voice lowered, getting all serious, it struck me all over again that he wasn't nearly as young as he looked. "There was no"—he made air quotes too—" 'doing it' involved. At least as far as we know. This was done good-old-fashioned test tube–style."

I shook my head, but Simon nodded his in unison. And so did Thom, Natty, Jett, and even Willow when I looked back at her. I was pretty sure I must've banged my head on something or been rufied or maybe I'd passed out again and this was all one big crazy dream.

Hybrids.

I let the word rattle around in my brain.

Up 'til now I'd been pretty open-minded, or so I thought. I'd accepted a lot: that I hadn't aged a single day the entire time I'd been gone, that I'd been "experimented" on and now would age ridiculously slowly, that my blood was now toxic to everyone who wasn't like us. But this . . . this felt like a whole different level of crazy. "Okay, yeah," I said, my voice rising another notch. "I saw that movie once. Isn't that the one where Jeff Goldblum accidentally turns himself into a giant bug by mixing his DNA with a fly?" I sounded unhinged; I knew that. But who wouldn't in my place? My mom and I had watched that movie too—*The Fly.* The scientist whose teleportation experiments had gone horribly wrong, and in the end, he'd morphed into something half man and half insect, and begged the woman he loved to put him out of his misery.

Was that what we were? Some genetic mutation that belonged nowhere? Is that why Agent Truman and his Daylight Division were so desperate to get their hands on us?

"This isn't a movie," Thom added, ending his silent streak. I tried to remember why I ever thought he was the voice of reason. "You knew we were different, you just didn't realize *how* different."

"So you're saying we're not even *human*?"

Simon tried to reach for me, but I batted his hand away. I couldn't stand the idea of being touched, not by him. Not by anyone. "We're still human," he said softly. "We're alien-*human* hybrids. We're . . . *both*." He tried again, and this time I let his hand stay on my knee. "It's what makes us—*you*—special. You need to believe that."

I crushed my palms against my eyes until I saw white spots. This was insane. I couldn't take any more of this talk about being some sort of . . . hybrid-whatever-we-were-supposed-to-be.

There was no way it was true.

Except, how was the idea that any of us was *less than human* any weirder than the fact that we'd been abducted by aliens and then returned? Besides, didn't that explain the strange things we could do—that we'd somehow been altered?

I squeezed my eyes even tighter as guilt choked me. If that was the case, what had I done to Tyler? What had I subjected him to?

Turning away from everyone, I pressed my head against the window.

I traced my finger around the ragged and bloody tear in my jeans. I thought about Agent Truman and what he'd said when we were surrounded: "She's the one we want."

She, meaning *me*. That, coupled with the guy down in the air ducts, the way he'd looked at me with those cold blue eyes of his. "It's you," he'd said, like he recognized me, even though we'd never met.

It's me . . .

What if that was it all along? What if this whole thing had never been about the rest of them—the other Returned—the way Simon suggested. What if Agent Truman had his sights set on me and me alone, and Willow had only gotten caught in the crossfire?

Agent Truman was still wearing that cast, after all; *he'd* been there that night at Devil's Hole and had seen what I could do.

Me. What *I* could do, not the others.

He probably knew I was the one who'd broken that glass tube in the central lab.

As much as I hated it, I couldn't help thinking Simon might've been right when he'd said the message from my dad had been a fake. I mean, if Agent Truman really did want to get his hands on me, why stop at Tyler when he could use my dad against me too?

From the front seat, Jett went back to work on his laptop as I watched the lights outside blur past.

"Get anything yet?" Simon asked Jett. It was clumsy, his attempt to switch the subject, and Jett paused before answering, "So far, all their files are encrypted, but nothing I didn't expect." I guessed that must've been what Willow had in her backpack when Simon and I had escaped the ducts below the central lab—hard drives or disks, password-protected files she'd stolen—but I was only half listening, unable to quit thinking about the other stuff—the aliens and the hybrids and genetic mutations Simon insisted we'd undergone. I pressed my finger to the spot on my shin where there was a bruise hidden beneath my jeans. It was the same bruise that had been there since I'd returned, and it had been there when I'd been taken too—five whole years ago. It hadn't changed at all during that entire time.

And it never would, thanks to whatever had been done to us. Thanks to what Simon tried to tell me was this alien DNA I was supposed to have in me now.

"Their security is Grade A," Jett told Simon, unaware I was freaking the hell out back here. "I can crack it, but I'll need heavier equipment to do it."

The SUV lurched to a hard stop, and I sat up, looking toward Natty. "What happened? Is something wrong?"

Natty leaned forward and shook her head from the ghostly shadows of the car's interior. "I don't know. Nothing, maybe. Looks like some kind of backup."

From the passenger seat, Jett strained to see around the traffic. "Whatever it is, it must be bad. I can't see where it ends."

I scanned the highway, too, on either side of us. All lanes were moving at a snail's pace. "Where are we?"

"Just north of Chehalis," Jett answered, closing out of the locked files for the moment and plugging something into one of the USB ports. "If it doesn't clear up soon, we won't cross into Oregon for another two, maybe three, hours." I watched as he pulled up a web browser.

Simon raised an eyebrow toward the computer. "Don't stay online too long. We don't want to give the Daylighters any way to track us."

Jett patted his laptop like it was a dog. "This baby's clean as a whistle. And I paid cash for the hotspot burner. If they track us, it won't be because of my Wi-Fi."

"Still . . . ," Simon said as I watched Jett search through news links and Department of Transportation websites.

I leaned back, avoiding Simon's gaze. I still felt weird about the way things had gone back at the Tacoma facility. I didn't fully understand Simon's reasons for agreeing to go in the first place. I mean, I knew why I'd gone—for Tyler—and I knew he said we'd gone because he wanted to know what the No-Suchers, this Daylight Division, was hiding in there, but was that really all there was to it? Or was it possible he felt guilty, too, that Tyler might have been there in the first place?

And what about the way he'd dragged me away after Willow was captured? Why me and not her? He'd told me I was special, but what did that even mean? Special to who . . . him?

Was that why I'd woken up with my head in his lap?

The whole thing was just too . . . weird. I pretended to be fascinated by the traffic so he wouldn't know how uncomfortable I felt around him.

Where were the fireflies when you needed them?

"Get off at the next exit!" Jett announced frantically

from the front seat. He snapped the laptop shut and was waving wildly toward the right side of the jam-packed highway. "Get over! Start signaling now. We need to get off the freeway as soon as possible!"

This couldn't be good. "Why? What is it?"

"It's us," Jett answered, twisting in his seat so he could face us all. "They've got roadblocks up ahead and they're looking for us."

CHAPTER EIGHT

"SO, WHAT NOW?" NATTY ASKED, HER EYES SHIFTing between the two leaders—Thom, who seemed to mean more to her than I'd realized, and Simon, who was lodged between us. I wondered if she was thinking the same thing I was: Which one of these guys was in charge now?

We pulled off in front of a driveway to a ranch of some kind. It was dusty and deserted and gave us exactly what we needed: privacy.

"The good news is that none of the reports mention us by name," Jett said as his eyes—that unusual mosaic of colors that looked like cut glass pieced together—fell on me. "Not even you, Kyra."

"Then how do you know the roadblocks are meant for us?" I wished he hadn't singled me out. I already felt responsible for this mess.

Something about the look Jett and Simon exchanged gave me a chill. "Because they *are* showing this picture." He spun his laptop so we could all see what he had. The shot was grainy, but there we were—me, Simon, Natty, and Thom. We were running across the blacktop toward the entrance of a top secret NSA facility. The image had to have been taken from one of the neighboring buildings' security cameras, right before we'd gone in to break Willow out.

Still, it didn't make sense. "So why not release our names? He might not know all of you, but Agent Truman definitely knows my name. And if that place, the Daylight Division, is such a secret, why are they so willing to admit we were even there?"

Jett shook his head. "They're not. Probably why they didn't put out a better image. As far as the authorities are concerned, at least the ones who've been alerted to look for us, we're just a bunch of animal activists who broke into a medical testing facility." He'd turned the computer back around and was reading right from the website. "It says here: they're holding us responsible for about a half-million dollars' worth of damage to some major pharmaceutical company." He shrugged, a sideways smile slipping over his lips. "It also says we did it in the name of animal rights. Kinda makes *us* sound like the good guys, if you ask me."

"We *are* the good guys," I pointed out. "*We* weren't the ones who started this."

Natty chewed on the side of her thumb. "So does this mean every police force in the state is looking for us?"

Jett closed his laptop and gave us a discouraged look. "Worse. Not just every agency in Washington, but Oregon, Idaho, and even the Canadian border patrol." He pressed his lips together. "They've got roadblocks on every major road and highway out of the state." He looked to Simon.

"Isn't that a little extreme for a bunch of animal lovers?" Natty asked.

"They have to come up with some cover story, and a half mill is nothing to sneeze at—" Simon started.

But Jett cut in. "That's not all. It says here we killed a security guard during our raid."

Killed?

I squeezed my eyes shut as I thought about just how far I'd been willing to go to save Tyler . . . and then Willow.

I'd caused a full-blown Code Red.

Just because I'd given them warning didn't stop the bile from surging up my throat.

"Do you think it's true?" I solicited, hoping for a denial. "That someone died?"

Natty's eyes were wide when she answered. "Maybe that Agent Truman guy." Her voice fell to less than a whisper. "He wasn't wearing a suit . . ."

Behind me, Willow's hand landed on my shoulder, reminding me he'd left me no other choice. I nodded, but my chest still burned, my stomach acids trying to eat their way out.

"So, why not put our faces out there?" I finally uttered. "Get the public involved? It seems like that would make things a lot easier for them, if everyone was on the lookout for us."

This time when Simon answered, I found I couldn't avoid looking at him. "They can't risk it. We all belonged somewhere once. We had families, friends, lives . . ." He shrugged, giving me a meaningful look. "*You* still do. They can't risk putting our real pictures on the news. What if someone recognizes us, even all these years and all these miles later? There would be questions. Some long-lost relative who looks *exactly* like their suspects . . . it would raise eyebrows at the least. They can't take the chance that some reporter might make the connection between all of us who were taken and then returned. It puts their little agency under the microscope. This way is easier, cleaner."

"So you think we're fine, then," I concluded. "No one'll even know it's us."

Simon shook his head. "Just because they haven't given decent pictures of us to the news outlets doesn't mean they haven't sent some to the authorities . . . along with some BS story about those pictures being classified information. Need-to-know, that kind of thing. But no matter how they're going about it, there's no way we're *fine*. Our faces are out there in some capacity, whether we like it or not. We gotta get someplace safe. Otherwise, if we do get picked up, we'll end up being handed over to the No-Suchers. Then we'll all be strapped to one of those stretchers, being lobotomized." He leaned his head all the way back and raised an eyebrow at Willow. "Too soon?"

Willow just snorted and punched the back of his seat.

Thom chimed in from the front. "He's right, though. They don't do anything in the public eye, not if they can help it. Those guys in the Daylight Division are about as shady as they come. And if there are already roadblocks, it means they're desperate to get their hands on us."

"So, what now?" I asked, wondering which was freaking me out more: the roadblocks or Simon's blasé mention of lobotomies.

"Well, we can't go back to Silent Creek. We can't risk that the Daylighters either know about the camp already, or that we'd be leading them right to it," Simon explained.

"Where, then? We have nowhere else to go." But as soon as I said it, there was this weird invisible wire that seemed to stretch between Thom and Simon, a look that passed between them that said I might be wrong. "Do we?"

Thom gave Simon a quick nod, and out of the corner of my eye, I saw Simon give one right back. A decision had just been made without a single word being exchanged.

"There may be a place . . . another camp . . ." But something about the way Thom was stalling made me think this might not be an ideal solution.

Willow gripped the back of our seat as she shoved her face between ours. "It's a bad idea. They won't take us in." There was a sharp edge to her voice.

"Sure they will," Thom assured her, still leaving the rest of us in the dark. "They might not like it, but they would never turn us away."

Jett, who apparently was as clueless as I was, squinted suspiciously. "Who we even talkin' about? *What camp?*"

Simon shrugged, like it was no biggie. It was the same kind of shrug Cat used when she was trying to convince me to do something she knew we shouldn't be doing. Like somehow that gesture would convince me that sneaking off campus in the middle of the day wouldn't land us in seriously deep shit with our parents, the principal, and coach.

Fool me once, my dad used to say.

So, seeing Simon try to pull that move made this whole thing seem like an even bigger deal. Especially since just yesterday he and Thom could hardly look each other in the eye. Yet now they were sharing private looks and making silent pacts.

They were one step away from secret handshakes.

"A place called Blackwater Ranch," Simon answered, finally filling in the blank. He nodded toward Thom. "It's where *we* met. A lot of the Returned end up there at some point."

A spark of recognition flashed in Jett's eyes, and he gave

a slow nod. "Yeah. I heard'a that place." His face contorted as though straining to recall more specifics. "Run by a Griffin something-or-other. One of those guys who thinks the Returned should rise up against the man. Give the No-Suchers a dose of their own medicine or something." He laughed at the notion.

"What, like some kind of army?" I asked. Sure, it sounded crazy, but who was I to question their ways? As the last of us to be returned, I'd barely scratched the surface of all there was to learn about the camps and alliances, and the scientists and agencies who were after us. I still had about a million unanswered questions about why, why, *why* this had even happened to us in the first place.

"Sorta like that," Jett answered. "From what I hear, they're like Returned activists. They have a reputation for being a tad on the zealot-y side, but stories tend to get exaggerated as they move from camp to camp." He glanced from Simon to Thom, still trying to get a beat on their whole look-at-us-being-friends bit. "Does all that sound about right?"

Simon gave that shrug of his, the one that made everything as clear as dishwater. "I think they just want to be prepared if anything goes sideways, is all."

In typical Thom fashion, he remained tight-lipped on the matter.

"So, where is this place? This activist camp?" I asked.

"About fifty miles outside Zion National Park. Basically, it's smack in the middle of the Utah desert."

Utah . . .

Awesome.

Geography wasn't my strong suit, but I knew Utah was nowhere near where we were. It was ten hours away. At least. And that was if we stuck to the main highways, which had already been ruled off-limits.

And we were supposed to get there with the NSA hounding us the entire way. Double awesome.

On top of everything else, it meant leaving my old life in Burlington even farther behind.

You'd think after everything I'd been through, and the way my world had been upended while I'd been away, the last thing on my mind would be missing my mom and her new husband and their new son, especially since they'd made it more than clear they didn't want anything to do with me. But the idea of being so far from them only made me so much more aware of how sick and tired I was of losing people.

I had to ask, "How are we supposed to do this? Get there . . . without being caught?"

Simon sighed, no longer looking bored or vague. "The only way we can. One mile at a time."

We drove twenty-four minutes to a gas station that was way, *way* off the highway. It was also super, *super* sketchy.

But just like when we were on the road to the Daylight Division's Tacoma facility from Silent Creek, we had to assume the sketchier the station, the less likely it was to have security cameras. It also didn't seem completely implausible that this throwback to the '70s was getting its mail by Pony Express, which we hoped meant the cashier hadn't been alerted to be on the lookout for a carload of kids matching our descriptions.

That was the other thing: our descriptions. There was no way we were getting all the way to Utah looking the way we did.

To avoid drawing attention, Jett went into the tiny store alone, and when he came back, he held out three boxes of hair color to Natty and Willow and me, like he'd just done us some huge favor.

"That's it?" I asked, turning up my nose at the selection. Our choices were jet-black, brown, and dark brown.

"You're lucky they had these. It's not exactly a Walmart in there." He passed Simon an old-school-style paper map, and Simon unfolded it as he began plotting our course from here all the way to Utah. GPS was out of the question, Simon had declared. It would be far too easy for the NSA to get a lock on us that way.

Simon glanced at the boxes in our hands. "Better get moving, you only have about half an hour."

Willow grabbed a box without even looking. Brown it was.

I was relieved because the girl on Willow's box had reminded me vaguely of Mandy Maxwell.

In the sixth grade Mandy Maxwell had sprouted a good

seven inches, and three bra sizes, past the rest of us girls, all within a matter of six months. There was something about the combination of high-water jeans and her brand-new C-cups that had left Mandy foul-tempered. So when I'd beaten her one too many times at tetherball during recess, she'd decided I deserved to have gum squished in my hair.

My mom had spent hours trying to pick the sticky wad out, but in the end she'd had to resort to scissors, leaving me with an unsightly bald patch. I'd hated Mandy long after the hair had grown back.

The idea that she and I might be walking around with the same hair color, natural or not, even this many years later . . . well, thanks but no thanks.

I turned to Natty, who was contemplating the other two options way too seriously, but at least she was putting some thought into it. I put my fate in her hands. "Go ahead, you pick first," I told her.

She bit her lip and shot me a questioning look. I shrugged because as far as I was concerned, it was hair. My natural color would grow back eventually.

But when her fingers clamped around one of the boxes, I was impressed by her bold choice. She'd chosen the one with the cover model who had sleek, cropped, intensely black hair.

I never would've called that one.

That left me with the darker of the two browns.

Willow had already gone into the gas station's restroom

with her package, so Natty and I followed, taking the new hairbrush Jett had bought us, along with the unopened pack of oil rags we'd be using as towels. Let the transformation begin!

Willow's blue eyes sparkled mischievously as she gave us a nod from where she was standing in front of the mirror, already hard at work on her own hair. Apparently she didn't need anyone's help.

I caught a glimpse of my reflection from behind her and was mildly surprised that I hadn't changed since the last time I'd looked. I still had freckles and eyes I thought were too big for my face—but not alien big, just regular-girl big.

I didn't want to be some half-breed alien anomaly. I just wanted to be regular old me again.

Averting my gaze, I fumbled with the instructions for the hair color. My eyes stung, making it hard to concentrate, but Natty just took the sheet of paper from my hand.

"Here, let me." She uncapped one bottle of astringent-smelling solution. Dumping it into the larger one, she shook them together like she'd done this a thousand times before. "I used to help my mom," she explained when she caught me eyeballing her. She pointed to the single toilet in the restroom, and I sat down on the closed lid.

"You never told me about your mom," I told Natty as she tipped my head back and began running the applicator tip through my hair in sections, squeezing the cold solution into my roots and rubbing it in with the fingertips of the cheap plastic gloves that had come with the kit. "You never really talked about your family." The pungent hair-color smell began to overpower the grungy bathroom smell.

Natty just shrugged. "You never asked."

She wasn't wrong. In all the time we'd spent together, I'd mostly just felt sorry for myself. It'd been all about me. Me talking about Tyler. Me talking about my dad and his drooly, mutty dog, Nancy. I'd probably even mentioned *my* mom. But I'd never bothered to ask Natty about her life before she'd come back as one of the Returned. "What was she like, your mom?"

Natty's fingers slowed as she massaged my scalp, her voice drifting. "Pretty," she said wistfully. "Funny too. The kind of person everyone noticed. When I was little, I would watch while she got ready to go out on dates. I'd sit on the edge of the bathtub while she put hot rollers in her hair and put her makeup on. And every time, she'd spray me with her perfume, while she told me all about whichever new guy was taking her out to whatever new place they were going."

"So your parents weren't married?"

She continued to work the dye through my hair. "My dad wasn't around much. He . . ." She sighed. "He couldn't keep out of trouble . . . got thrown in jail a lot. Sometimes, when he was out, he'd promise to visit or send presents, that kind of thing. But it never happened. My family wasn't like one of those TV families." She didn't say it like she was sad or anything—instead she smiled a faraway smile. "I always wanted my dad to be like Pa Ingalls."

I wrinkled my nose. "Who was that?"

Willow did a double take and let out a whoop that passed for a laugh. It was maybe the first time I'd ever heard her laugh and I definitely didn't hate it. "Are you for real?" She shook her head like she was shocked, or mock-ashamed, by my lack of knowledge. "He was the dad on a little show called *Little House on the Prairie*. Ever heard of it?"

Okay, yes, I'd *heard* of it, but I'd never actually *seen* it. "You know that was before my time, don't you?"

Natty went back to work, shrugging. "I guess that makes sense. But it was my favorite. I didn't understand it back then, but I guess *my* dad wasn't interested in having a family," she lamented. "Mostly, he just called when he was broke or in a fix. Him and my mom would fight over money, and then we wouldn't hear from him again until he needed something else."

I tried to imagine what that would be like, not having a real dad, the kind who was there every day, helping with homework and cheering the loudest at your games, or even being pissed at you when you snuck off campus with your best friend—all the things a dad should do.

Natty had gotten screwed in that department.

"Sorry," I told her lamely, because what more was there to say?

She just went on massaging the last of the solution into my hair. "We've all got a story, don't we?" She said it like it was a fact, and I guess it was. The Returned were interesting, to say the least.

It made me wonder about Willow—her family, her past

before all this. "What about you?" I asked.

"Yeah," Willow said, showing me her teeth in a flash of white as she smeared the chocolate-brown goo through her already brownish hair. Not much of a disguise, if you asked me. "I watched *Little House on the Prairie* all the time."

Smartass. Apparently saving someone's life wasn't enough to make her open up to you. Fine. I didn't regret going back for her; we didn't have to be besties or anything.

"So what about you and Thom?" I finally asked Natty, and when her fingers stilled, I knew I'd thrown her for a curve.

"What about us?"

A hint of amusement shone in Willow's eyes. "Don't be stupid. You know *what about us.* Everyone saw the way he jumped in the car the second you decided to come with us. Dudes don't do shit like that unless they're whipped. And, girl, he's seriously whipped."

I'd stopped to study Natty, and her lips drew into a tight line. "I don't know what you mean. He's my leader. And my friend. End of story."

Willow laugh-whooped again. "Whatever, dude. Fine, don't tell us. But we're not blind."

I gave Willow a warning look. "*It's fine,*" I said between clenched teeth. "She doesn't have to tell us if she doesn't want to."

There was a stretched-out silence during which I wasn't sure who was in more trouble—Willow for prodding Natty, or me for silencing Willow.

Then Natty shrugged and pasted on a phony smile. She stripped off her gloves and tossed them in the overflowing trash can. "Now you do me," she said, effectively ending the whole are-they-or-aren't-they conversation.

As I got up, I grinned an *I told you so* grin at Willow.

Catching a glimpse of myself in the grimy bathroom mirror, with my too-giant eyes staring back at me, I sort of looked like one of those characters from a Japanese manga. My head was slicked over with the sludgy-looking gunk that would eventually turn my dishwater-blond hair a deep shade of brown. *My* disguise would be *way better* than Willow's.

I checked the time on the wall clock as I started following Natty's instructions. I didn't want to lose track of how long I kept this stuff on my head because already my scalp was tingling.

Simon was leaning against the wall when I came outside again exactly thirty-seven minutes later. Willow had given up waiting for her hair to process and had rinsed it too soon, leaving it with the kind of coppery sheen that was nothing at all like Mandy Maxwell's. She'd also given up on letting Thom drive, mostly because, in her words, he "drove like a blind grandmother." She was in the SUV now, waiting impatiently for us as she thumped her fingers against the steering wheel.

Inside the bathroom, Natty was still crouched beneath the electric hand dryer, trying to dry her newly ebony hair.

I was surprised by how *not* dramatic the look ended up being on her, as if she'd been born for the color instead of being washed out by it. Something about the contrast of black hair against her ultra-pale skin gave her the flawless complexion of a china doll. And even her eyes, which were already striking, seemed less hazel and more the color of golden honey now that her mousy locks shone like glossy ink.

"That was longer than half an hour." Simon flashed me a smug look from beneath the flat brim of the brand-new trucker's hat he was sporting. As if I wasn't totally aware of the time. He pushed away from the wall. "Here. Jett got you these." He held out a plastic bag.

Inside were powdered doughnuts, one of the few things that *sorta* tasted the same since I'd been returned. Probably because they were coated in a thick layer of pure sugar.

Somehow it was even better that Jett remembered I liked the mini-sized ones.

I was looking around, meaning to thank Jett, when Simon surprised me by taking a strand of my hair between his fingers. "I like it. It's . . ."

"Dark," I finished, and self-consciously brushed his hand away.

Unlike Natty, it had been weird looking back at the brunette in the mirror. It was like seeing a stranger, almost like when I'd first come home after my disappearance and I'd scoured every inch of myself for signs I'd changed. This time I most definitely had.

Except, I wasn't gonna lie, I didn't hate it. My hair had always been so . . . so *plain*. Boring even. Cat was the one with the cool hair—super blond and fierce. Mine was just . . . there.

But now . . . now it sort of popped. It was brown like on the box, but in real life, in person, it was more vibrant—it had this cool undertone of red or auburn that made it shimmer like bronze. Or fire. And sure, my freckles stood out a little more, but not in a bad way.

I was like Natty—a bolder version of myself.

I would probably spend as much time looking in the mirror over the next few days as I did checking the time.

"It's a good look on you. It'll make getting to Blackwater a whole heckuva lot easier." Only the way his eyes stayed fastened on mine, never actually straying to my hair at all, made my stomach flutter nervously.

I lifted my chin, hoping to deflect some of his unwanted attention. Hoping to fluster him for once. "I've been thinking—why Silent Creek? Why'd we go to Thom if there are other camps out there?"

Mission accomplished, I thought, relishing the way Simon blinked and then sputtered, "Kyra, this really isn't the time. Don't you think we have enough to deal with right now?"

I shrugged one of Simon's *no biggie* shrugs. Seemed like the perfect time to me. "If we're really in this together, then we shouldn't have all these secrets." I challenged him with my eyebrows. "Anyone can see you two have some kind of history. And whatever happened between you, it was obviously crappy. So, why take us there in the first place?"

He scowled at me. "You're a pain in the ass, you know that?"

It wasn't the worst thing I'd ever been called. "If you say so."

"*Not* a compliment."

"So . . . why Thom?"

He paused, sweeping his gaze toward Thom, who was at the SUV, impatiently watching the restroom door. I wondered if he was waiting for Natty the way Simon had been waiting for me. "I guess because I knew he would protect us. I might not like him, but I trust him."

"And does that feeling go both ways? Does *he* trust *you*?"

Simon's expression darkened, and it wasn't hard to guess this was still a sore subject for him. "He does. But we have . . . a *complicated* history," he admitted. "All you need to know is that we're putting everything in the past. At least for now. Look, that wasn't what I came here to talk about. Can we have a minute? Alone?"

We were already alone, but I lifted one shoulder. "Go ahead. Talk."

He reached for my arm, drawing me farther away from the restroom door. My stomach sank because I was pretty sure I knew what this was about, and I suddenly wished Natty would hurry the hell up so we could get on the road again. At least inside the SUV, Simon couldn't pull me aside.

When we stopped, I ran my hands along my arms, even though I wasn't the slightest bit cold.

"I should've told you. About the DNA stuff," he said when there was no chance anyone would overhear. "It's just . . . it's a hard thing to explain."

"Yet somehow you managed." I didn't wait for a response. "How can you even live with it? How do you not freak out every single second of every single day? Don't you feel . . . like . . . like a monster?"

"Kyra. Try to understand. You're still the same as you were before. I mean, yes, we all age slower and need less sleep, but isn't that what most people dream of?" he said. "Think about it, how is what *they've* done to us any different from all the medical techniques and cosmetic procedures people go through to look younger and live longer? People take drugs, get plastic surgery, and inject Botox in their faces to slow the aging process. Pharmaceutical companies do research on everything under the sun to improve health and cure illnesses, and even just so consumers can *look better.*" His eyes ticked skyward. "So . . . *they've* perfected it before we have, so what?" His smile was uncertain as he chewed his bottom lip. "It doesn't change *who* you are."

I thought of the way Tyler had told me I was the same girl I'd always been right after I told him I hadn't aged while I'd been experimented on.

Simon took a step forward, and this time, instead of touching my hair, his fingertips skimmed mine. It wasn't accidental, the touch, and I told myself that the thunderbolt that ricocheted through my belly had more to do with my own pangs of self-doubt than that momentary brush of his skin against mine. "You're perfect, Kyra."

Tyler had said that too, and I had to wonder if he'd still feel the same way now, knowing that those aliens had somehow changed the foundation of who I really was.

I squeezed my fingers into a tight fist. "Don't," was all I managed to say back to him.

"And I want to apologize . . . for what I had to do back there," he said at last. And it was strange because I guess I knew he was talking about the Tacoma facility, even without him having said so. I hadn't expected him to say he was sorry. It wasn't like Simon to admit he was wrong, especially since I hadn't asked for it. "It wasn't easy"—he squared his shoulders—"leaving Willow behind like that, but I had to do it."

"Why?" I lowered my voice because even though Willow was all the way across the parking lot in the SUV, there was no way I wanted to risk her hearing us talk like this. "How could you just . . . *abandon* her like that?"

Simon glanced to the vehicle too. He watched it for a long time, and then he blew out his breath. "It wasn't about abandoning Willow." He waited for me to return his gaze, and when I finally did, his jaw tensed. "It was about you. I couldn't let anything happen to *you*."

He may as well have punched me in the gut. There were only two explanations for his actions back there in that alley.

One, those extra abilities of mine, the ones that the

others didn't have, made me worth saving.

Or two, and this one was without question more frightening . . . Simon had feelings for me that there was no way I could return.

Neither answer was acceptable.

CHAPTER NINE

Columbia Basin, Washington State

IT NEVER REALLY BECAME CLEAR WHO THE leader was, Thom or Simon. Neither was totally in charge, but both of them were in a weird kind of way.

They became co-leaders of sorts, deciding our fate in this almost eerie shorthand that involved nods and meaningful looks that made it seem as if they'd been doing this forever. The rest of us were still in the dark.

More secrets.

Staying clear of the major highways wasn't as hard as we thought it would be; there were more than enough lesser-traveled side roads to keep us clear of any potential roadblocks.

Thom wanted to stop at another hole-in-the-wall gas station to pick up a burner phone so we could let the Silent Creekers know we couldn't come back, but Simon declared it was too risky to contact them or anyone else by any means, even burners. We couldn't risk anyone's safety, so, for now, we had no way of knowing if the Silent Creek camp had been compromised, or if the NSA was already on our trail.

We were operating in the dark both figuratively and literally. At least one would end soon.

Even before Thom pointed out, "Sunrise," I'd felt it, and had to bite my tongue to keep from gasping against the sharp knife of pain.

Within seconds, the stabbing sensation passed, but I realized it was just one more thing that made me different, set me apart from the others.

From the way the deep black sky in the distance was barely transitioning to a murky shade of gray, we probably had less than an hour until the remaining night would no longer be blanketing us. We hadn't seen many cars on the road, but daylight would bring out more drivers . . . and make us far too visible.

It seemed impossible we'd only just left Silent Creek the day before, and here we were totally cut off from all the other Returned, completely on our own.

On the run.

But I was finally starting to feel better about our

circumstances. To process it and file it away and cope with the realities of everything we'd been through.

True, we'd been lured to the Tacoma facility by Agent Truman, only to discover Tyler hadn't actually been there at all. And also true, we'd nearly lost Willow in the process.

But the more important thing was we'd gotten her back.

Simon tapped his finger on the map as he leaned over to show Willow. "It looks like there's a town up ahead. Maybe we can find a place to stash the car and get a room where we can lay low for the day."

Jett caressed his forearm. "Won't the six of us together draw attention? Especially if the police here have been notified about us?"

"He has a point," Thom said, looking decisively at Simon. "We need to split up when we get there. Meet again at sundown."

Simon had been right about the town being small. And Jett had been right about us sticking together—it wasn't exactly the kind of place six kids could blend and go unnoticed.

But at least it wasn't Silent Creek–small, which was damn near invisible.

This little town, just east of the Cascade Mountains, was bigger than Silent Creek, but just barely, and our hopes of finding a motel we could check into, someplace we could hide until nightfall, turned out to be wishful thinking.

There wasn't a hotel, motel, hostel, or inn for miles and miles, and we needed to get off the roads . . . fast.

Our best hope was that we could make ourselves scarce for the next fifteen hours of daylight.

"How are we planning to split up?" Jett asked.

Simon and Thom did that weird looking-at-each-other thing, and then Thom came back with, "How about Team One and Team Two?"

But Willow's lips pressed into a tight line. "No offense, but that didn't work out so well for me last time. How 'bout I take Kyra and Jett?"

Okay, so that wasn't exactly the way I wanted to spend my day either.

At first I'd thought it was cool that Willow was no longer glaring, or even growling, at me. But what had started happening was almost worse, and it was getting stranger by the mile.

Whatever life debt Willow thought she owed me after I'd shot myself in order to save her had morphed into her strange attempts at girl talk. And frankly, Willow sucked at girl talk.

During this last stretch, she'd asked about my favorite music, and who was my first kiss, and whether I'd ever tried putting chocolate frosting on my pancakes. It was seriously weirding me out.

I sent a *Help me* glance to Natty—a little silent message of my own—thinking I'd rather play third wheel to her and Thom than play another round of *Let's Be Best Friends* with Willow.

"Sorry," Natty jumped in. "I already called dibs on Kyra."

"Fine. It's settled, then," Simon announced. "I'll take Kyra and Natty. Willow, you can go with Thom and Jett." He glanced around at everyone like he was the coach and we were his team. I half expected him to make us put our hands in for a cheer. "We all good?"

Thom looked like he might argue, but it was Willow who looked downright dejected. I almost felt bad for her.

Almost.

On the other hand, spending an entire day with Simon, away from the others, sort of defeated my whole not-wanting-to-be-on-Team-Two plan, since he was one-half of the reason I didn't want to be on that team. Willow might be weirding me out, but not knowing how Simon felt still made me uneasy.

I ignored the frenzy in my stomach as we parked the SUV in a church parking lot. Ours didn't stand out among the rest, so hopefully no one would give it a second glance. With any luck no one would notice our out-of-state plates or call the police, and when we came back, it would still be here.

Just in case, we gathered our necessities.

I cringed when I realized my jeans were still shredded, and disgustingly bloodied. "Someone will for sure notice if I walk around in these."

From out of nowhere, Simon produced a box cutter and tossed it to me. "You'll have to turn them into shorts for now." He counted out some cash and divided it out. "We'll try to find a place to get you something else to wear."

There wasn't time for modesty as I hid behind the SUV and stripped out of my jeans. I did my best to hack through the denim with the box cutter, but it wasn't pretty. The legs weren't even close to even, and there were still spots of blood visible above the hemline. But at least without the gaping hole, it was unlikely anyone would guess what the splatter was. When I came out again, I raised my hands. "So? Can I rock the cutoffs, or what?"

Natty giggled while Simon passed out our fake IDs, and not for the first time I found myself staring at my face on Bridget Hollingsworth's driver's license. It was the same ID Simon had given me before, when I'd been on the run from Agent Truman and the No-Suchers.

Thom signaled to me that he wanted a minute alone. I followed, wondering what this could possibly be about. "I almost forgot," he told me when we were out of the way of the others. "I got you this . . . at the gas station we stopped at."

I stared down at his offering in surprise. Thom had always been nice enough to me, but this was different, and all of a sudden I saw him the way Natty must—handsome, sweet, thoughtful.

I shook my head. "I can't . . ." I tried to wave him off as I blinked furiously. "How . . . how did you *even know*?" My last words came out squeaky, like someone had pinched the end of a balloon and was letting the air out super slow.

"Natty's not your only friend at Silent Creek, you know? Besides, you're a little obvious—always checking the time. This'll make things easier for you." He nudged his hand closer. "Here. Take it. I don't think the place I got it from has a return policy, so if you don't accept it, then *I* have to wear it." He glanced meaningfully at the pinkness of it, letting me know which option was out of the question.

I wasn't used to being embarrassed, but his gesture took me totally off guard. Thom wasn't my friend, and he wasn't my leader either. I was just someone who'd landed on his doorstep in need of a place to stay. If it wasn't for the fact that the present was calling to me, I would have held firm in my I-can't-accept-it stance. But I seriously wanted it, so I held out my wrist, trying not to be all wigged out by the fact that my obsession had been so obvious.

Thom wrapped the rubbery pink band around my wrist and secured the clasp. It wasn't fancy or anything, but the time had already been set.

Dragging my eyes from the rhythmic advance of the second hand as it ticked around the face of the watch, I couldn't stop myself from grinning like an idiot. "It's perfect," I told him.

"Do me a favor, will ya?" he asked. "Keep an eye on Natty today. Don't let anything happen to her."

I frowned, because of course I wouldn't let anything happen to her, not on purpose anyway. "Yeah. Sure."

The scrunched muscles between his brows softened, just a tad. "Thanks. It's just . . ." He shrugged. "Well, you know . . . thanks," he finished, running his hand through his black hair. Then he put his watch beside mine so I could see that the two were in sync. "Seven o'clock," he told me, and something as seemingly insignificant as having a plan to meet—*a set time*—made me feel . . . *right.* As if I had a purpose.

And then Thom, Willow, and Jett wandered away from us, leaving me alone with Simon and Natty. I grinned at my new team, feeling a sense of determination to make the best of our forced time together. "Now that those losers are gone, what should we do?"

Bowling.

That's how we spent the better part of our afternoon, in a noisy bowling alley where we watched the Thursday afternoon leagues fill up the lanes—a lot of old men, and some women too, who wore matching shirts and had fancy, shiny, and even colored bowling balls that they polished before they threw them and then again when they plucked them off the automatic return. They razzed each other about gutter balls, and even more when someone got a strike or a spare—*Lucky shot!* someone would yell almost every time—and in general they gave the impression that they'd known one another for a very, *very* long time.

The whole thing made me homesick for Cat and all the girls from my softball team who I'd spent hours and hours on the field with. I was even a little nostalgic for Austin, since he and I had grown up together.

But most of all, I missed Tyler.

I picked at the deep-fried cheese sticks and onion rings we'd ordered while we waited for a lane to open up for us.

Unlike the doughnuts Jett had gotten for me, this food tasted the way almost everything had since I'd returned: bland. But it gave me something to do with my hands and it made us look like normal teens, which was our primary goal. To blend.

There hadn't been any real stores in town, not like a Target or a Walmart, a superstore that had racks and racks of clothes I could choose from. There wasn't even a grocery store that carried clothing, like a Fred Meyer. I hadn't planned on being choosy; I just wanted something not of the cutoff variety, preferably without chunks of my own flesh stuck to it.

But obviously, in a town without a flashing stoplight, that had been too much to ask for.

We'd walked through the miniature-sized "downtown" area, which consisted of a gas station, some old-fashioned-looking buildings that housed a bakery–slash–coffee shop–slash–hardware store, a butcher shop, and a liquor store that was, not surprisingly, the biggest shop of them all.

It was in this section of town that we also came across a small consignment shop.

The place was jam-packed with all kinds of clothes, hats, shoes, and purses that smelled vaguely like disinfectant. The racks were arranged by clothing type, and I was starting to think I was either going to be stuck with my cutoffs or something of the polyester variety, since that's what they mostly had, when I actually managed to find one pair of jeans in exactly my size. And bonus, not only did they fit me, but they only had to be rolled at the hem one time.

Plus, we'd killed nearly an hour and a half in the process.

When the bowling lane we'd requested, the one farthest from the door and away from the bar and the check-in counter, finally came available, we traded our shoes for the well-worn rentals and picked our not-fancy-or-polished balls from the racks against the wall. I bent down and laced my shoes as I watched Simon try to explain to Natty the finer points of knocking pins down with a ten-pound ball.

Her first approach was comical, and her release was less than impressive. She took three awkward steps and launched the ball as hard as she could, which was also entirely too late, resulting in a loud, and totally attention-grabbing, crash against the hardwoods.

She definitely wasn't a natural.

Nervously I glanced around, but only a few disinterested gazes even drifted our way, and it was clear it wasn't the first time someone had mishandled a bowling ball in this place.

Her ball rolled listlessly toward the gutter, and as if she'd expected a strike her first go-round, Natty stomped her foot and muttered, "Darn it!" which was probably the equivalent of a swear, coming from Natty.

"Really?" I scoffed, because how could she not have known that thing was headed to the gutter?

She shrugged, and we both sat on our bench and watched as Simon took his turn. He was actually pretty good. A million times better than Natty, and he probably could've given some of the leaguers a run for their money.

His first roll wasn't a strike, but on his second, he bowled a split, sending one of his two remaining pins careening into the other and clearing the lane. Even if he'd done it by accident, he was taking full credit for the maneuver as he strolled back confidently, his chest all puffed up. "Time to see what you can do, Hollingsworth."

Natty nudged me, reminding me that *I* was Hollingsworth, and I sprang into action.

I doubt it would surprise anyone to know I was competitive . . . or at least that Kyra Agnew, all-star pitcher, was competitive. There wasn't a chance in *H-E-double hockey sticks* I was letting Simon one-up me, not if I could help it. And the fact that I'd grown up in Burlington, Washington, where sometimes the only thing to do on a rainy Saturday afternoon was go to the bowling alley with your parents, probably didn't hurt any.

I clutched my bowling ball against my chest as I took my first step.

One . . . I took a step and eased my arm down in front of me, letting it fall to my side. Two . . . Another step as I lunged with my left knee and I began the forward arc of the ball. Three . . . I released it, not early, and not late the way Natty had, but just as I reached the line at the top of the lane.

I knew the moment I let it go, though, that I'd done something wrong. I was stunned as I watched the heavy ball barrel down the lane so fast it was a singular black smudge.

It reached the end of the lane and ripped through the pins on the right side, exactly the way it should have. But instead of landing in whatever opening was back there waiting to swallow it and carry it back to the return the way the rest of the balls did, this one just kept going. It hurtled right over the top of the chasm.

The sound that followed was a terrible screeching noise. Not a crash, but almost like metal scraping, or crunching, or collapsing. It was loud and harsh.

I heard Natty gasp, and even without looking, I knew Simon had jumped to his feet behind me.

This time the eyes that turned our way were not disinterested in the least.

They were interested-fascinated-*downright stunned.* And I couldn't blame them.

"Kyra?" Even Simon forgot to call me by my fake name as he appeared at my back.

I stammered, "I don't know . . . I didn't mean to . . ." How could I make him understand? It was like the time I'd jokingly chucked the softball at Tyler, only it hadn't been funny when the ball had rocketed toward him rather than lobbing the way I'd meant it to. I'd nearly torn a hole through the backstop that day.

"Crap," Simon—whose new ID said his name was Barry Pomeroy—whispered as he gripped my shoulder and dragged me stumbling back to where Natty was already frantically stripping off her rental shoes and looking around anxiously. "Take these back and get ours." He handed his shoes to Natty while I kicked mine off too.

Natty had just gathered all three pairs when the

scoreboard over our lane began to flash. Clearly whatever had happened back there, where that god-awful sound had come from, my ball had caused a malfunction of some sort.

Nice. Way to *not* draw attention.

"It's fine," Simon told me while my heart hammered and my gaze slid uneasily around to the other lanes, to where everyone had all but stopped what they were doing, and their watchful stares were pinned to me now. "We'll just get our things and go. No one'll ever even know we were here."

Except he was wrong.

The guy trudging toward us had a look in his eyes that made my heart stutter. And from the way his nostrils were flaring as those eyes locked on us, I knew we were in seriously deep shit. His blue-and-black bowling shirt—the same color-blocked kind the waitress and the guy behind the shoe rental counter had been wearing—strained around his bulging belly with each heavy step he took. But he had an air about him that made it clear: this was the guy in charge.

"You goddamned kids!" he bellowed before he'd even reached us. "Always breakin' things! Always up to no goddamned good! What'd you do this time?"

Simon stepped forward, but I slipped in front of him, pasting on my most innocent it-wasn't-my-fault expression. It was a look I generally reserved for crisis situations, and even then only pulled out for those of the male persuasion—I'd used similar looks on my dad, Austin, and on guy teachers and coaches. Women tended to be impervious since most of them kept similar looks of their own for just such an emergency.

"It was an accident," I explained, wrinkling my nose and hoping I looked distressed rather than like I was sniffing something revolting. "I have no idea what happened."

He just scowled back at me, propping his ham-sized fists on his hips. He wasn't buying my little damsel-in-distress display. "All I know is, I just got lane one up and running again, and now you kids"—he eyeballed Simon behind me, his bulging eyes getting even bulgier behind his greasy cheeks—"you come in here and fuck it all up again. Do you know how much trouble you just cost me? Not to mention how much goddamned money?"

Natty came back and was holding our shoes. She kept glancing toward the door and then back at the people—at the crowd that was gathering around us—and back to me and the boss man. She reminded me of a frightened animal, which irritated me since she was part of my team, and I was counting on her to have my back. Cat would've had my back.

Simon had had enough, and he finally tried to smooth things over. "Look, we don't want any trouble. Can't we work something out?" He reached for his pocket, and I thought that would be the end of it. He would buy our way out of this.

Natty must've thought the same thing I did, and she took a step toward me, handing me my shoes.

But the boss guy didn't even blink. He wasn't interested in making any *deal* with us.

When I reached for my shoes, it set the guy off. Rage sparked behind his eyes. He'd had enough of us *goddamned kids*, and one of his ham hands snaked out, his fat fingers closing around my wrist. I had to give the guy credit—he was strong. Not super strong like me or anything, but strong enough, and when he squeezed, I felt my bones pop.

"Where d'ya think you're going?" he sneered in a menacing voice.

Dizziness surged through me, and I realized that no amount of sweet-talking or cash was going to get us out of here unnoticed.

"Get your hands off her!" Simon insisted, forgetting all about trying to pay the guy off as he tried to shove him away from me. But Simon couldn't stop what had already started, and the scene we were causing made us a million times more interesting as several more of the nosy bowlers packed in around us.

The boss guy started dragging me toward the shoe rental counter. "We'll see what the sheriff has to say 'bout all this." He nodded to the pimply-faced kid who'd taken our shoes. "Call Sheriff Hudson. Tell him we got trouble here."

When the kid picked up the phone, it felt like the guy had just wrapped his hands around my throat instead of my wrist. I couldn't swallow. I couldn't breathe.

If they called the sheriff on us, eventually someone might realize we weren't who our IDs said we were. They might even figure out who we really were. And if Agent Truman was notified . . .

There were people standing in our way, and not just Simon and Natty, but a full-blown crowd now too. I wondered why none of them jumped in or tried to tell this guy he'd crossed a line by manhandling one of us "goddamned kids," let alone a girl, but they all just stood there, gaping with morbid fascination.

Chicken shits! I wanted to scream at them, but all I could think was that they were all seeing our faces. With every second that passed, the chances they could identify us grew.

The guy didn't slow, and as much as I wanted to try, I was afraid that if I did try to hit him or kick him, that I might not be able to control my own strength and it would end up like the bowling ball incident all over again. What if I hurt him? Or worse?

What if that just gave these people even more reason to recognize us?

"Please. She didn't mean it," Natty begged, getting in front of us and trying to slow him down.

But Natty was no roadblock, not for this whale of a guy, and she might as well have been a bug in the path of a car. He swept her aside with his free arm, sending Natty sprawling backward. Her head made a hollow *thwack!* sound against the hardwood.

Seeing her on the ground like that triggered something in me. "Lemme go." I thrashed, wringing my wrist in the circle of his unflinching grip. "I can explain. This was all a big mistake." I couldn't dislodge myself. All I managed to do was make him yank my arm even harder.

"The only mistake is letting *you kids* in here . . ." *You kids.* We were all alike to this guy. "Little fuckers are always messin' things up, thinkin' you can call your daddies and have 'em bail you out." He was muttering as he half shoved, half dragged me. "Not this time. This time you can answer to the law."

Hot sparks exploded behind my eyes. It wasn't pain, though, not this sensation. It was sheer-complete-*utter* panic.

Above us, the monitors and TV screens began to blink, flashing erratically.

Somewhere, down on the lanes, several pins crashed together loudly. The jarring and unexpected sound was followed immediately by another set of pins falling, then another and another. And after each crash, there was the mechanical whir of the automatic pin machines as they worked to set the fallen pins up once more.

Heads whipped around to see what—or who—was causing all the pins to collapse, but the lanes were all deserted since everyone had gathered around us.

Now we weren't moving at all—me, the boss man, no one in the bowling alley.

"What the—" he whispered, but instead of loosening, his grip on me got tighter, more painful.

He was going to turn us in and Agent Truman would put us under a microscope . . . body part by body part.

My skin felt like it was on fire, and just when I thought I might combust from the inside out, the trophy case erupted like a bomb had been set off within it. Pieces of glass flew outward, sailing in every direction. The kid behind the counter barely ducked in time to avoid being impaled by one of the trophies—an enormous green one with a giant gold star on top—as it hurtled end-over-pointed-end right for him. It smashed into a gazillion plastic bits against the wall behind him.

"Kyra." The warning in Simon's voice made me pause as I searched for him among the sea of faces.

He was scolding me, like I'd done something wrong.

I wanted to tell him he was confused, that it was the other guy—the one who had me in his death grip—who was the bad guy here. But I knew what he meant. The truth was reflected on every aghast face staring back at me, every O-shaped gape and horrified gaze. Even they knew.

I'd done all this—the blinking monitors that were still flashing wildly, the unexplained pins toppling over, the shattering trophy case.

Me.

"Crap," I said, and then looked up at the boss guy, who'd finally released me so he could pick a small fragment of glass from his forearm. "I'm sorry."

Natty gathered our shoes and gave me a pointed look. "Let's go."

This was our chance, she was telling me. While everyone was too dazed or too afraid to realize they could still stop us. They didn't know my limitations.

And no one even tried, not even the boss guy. The crowd just parted. But there was no mistaking the whispers of "*Did you see that?*" and "*What is she . . . ?*" all jumbled together.

I'd gone from minor spectacle to full-blown freak show in the space of less than ten minutes. Must be some sort of new world record.

And now we weren't just trying to go unnoticed in this nothing of a town until it got dark. Now, because of the scene I'd just caused, we had to seriously lay low, since I was pretty sure every single person in that bowling alley could probably describe all of us to a police sketch artist if asked.

Impressive.

CHAPTER TEN

WE HEARD THE COP CAR, WITH ITS SIREN BLARING, before we'd even cleared the parking lot of the bowling alley. If only that pimple-faced jerk behind the counter hadn't been so quick on the dial, or if his asshole boss would have just made the deal when Simon had offered it . . .

Then we wouldn't be in this mess now.

The black-and-white car turned into the parking lot just as Simon and Natty and I rounded the corner and disappeared from sight. I didn't even have my shoes on yet before we were sprinting down a crushed gravel road, dust flying behind us. I could feel the sharp rocks poking at me beneath my socks. But we didn't slow down.

Simon slammed into the wobbly wooden fence at the end of the road, scaling it in a single, nimble leap. Without hesitating, I followed, although I was far less graceful and suddenly wished I'd focused more on track over softball. When I landed in more gravel on the other side, I gasped, but Simon covered my mouth to shush me.

I stayed low, crouching the way he was as I searched the shabby-looking houses around us. Laundry waved on drooping clotheslines, and somewhere, inside one of the houses, a baby wailed. But other than the baby, it was silent. There were no dogs barking, no people talking, not even a television or radio in the background. No reason to think anyone knew we were back here.

Natty landed beside me and stared at me with her ginormous saucer-sized eyes.

"I'm sorry," I said to Simon, because I *was* sorry, for messing up something as simple as trying to stay hidden for just one day.

Apparently that was all the confirmation Natty needed. "So it *was* you? You did all that back there? The breaking glass and flying trophies? All without even touching them?" She didn't ask it like she was accusing me of doing something shady. Instead, there was this hint of amazement, like she thought I'd done something really, *really* right.

"I'm pretty sure."

"Holy crap," she breathed. "And what about at the lab? That giant tube thing? That was you, too?"

"It's not as cool as you think," I whispered.

At any other time, I'd have been lying. The fact that I could make things happen—move things with my mind—even when I didn't mean to, was sort of awesome. It was the part where it happened outside of my control that made it disturbing.

Besides, it was bad enough having Willow mooning over me because I'd saved her. I didn't need Natty acting all weird too.

"Can you do it again?"

"I have no idea. It's not the first time it's happened, but I can't figure it out. So far, I don't know how to control it. I've been trying to move things for weeks." I cringed, thinking of the scene back at the bowling alley, not exactly rolling a pencil across a table. "I have no idea why this was different from all those times."

"What about the bowling ball?" she asked. "I saw you *throw* that. That wasn't the same."

Again, it was something I didn't totally understand. "For some reason, if I'm not overthinking it, I can throw super hard, too. But like the moving things without touching them, it doesn't work just because I want it to." I'd practiced that too. After a successful attempt, in which I'd done some major damage to one of the storage buildings at Silent Creek, I'd moved my target practice into the woods and tried honing my skill there. But the results had been less than encouraging.

To prove my point, I punched Simon in the arm. "See?

Just because I can throw hard sometimes, it doesn't mean I can just turn it on and off. And it doesn't seem to work for things like hitting." I eyed Simon, who was dramatically rubbing his arm.

"What if you'd been wrong?" he griped.

I shrugged unrepentantly. "Then I guess we'd be having a very different conversation." Turning back to Natty, I said, "Seriously, though, you can't tell anyone. Not even Thom or Jett. And especially not Willow." I didn't want her to have any more reason to worship me. "Simon's the only one who knows." I gave her a serious look to let her know I meant what I said. "And now you."

Simon threw my shoes at me. "And now half this town. Since they know what we look like, we need to find someplace to stay hidden for the next . . ." He hesitated, clearly irritated that I'd put a kink in our plans.

I glanced at my new watch, trying to be helpful. "Two and a half hours," I offered.

"Two and a half hours," Simon huffed, shoving his feet into his own shoes and pulling me up by my arm. I'd clearly landed on his shit list.

He dragged us behind the run-down houses, keeping close to shrubbery whenever possible.

We hid behind garbage cans and cars and anything else big enough to conceal us. I was anxious, because what if it was already too late? What if the sheriff, or whoever had been called to the bowling alley, had put two and two together and figured out we were half of the missing teens the Daylighters were searching for?

For all we knew, Agent Truman was already on his way.

When we made our way back to the main road, just a few blocks from "downtown," I pointed at a house that looked like something straight out of a fairy tale. "There." It had pink trim and light blue shutters, and on the large wrap-around porch there were two rocking chairs painted a bright shade of yellow. It was cozy, in a gingerbread house kind of way, and made me wonder what kind of life-sized Barbie doll might answer if we knocked. Except we wouldn't have to knock on those doors to get inside this Dreamhouse.

Columbia Valley Library, read the pink-and-gold sign planted in the front yard.

"The library?" Simon asked skeptically.

But I was already dragging Natty across the street. "Think about it—it's perfect. The cops probably won't look for us there, and if we're lucky, whoever works there won't have a clue what just happened at the bowling alley."

Natty chimed in. "Besides, it wouldn't be weird for us to be hanging out in a library for a couple of hours. That's what they're there for, right?"

"I don't know . . ." Simon hesitated. "I'm not much of a reader."

"Okay. Sure. I understand." But we were already on the porch, and I grinned at him over my shoulder. "If you need help, let one of us know. We can help you sound out the big words."

* * *

The inside of the library was nothing like the outside. And while it barely resembled a Barbie Dreamhouse, it was hardly like a library either, at least not the library we'd had back in Burlington, which had these enormous windows and tall ceilings, state-of-the-art computers, and neatly organized shelves and displays.

This place was dark and dusty, and the books were scattered around in almost total disarray. If there was a system—Dewey decimal or otherwise—it wasn't apparent. The only similarity I could see between this and the Burlington Library was the fact that it called itself a library. That, and the fact that there were, indeed, books.

Still, I was surprised by the guy who came down the stairs to greet us. He didn't look all nerdy and bookish, which despite not being library-ish, was the kind of Norman Bates vibe I'd expected in a place like this. But instead of wearing a sweater vest and bow tie, this guy had on baggy jeans and a faded Rolling Stones T-shirt. He looked like someone's slacker brother who should be stuffing his face with Cheetos and playing Xbox in the basement.

"So, let me know if you need help finding anything. Nonfiction's in the back . . ." He pointed through an opening that might have once been a dining room or a living room, but now had stacks of disorganized shelves covering the walls. "And fiction's through there." Again, he pointed, this time through another opening, on the opposite side of the stairs. "If you need to use the computer, lemme know—I'll give you today's password." He nodded at a desk in the corner. Next to the desk, a sign read:

We're sorry!

Due to national security concerns, we are unable to tell you if your internet surfing habits, passwords, and email content are being monitored by federal agents; please act appropriately.

My breath snagged in the back of my throat at the mention of federal agents, but the guy just shrugged and said, "Patriot Act," like that explained everything. Then he threw in, "Just try to stay off the porn sites. Gives us all kinds of viruses."

I raised my eyebrows at Simon, just the tiniest bit, making it clear I doubted the guy was talking to Natty and me. Simon scowled back, letting me know he didn't think I was funny, even the tiniest bit.

Natty didn't hesitate, and took off toward the fiction section, while Simon stayed with me. I was tempted to ask for the computer password so I could maybe go to my dad's old online forums, those weird conspiracy theory sites he used to frequent. I doubted he'd risk visiting them now, but there was a part of me that thought if only I could spend a minute or two in the places he used to spend hours-days-months of his life before I'd returned, maybe the ache I felt to see him might dull, even if it was only temporary. Even if whatever connection I'd feel wasn't real.

But I was equally nervous that somehow Agent Truman might expect it and be monitoring those sites, waiting for me to slip up like that so he could track us down.

"Thanks," I told the librarian politely as I made my way, instead, to the nonfiction section.

I examined the jumbled collection of books that included everything from local history to crafts to finances. I paused when I reached the meager section on relationships, and I ran my finger over a spine with an image of a couple kissing.

"Can I ask you a question?"

I hadn't even realized Simon was standing right behind me until then, and I dropped my hand.

"What if he doesn't come back?" He went on, not waiting for me to admit that I knew exactly who he meant. "I know you don't want to hear this, but eventually you have to ask yourself: When is enough enough? When do you give up?"

I hugged myself tightly as I turned to face him, wondering why he was bringing this up now. My stomach and my throat clenched painfully.

I'd already asked myself that same question a hundred times: *When* would *I give up?* Problem was, there was no good answer.

I took in every detail of Simon's face, like it might somehow make a difference in the way I answered—his dark lashes, the golden specks that floated in his strange eyes, the curve of his full lips. He watched me with a kind of fascinated intensity that made me hyperaware of the way I held myself, and made me notice the way I pressed my toes against the bottom of my shoes. I traced my tongue back and forth along the roof of my mouth—a nervous habit.

"It wasn't your fault," he said. "You didn't know what would happen to him. I should have told you what they did—the DNA replacement—so you could make an informed decision."

I shuddered, because I wasn't sure it would have made a difference. Tyler would have died if I hadn't let him be taken. Could I really have let that happen, even knowing he wouldn't come back fully human?

"You did what you thought was best." Simon's voice was lower, huskier now. "But at some point you have to forgive yourself." His words were hypnotic.

The moment I licked my lips, I regretted the action. There was something about the way Simon was looking at me, about the way he was watching my mouth a little too closely, his eyes darting back and forth to mine, almost like he was asking—no, begging—me for permission. I didn't want him getting the wrong idea, and I was afraid I'd just sent out some sort of *kiss-me* signal. I swallowed super hard, my mouth feeling like it was suddenly stuffed with cotton. "What if I can't forgive myself?"

"Kyra." His hand nudged my chin upward and I literally thought my heart would explode like the trophy case at the bowling alley. "You get that the two of you weren't together for that long, don't you?" He scowled down at me.

It took several seconds before his words finally penetrated

my brain, probably because my feelings were so mixed up. But once they did, I recoiled, shoving away from him. "Wait. What are you trying to say?"

Simon wasn't nearly as confused, and he repeated, "I said, it's not like you were together all that long, you and your boyfriend."

"Are you being serious right now? You think that makes a difference, *how long* we were *together*?"

"I'm just saying isn't it possible your feelings for him . . . *how strong* you think you feel might have at least something to do with guilt?" His shrug was almost too much, and my mood shifted. "Think about it, Kyra. You almost killed him, and then you had to send him away to aliens to be forever transformed. That would be tough on anyone. It would make anyone see things . . . *differently*. I can see why you're having a hard time moving on." His smile was probably meant to be sympathetic, but it had the exact opposite effect, and I felt myself losing it.

"And by moving on, you mean getting over him, is that it?" I poked Simon in the chest, glad when he winced. "And then what? You think you can just jump in and take his place? What do you want me to say, Simon? That I'd rather be with some bossy jerk who keeps secrets and thinks he knows what's best for everyone? That if you just give me a few more days, I'll be over Tyler and you can step in and take his place?" My hair whipped against my cheeks as somewhere in the room I heard something crash to the ground. "Well, I won't. And you can't. It's not that simple.

I've known Tyler his whole life. His brother and I were best friends *way* before he was my boyfriend. Not everything is about—"

I was about to explain a hundred different reasons why I'd never get over Tyler, when I saw the book slam into the back of Simon's head. "Jesus—*what the* . . . ? Did you see that?" His hand shot up to the base of his skull. And then with an incredulous look, he asked, "Did . . . you . . . did *you* do that?"

I was about to deny it, because there was no way it was me, when I looked down at my hand. It was still outstretched.

My eyes got huge when I realized what I'd been thinking right before that book had pegged Simon in the head. Because that was almost exactly it, what I'd been wishing for: something to throw at him.

Okay, so maybe it hadn't been the softball I'd imagined, but I suppose a book was a pretty good substitute.

He stood there watching me, and his eyes moved from my face to my hand and he stopped rubbing the place where the book had smacked him. "You were pissed, weren't you?" He took a step closer. Too close. "Think about the other times it happened—today at the bowling alley, yesterday in the central lab, that night when Agent Truman had your dad at gunpoint. Were you mad then, too?"

I tried to think back. *Mad?* Was it really that simple? It made me sound like a Neanderthal, but that didn't make it untrue.

I was always sort of pissed at Agent Truman.

But what about that first time it had happened? At the minimart, when Tyler had been back at the motel burning up with fever, had I been pissed then, too?

No, not pissed, just out of my mind with worry, and completely racked with guilt because it had been *my fault* he was sick. I'd been absolutely-utterly-*hopelessly* desperate to get my hands on some Tylenol to bring his fever down. I'd been frustrated . . . almost to the point of being panicked.

Maybe that was the key. Maybe it didn't have to be angry so much as just worked up in general. Pissed . . . panicked . . . agitated . . . whatever it was that made my adrenaline pump.

So why, then, hadn't this uncanny ability of mine manifested itself in the alley when Agent Truman had Simon, Willow, and me cornered? What had been different about then?

It took me a second to put my finger on it, but it was there: *fear.*

It hadn't been anger then, it had been full-on terror—a tail-between-my-legs, cowering kind of fear.

At the bowling alley, when I'd been freaking out that Agent Truman might find out we were there, I'd been . . . *desperate* to stop that from happening.

Desperate. Panicked. One hundred percent freaked out.

It was as if I'd been zapped with ten thousand volts and juiced up with steroids, all at the same time.

"Try it again," Simon coaxed.

I whirled around, concentrating as hard as I could on the haphazard stacks around me. At a row of old encyclopedias, and magazines and journals, at the uneven spines of hardcovers and paperbacks all shoved in together.

"Get mad," Simon coached, as if I hadn't thought of that myself. I conjured up an image of Agent Truman as I squeezed my hands into fists, thinking of all the things he'd done to ruin my life—convincing my mom I was hazardous to be around, hauling my father up to Devil's Hole that night and using him the same way he'd used the promise of Tyler being alive to bait me. I pictured his smug face and the way he'd looked, standing on my doorstep that very first day in his starched suit, which was almost the exact same way he'd looked when he'd shot Willow with those beanbag bullets.

I glared at the pages of the open book at my feet, the one that had hit Simon in the head, as I pictured the agent's arrogant face, but nothing happened. The pages didn't budge. Not so much as a rustle.

"Get pissed, Kyra."

"I'm trying," I shot back. I didn't need him telling me what I should do—I understood what he'd said. Maybe I just wasn't the kind of person who could get mad at the drop of a hat. Maybe I didn't have a big enough chip on my shoulder.

He got in my face. "You know he's never coming back, don't you? Tyler? And it's all because of you." His words were crisp and cutting. I recoiled. And when he said, "*You* killed him," I felt my fists clench into tense balls.

I wanted to hit him, and I wanted to turn away so he couldn't see the way my eyes burned. His face blurred in front of me. It was bad enough that I'd beaten myself up about Tyler, and what might've happened to him, every single second he'd been gone—I didn't need Simon shoving it in my face.

The book tore through the air from behind my head, whizzing past my ear so fast I could feel the draft. It slammed hard against the wall, sounding like a rock, and then it dropped to the floor.

I tried to tell myself to stop, but all I could think was: *I killed Tyler . . .*

. . . I killed Tyler . . .

. . . I killed Tyler . . .

And each time those words rang through my head, another book shot off the shelves, and another . . . and another.

Footsteps shuffled upstairs, and Simon's fingers closed over mine. "Okay," he said. "Enough for now. We can't let anyone see you." He squeezed my hand, silently telling me I'd done well.

I didn't know about that because all I could think was that other thing: I'd killed Tyler.

"I didn't mean it," he whispered, as if he'd read my mind, and he didn't let go of my hand, even when Natty came into the room, her eyes wide.

"What's going on in here?" Her nervous glance shot to the books strewn around the floor, and then over her shoulder.

"You kids okay down there?" the librarian called from the top of the stairs. "Need anything?"

My pulse echoed in my ears, and my throat felt tight and raw.

"We're okay!" Simon called back to him. "We'll let you know if we need help!"

We were all still for a second as we waited to see if he might come down anyway. But then there was more shuffling, and his footsteps, along the creaky old floorboards, moved away from us.

"This might not've been the best place to practice. We probably should've chosen someplace a little more . . . soundproof," Simon said, shifting into action and picking up fallen books. "We need to clean this mess up and get out of here. Who knows what he heard and who he might've called."

We did our best to put everything back where it belonged, but the order was tough to figure out. There was a book on military strategy that I dropped on a table on our way out the door, and another that totally didn't belong in the nonfiction section at all.

It was a small paperback that I recognized right away, a book I'd seen in school probably, but that I'd also heard Tyler mention: *Slaughterhouse-Five*. I had no idea what it was about, but without thinking, I shoved it in my back pocket.

"Oh, shoot," Natty said, pausing when Simon and I were already on the porch. "I left the backpack."

We definitely couldn't leave the backpack behind. It had our fake IDs, some cash, and a few other things Simon thought we might need if our vehicle was discovered and we had to make a run for it. "I'll be right back," Natty said as she disappeared back into the library.

Outside, it was still daylight, but according to my new pink wristwatch, we were down to our last thirty-six minutes. Totally manageable.

Nervous to be alone with Simon again, especially after what had just happened back there, I cleared my throat, then crossed and uncrossed my arms. "Look," I started, meaning to bury the hatchet once and for all. "I'm sorry about that. Back there. With the book . . ."

"I guess we'll have to work on that temper of yours." Simon was lounging with his back against one of the tall pillars of the porch, and watching me closely.

I meant to tell him he had it all wrong, that I'd have to find some other ways to tap into this weird ability of mine because I couldn't walk around being all wound up all the time, but I never got the chance because that's when I spied the patrol car. Not that it was hard to see, coming right down the street the way it was.

I had no way of knowing if they were looking for us because of the incident at the bowling alley, or if the librarian actually had heard the commotion downstairs and called the cops, or if it was just a giant coincidence, and these guys were on their way to someplace else entirely. But panic set in, making it damn near impossible to breathe.

Simon and I were sitting ducks. We had no place to go, and whoever was in that car would easily spot us.

So, I did the only thing I could come up with.

"Follow my lead," I gasped as I launched myself at

Simon. I wrapped my arms around his neck and crushed myself against him. I pressed my lips to his, pretty much demanding that he kiss me back.

I thought he might protest, maybe even ask what the hell I was doing since he hadn't seen the cop car the way I had. But he didn't. He was either smart enough to recognize I had a plan, or he was completely willing to disregard the fact that I'd just assaulted him with a book, and he let me kiss him.

But I was the one who was really taken by surprise.

Simon's lips were a million times softer than I expected they'd be, even though I told myself I'd never thought of them at all. And there was this brief moment, just the shortest of pauses, during which I swear I felt his breath catch in the back of his throat, right before his entire body relaxed and one of his arms slipped around my waist. That was when he tugged me even closer to him.

When his lips parted, and his tongue brushed mine, I nearly abandoned my plan altogether—to hell with saving our asses!

Simon totally should've known better. Everyone knew the first rule of fake kissing: no tongue.

But my instincts for self-preservation kicked in, and I knew there was no backing out now. Not without knowing for sure if we were still being watched or not. The only chance we stood of pulling this off was to fully-totally-*absolutely* commit.

We had to *become* one of those couples I'd always rolled

my eyes at in the school hallways—the ones who went at it so unabashedly, they made you wish you could stab your own mind's eye out.

Slipping my hand from the back of his neck, I tested the feel of his skin, tracing the line of his jaw, which was slightly, but not totally, stubbled. I ran the pad of my thumb over it, and breathed in the scent of him—something like leather and cigarette smoke from the bowling alley and the onion-y taste of his breath.

Simon explored as well, letting his tongue trace the inside edge of my lower lip.

I trembled, which had nothing at all to do with the way his fingers feathered along my spine, or the way his teeth grazed my lip, or the feel of his body pressed against mine, and I swore I heard him let out a low, breathy chuckle. Part of me wanted to stomp on his foot for being so bigheaded, but I was too busy trying to play the hero, so instead I kept up the performance of two teens who couldn't keep their hands off each other.

I pressed my palm flat against his chest, mapping the hard lines and lean muscles, probing and testing. The swirling in my stomach was surely a bad reaction to the fried foods I'd choked down at the bowling alley, and definitely not at all to Simon.

"Ehem!" Natty shouted, a sound that was so obviously *not* her clearing her throat that I probably would've laughed if I wasn't already dying of embarrassment over the part where she'd caught the two of us kissing. "You two need some privacy?" Even without looking at her, I knew she meant the thing where I was still draped all over Simon.

"Are they gone?" I asked against Simon's teeth, while Simon kept his arm secured around my waist.

Natty sounded uncertain when she answered, "Are *who* gone? I have no idea who you're talking about."

"The cops." But from Natty's bewildered tone I already had my answer, and I shoved away from Simon.

I told myself that it was normal to feel a little tingly, my head just a tad—a tad!—fuzzy, after such close contact. It would be weird if I *didn't* feel that way.

"Cops?" Natty asked, and I got the feeling this was her version of the third degree. "Is that what this was all about?" She waved at us, like she was waving at something disgusting and unnatural. Like now she was the one who needed something pointy and sharp to poke out her mind's eye.

But Simon just shrugged, crossing his arms over his chest and flashing me a know-it-all smile. "*I* didn't see any cops."

I crossed my arms too, but not all show-offy and full of myself, the way he was. I cocked my head to the side and gave him an exasperated look. "Really? So you, what, you thought I just couldn't keep my hands to myself another second? That I *had* to have you?"

His grin widened as he raised one eyebrow at me. "Pretty much."

"Ugh!" I stomped down the porch steps to the sidewalk below. "You're such an ass!" I shouted over my shoulder. "You knew what I was doing. You knew it was all an act so we wouldn't get caught," I insisted, wondering if it was him I was trying to convince, or Natty.

Or maybe it was me, I wondered, pretending to wipe away the memory of what we'd just done from my lips, because my body was still buzzing, and my lips still burned in all the places his had touched seconds earlier.

PART TWO

And so it goes . . .

—Kurt Vonnegut, *Slaughterhouse-Five*

CHAPTER ELEVEN

Day Twenty-Eight

Just outside Zion National Park. Somewhere in Utah.

DRIVING AT NIGHT SHOULD'VE BEEN PEACEFUL, and in a way I guess it was. Thom and Simon sat in front, with Simon doing most of the driving and only handing over the wheel for a two-hour stretch somewhere between Twin Falls, Idaho, and Salt Lake City. That part wasn't relaxing, though, since Simon muttered beneath his breath almost the entire time about how slow Thom was driving, even though the speed limit on the side roads was well below the fifty Thom was going.

Natty sat next to me, and continued to gawk at me with that weird fascination that made me worry she was gonna blurt out that I was some kind of superhero, the same way Tyler had when he'd learned I could see in the dark and hold my breath for crazy long. Or that she was going to ask me to levitate something, like it was some parlor trick I could conjure on command. If only it were that simple.

I kept frowning at her, reminding her it was our secret and that she needed to keep her mouth shut. Then she'd just nod, like she'd known that all along and I could totally trust her.

Her lips were sealed, she'd tell me with those placating looks.

It went on like that for hours and miles, but at least I wasn't forced to talk to Simon, to rehash those last few minutes we'd spent alone together in front of the library, because whenever I thought about *that*, the tops of my ears burned and my toes curled tightly.

What had I been thinking, kissing him like that? Had it really been the only way to avoid being noticed by those cops?

Because now . . . now all I could think was: *I'd kissed Simon.* And not only that, but he'd kissed me back.

Even worse, I felt guilty because Tyler might be out there somewhere, newly returned and trying to find me the way I was trying to find him. I was ashamed because maybe, just maybe, there was a tiny part of me that hadn't hated that kiss. Did that make me the worst person ever?

Probably.

Whenever I caught Simon shooting me glances from the

rearview mirror, I pretended not to see him. I picked my fingernails and acted like the darkness and the scenery outside were the most fascinating things in the world. Pretty much anything to avoid his gaze.

I didn't want to know what he was thinking, and I definitely didn't want to give him any idea what was going on inside *my* head.

"We're getting close," Thom said as he sat up. "Keep your eyes peeled."

I looked around. We were surrounded by desert that was hardly at all like the desert we'd left behind in Washington, which had long, flat stretches that seemed to last forever.

Here, the land was uneven and rocky, with tall cliffs that sprang up on both sides of us. The rock sheers looked like they'd been hand carved, and even in the darkness I could make out intricate ridgelines and seams that felt like they had a story to tell, marking their passage throughout time. I wondered what they'd look like in the light of day.

"What are we watching for?" I asked, scanning for signs we were no longer alone. It seemed unlikely, though. We were on the only visible road—with no obvious signs or manmade structures in sight.

"Trouble," Simon warned, raising the hair on the back of my neck.

Natty leaned over the top of me, her breath fogging the glass as she searched too.

"Why would there be trouble?" I asked. "I thought you said they would help us."

From the passenger seat, Thom was looking too, but I wondered if he could see anything but blackness. "We had no way of letting them know we were coming. Far as they're concerned, we're trespassers."

"It's late," Jett said quietly. "They probably don't even know we're here."

"Oh, they know, all right." Simon's ominous whisper sent a shiver of trepidation down my spine, as an eerie hush cloaked us.

The ambush, when it finally came, struck Simon's side of the SUV first. It made sense, I suppose: if I were planning to ambush a vehicle, I'd go for the driver first.

The driver's-side window shattered, and Simon flinched the way anyone would if the glass next to his head had just exploded without warning. The SUV swerved hard to the right, driving all the way off the road and leaping wildly over the rocks and bushes beside the smooth asphalt.

Simon regained control quickly. But then something solid and hard struck the windshield as well. It was crazy loud, and even though it wasn't totally unexpected this time, I flinched even harder than the first time. I couldn't tell whether we'd been hit by a rock or some kind of ball bearing, or whether it was something even more dangerous, like a bullet, but it didn't matter. The windshield began to fracture, splintering from a point directly in front of Simon's face and spiderwebbing out in all directions, looking like cut-glass lace.

"Get off the road!" Thom yelled, and before Simon

could react, I felt Willow climbing over the top of us, her boots gouging into my thighs as she clambered past us, and into the front seat between Thom and Simon.

She gripped one of the weapons we'd packed before leaving Silent Creek, a long black rifle-looking thing that was as foreign to me as one of Jett's motherboards.

Thankfully, I wasn't the one who had to fire the thing.

"I told you this was a bad idea!" Willow shouted as she shoved Thom against the passenger-side door.

Neither Simon nor Thom answered. Simon kept his head low as we barreled along; only his eyes were visible above the dash. Willow leaned over the top of him and aimed the nose of the gun out the shattered side window.

"Cover your ears," she called out absently, and it was hard to tell if she was talking to Simon, who could only cover one of his ears since he was driving, or to the rest of us.

I didn't take any chances, and stuck my fingers in my ears just as she pulled the trigger.

It turns out, fingers make poor earplugs, especially in tight quarters. The sound rattled the inside of the car, and my ears rang in a way that felt like I might have suffered permanent damage. Still, as long as Willow was playing Annie Oakley, I kept them plugged.

"Why are they shooting at us? Can't we just surrender?" I yelled, wondering if anyone could even hear me.

We drove in a crisscrossing pattern that I assumed was meant to give whoever had ambushed us a less . . . *stationary* target. One second I was colliding against the glass on my right, and the next I was crushing Natty as she was shoved against Jett on the other side of her. I was grateful I'd never been prone to motion sickness because this was like being on the world's worst roller coaster.

Willow, who was on her knees now as she crouched over the top of Simon and used his shoulders to support her elbows, hollered back at me, "That's what we're doing!"

It took me a second to process what she'd said. Surely I'd misheard her—maybe my ears really *had* suffered permanent damage.

There was a brief pause, and then Simon answered me. "Trust us—" he called back.

He was about to say more, but was cut off when a sudden jolt came from the front of the car. The entire vehicle shook, and then it wobbled hard, and eventually it just seemed to lose steam all at once.

Willow fell forward, smacking her head against the dash, and before she could regain her own balance, Thom reached around her waist and dragged her up again, so she was out of Simon's way while he wrestled with the steering wheel. This time, when the SUV bounced over the rocks at the side of the road, we rapidly lost speed, and the roller coaster felt more like bumper cars.

"What was that?" Natty asked.

"Spike strip," Simon replied. "They just blew out our tires." He slammed the brakes and shoved the car into park, his fingers working deftly to unbuckle his seat belt as he whipped around to face us. "Everyone, out. Now!"

But before I'd even released my own seat belt, I saw them. Coming out of the dark, and not just a few of them. We were surrounded.

"Kyra?" Jett said, glancing over at me, my hand frozen in place on my seat belt. "What is it?"

The rest of them couldn't see what I did. They couldn't see in the dark the way I could, and didn't know there was a legion of soldiers approaching, armed way beyond anything we had packed inside this car. "There are so many of them," I whispered, my voice shivering as I worried that those people out there might somehow be able to hear what I was saying. "They have guns. A lot of them," I relayed to my friends inside the car, not wanting anyone to get hurt.

"When you get out, keep your hands in the air," Simon ordered. "Don't make any sudden movements. These guys aren't messin' around."

I studied those approaching us. Some were shielded behind bandanas that masked their noses and mouths, looking like Wild West bandits, and others wore nothing over their faces, just leers.

Thom added, "Do as he says. Get out slowly, arms raised. Follow their orders." He opened his door, leading the way as he lifted his hands up in surrender. His last word was almost inaudible as at least five of those surrounding us descended on him. But I heard him call out, just before he landed on the ground, face first. "Submit."

Me, Natty, Jett, and Simon got out on our own, and were all thrown down the same way Thom had been, and suddenly all that scenery I'd been admiring—the desert—was in my nose and my eyes and inside my mouth, tasting a lot like the modeling clay I'd once licked off my fingers in first grade.

Willow had to be dragged out, and even though she'd just told me we were surrendering, she went down exactly as I'd expected her to: combatively. It wasn't pretty.

"They were warning shots, you idiots! Do you not know the difference?" she screamed when they finally pulled her, flailing, from the SUV. "Take your hands off me!"

I tried to see what was happening, but there was a knee digging in the center of my back, pinning me to the ground. All I could make out were the two front tires of our SUV, which were torn to scraps by the "spike strip" Simon said they'd used. I had to blink against all the sand being kicked around, scraping my eyes.

Above me, I heard the murmur of voices:

" . . . Griffin won't like this . . ."

"You freaks lost or somethin' . . . ?"

. . . and something about *" . . . familiar . . ."* but Willow's shouts made it impossible to hear the rest of what they were saying.

"*Let. Me. Go!*" Willow insisted again. There were boots grinding in the sand and bodies bumping together and grunting, lots of grunting. I couldn't pinpoint where any of it was coming from. One second it seemed far away, and the next it was right on top of me. But the entire time I heard Willow, screaming indignantly to be released.

I told myself this would be the perfect time to "get pissed" as Simon called it. Except I wasn't so sure what I would do, exactly. Move some sand around? And against what . . . an army of weapons?

Besides, those weapons they had weren't just aimed at one person. Even if I could manage to knock one of these guys out with a rock, or some other suitable object I just so happened to find lying in the middle of the desert, then what? Wouldn't that just make the others trigger-happy? I couldn't risk putting my friends in danger just to prove I had some control over this strange ability of mine.

After several seconds of struggling, there was the sickening flat and hollow sound of meat slapping against meat—and I knew someone had struck Willow. Then she was silent too.

I tried to roll away from whoever had me pinned, but Simon was right, these guys weren't messing around. And before I realized what happened, I felt a sharp slam against the side of my head. Stars swirled behind my eyelids and it took several attempts before my vision cleared. But unlike Willow, I only had to be warned once to stop my struggling.

When I was yanked to my feet, I saw Simon shoot a concerned glance my way.

"What?" I mouthed, trying not to draw any more attention than necessary.

Simon lifted one shoulder, indicating the right side of his face. But he didn't mean his face, he meant mine.

My face.

The guy who'd had his knee digging into my back let

go of my arm. I brushed my fingertips across my temple, to the place where he'd smacked me with his rifle. Tentatively, I pulled my fingers away and glanced down at them.

There was so much blood.

"Oh, no," I breathed. I glanced uneasily at the swarm of people who'd just disabled our vehicle and were holding us at gunpoint. "You're not . . . ," I started to ask the guy almost absently, and then my eyes shot back to Simon as I mouthed, "They're all . . . ?"

There were so many more of them than us, and they so didn't fit the image I'd conjured in my head ever since Jett had used the word "activists." I expected throwbacks to the Flower Power communes of the '60s rather than the militant-looking, gun-wielding combat mongers they'd turned out to be.

But now that I was looking—*really looking*—they appeared too much like normal people. The idea that I might have just poisoned them, the same way I had Tyler, made my knees wobbly.

Simon just shook his head, looking around at our abductors. "Returned," he mouthed back.

I exhaled audibly. They'd be okay. And then I realized that the kid next to me, on closer inspection, really was just a kid . . . a boy. He wore a sleeveless shirt and flexed biceps that were a little too defined for how short he was, almost like he had a kid-sized head on a man's body.

I realized then that my first impression of them was somehow . . . *off*.

It wasn't that they didn't have a military vibe, because they sort of did. But only in the sense that they all carried guns—rifles, handguns, that sort of thing. It was more the way they were dressed that I'd gotten wrong. These kids weren't dressed for combat, not like the guys back at the Tacoma facility, the ones wearing fatigues with the black grease paint smeared over their faces.

Heck, not even like Natty had dressed for this operation.

No, these kids looked more like they were heading out into the wilderness, ready to go backpacking or mountain climbing. They wore hiking gear—boots and vests. Plus there was that whole bandana thing. I didn't think it was Old West–y. Instead, I wondered if it wasn't for keeping the dust out.

I glanced uneasily at Simon, and then to Thom, silently letting them know what I thought of their having brought us here. Returned or not, we didn't belong here.

"How'd you do that?" the kid next to me asked curiously, when I'd healed in less than thirty seconds. "Never seen anyone do that before. Not that fast."

I was saved from having to explain when a girl with a shaved head shoved Simon from behind, giving him the *Start moving* signal.

"Where we going?" Simon asked, even as his shoes started crunching softly in the sand beneath him.

The girl shoved him again, harder this time. "No questions."

I got the same nudge, and without looking, I was pretty

sure Thom, Natty, Jett, and Willow had gotten it too. Since there were no more arguments coming from Willow, I assumed she'd finally taken Thom's advice and submitted.

Around us, the footfalls of dozens, maybe a hundred or more, fell in sync. We didn't bother trying to run. Our car was out of play and there was nowhere to go for miles. Even if there had been a town, who would we run to? The authorities were out of the question. Our parents, those of us who even still had parents, were just as bad—my own mom had tried to hand me over to Agent Truman in the first place. My dad . . . well, who knew where he was now.

We were on our own, and our best hope was here, holding us at gunpoint.

Seventeen minutes into our trek, Thom finally broke the silence. "Where's Griffin?" he asked.

We hadn't passed through any gates or enclosures of any kind, nothing to indicate that we'd entered their camp at all. As far as I was concerned, we were still in the middle of the desert.

"Busy," a boy I couldn't see answered, and a round of laughter rumbled through the group. I wasn't sure why, but for whatever reason, we were the butt of some joke, like our very presence was somehow amusing.

"Not too busy for us," Simon said. "Make sure Griffin gets word that Simon and Thom are here."

The girl pushing Simon along gave our two camp leaders the once-over. I couldn't tell if she was trying to be one of the boys with her hair cropped close like that, or if she just liked the way it looked. Her scalp was visible, but even that wasn't enough to make her pass as a guy, not with such delicate features and thick, black lashes. Somehow, she managed to make a shaved head look good. "I knew I recognized you," she spat, playing up her whole macho routine. "How you even gonna show your face here?" She looked around at the others—her cohorts. "Dude used to be one of us. But he couldn't cut it here, so he had to start his own camp," she explained before turning back to Simon. "These your pussy soldiers, leader boy? You thought you could take us in our own house?" She snorted, and so did the rest of them, laughing at us again. "Joke's on you, isn't it?"

"You come up with that theory all on your own?" Simon popped off. "You really think we came here to attack you?" He turned to Thom. "Nah. That can't be right. Griffin wouldn't let 'em think on their own." His skeptical gaze turned back to the girl. "That'd be dangerous. You don't wanna hurt that pretty little head of yours, do you, darlin'?" He winked at her then, which was definitely a mistake.

Her dark blue eyes flashed and she came at him. "I'm not your darlin', you piece of . . . ," she grunted as she rammed the butt of her rifle into his face.

Simon didn't even try to defend himself. I flinched as I heard that sound—which wasn't so much the sound of bone crunching as it was the surreal sound of Simon's nose as it dislocated when the base of her weapon smashed into it from the side.

He crumpled to the ground in front of her, falling on his

hands and knees, while she stood poised above him, panting and looking satisfied with herself. Blood pooled into the sand beneath him.

I couldn't tear my eyes away as I waited for one of them to move first. Either for Simon to retaliate, or for her to decide she hadn't satisfied her bloodlust just yet.

But they both stayed where they were. Eventually, Simon spat a mouthful of his own blood into the dirt. "The thing you haven't figured out yet is, Griffin's truth is twisted. The Returned should be working together, not turning on one another." His words came out mumbled, but we could understand him all the same.

Except no one cared what Simon had to say, and he was hauled to his feet once more, his face a bloodied and mangled mess.

"Move it!" the boy next to me said, pushing me in case I got the wrong idea and thought I had something to say too.

"What is this place?" I pressed my hand against the dirt-smeared window and looked outside.

This camp was nothing at all like sleepy Silent Creek. This was more like boot camp, with tents everywhere. Only these weren't the fun camping kind you slept in during summer excursions with your family. These were the heavy canvas tents of war. The ones with beat-up Humvees, or maybe even tanks, parked out front.

There were obstacle courses, too. Tall rope walls, and orange cones set up at regular intervals, and rows of tackle dummies—similar to the ones the football players used at my high school during practice. And even at this hour, several people were running in formation, their paces perfectly timed, military-style.

We were so not in Kansas anymore.

Thom's voice came from behind me as I stared out to the field beyond, watching the predawn drills. "To the outside world, it's one of those camps for troubled teens. The kind of place parents spend a small fortune on when they think their kids are doing drugs or being delinquents. Utah has a ton of those places since the laws are more lenient here for that kind of thing."

I moved out of Jett's way when he nudged me aside so he could pry yet another faceplate off one of the outlets, this time the one beneath the window where I'd been standing. He was on a mission to find some way to tap into their communications system. So far he'd pulled apart every outlet, wall plate, and even the overhead lights, trying to find the right combination of wires he might use to get a message out to the Silent Creekers so we could let them know we might be in over our heads here.

"It makes it easy to hide a bunch of teens in the desert," Thom went on. "Plus, no one ever questions why a group of minors always has cash for supplies when they do have to go into town."

"What about the guns?" I asked. "No one questions that either?"

Simon stopped pacing the creaky floorboards long

enough to answer. "The kind of people they buy weapons from don't care where they get their money."

Good point.

"How much longer do you think they'll hold us here?" All of us except Willow had been confined to a room with two army-style cots, a sink, and a toilet that sat smack between the two cots with absolutely nothing to shield it from view. As in, zero privacy.

It was suspiciously like being in jail, minus the bars and the supersweet orange jumpsuits. No one would tell us where Willow had been taken, and we were in no position to lodge a complaint.

"Not long," Thom said. "Griffin'll want to know exactly why we're here and what our end game is."

Natty looked up from the cot she was sitting on. "End game? Why does there have to be an end game?"

Simon and Thom shared a look. "There always is with Griffin."

"What aren't you telling us?" I asked, frustrated by this constant looking thing they were doing between the two of them. "What's the big mystery? You clearly have issues with this Griffin guy. And what was with that overblown welcome party? Who does that?"

Simon's grin was arrogant, and I braced myself for what was about to come. "It's safe here, Kyra. You don't need to be afraid. I'll take care of you."

I scowled back at him. "I don't need you to take care of

me, and I didn't say I was afraid." Even if I had been, there was no way I'd ever admit it to Simon. Especially not after he'd just landed us in Returned jail.

He crossed the crude planked floor and planted himself directly in front of me. I suddenly felt weird all over again, the same way I had right after I'd kissed him in front of the library. Like if I let my guard down, or gave him the right opportunity, he might take advantage and try to re-create that moment again.

Like he had feelings for me there was no way I could ever return.

Even though there was still blood crusted around his nose, from this close I could tell his injury was fully healed now. Still, I had to stop myself from reaching out to touch it . . . from asking if it still hurt. But I couldn't give him the wrong idea.

He reached for my hand and I started, not meaning to, but doing it all the same and then feeling like a jerk for making it seem like I was repulsed by him.

I wasn't. I just didn't want him touching me.

He didn't feel the same way, and he took my hands and drew me aside, looking at me so hard, so intently, my pulse throbbed. He lowered his voice. "Look, I know you think I'm joking, but I'm not." He glanced toward the others, and I did too.

Thom was still staring out the window. Natty stood quietly beside him now, but she was watching us. When she caught us looking, she ducked her head and turned away quickly, making me feel like we'd been caught doing something wrong.

My stomach twisted. Simon didn't seem to notice Natty's scrutiny, but then I felt his thumb stroke the back of my hand, and the twist turned to a full-blown tangle. I tried to pull my hand away, but his grip tightened.

My eyes widened and shot to his, but he just grinned in response. He moved closer until there was almost no space between us. His lips were right at my cheek, tickling my neck. His voice, though, was serious, and deadly quiet—the complete opposite of his playful veneer. "I need you to promise that whatever happens, you won't tell *anyone* what you can do. The moving things. You need to swear to me that you'll keep that a secret."

I closed my eyes against the feel of his breath on my skin. "What about . . . ?" It was an effort to reopen them, but when I did, I looked past him, past his shoulder, to where Natty was held rapt by Thom now. I could hear the low timbre of his voice, but not his words, as he stared down at her.

Just a few feet from them, Jett fumbled inside the wall, pulling away pieces of drywall in an effort to get at the cluster of wires.

Simon just shook his head, and his nose brushed against my hair. "We have to hope she doesn't say anything. Griffin can't find out." His fingers closed around mine, strong and firm. He was begging me to promise.

But I wanted something else. "Why did you and Thom

bring us here?" I whispered back.

"We had to go someplace. We had to get you guys off the road, and out of harm's way." His brows squeezed together, his copper eyes searching my face. "Griffin's unconventional, but we have allies here. I swear it."

His palm slipped up and cupped my cheek.

I bit back a gasp. "Simon." It was as close as I could manage to a rebuke.

I couldn't let him do these things . . . touch me this way. It was hard to even say that one word, though, and I was worried that if he pushed the issue, I might not have the strength to elaborate. To tell him I needed him to stay away from me. Or that I would never, ever like him the way I thought he wanted me to.

My heart was crashing so hard, and so forcefully, that I almost didn't hear the door when it was flung open . . . not until it collided against the inside wall.

The blue-eyed girl with the shaved head—Simon's new BFF—stood in the doorway, glaring at us . . . at Simon most of all. I moved my face away, so he was no longer touching me, and pulled my hand from his.

But I was too late—she'd noticed. Her condemning glare moved from my hands to Simon. "Come on," she dictated to him.

"Wait!" I said in a rush. "What about the rest of us? You're not leaving us here, are you?"

Jett jumped up, doing his best to block the gaping hole he'd made in the wall. "Where are you taking him?"

"None'a your business," she shot back.

"Don't worry. I got this." Simon gave me an overconfident nod, and then turned his less-than-convincing charms back on the girl. "So, that's it? No '*Nice to see you*' or '*I've missed you*' or '*Where have you been all my life?*' Just '*Come on*'?" he taunted her, and I wanted to tell him to just, for once, shut his mouth and do as he was told. But it was useless. He was Simon—it wasn't in him to leave well enough alone.

"And you," Buzz Cut told Jett before closing the door behind them. "Stop messing with the wiring. If you start a fire, no one's comin' in here to save your asses."

When the lock snapped into place, Jett's gaze shot around the room, moving from one place to the next as he searched for something. "Dammit," he cursed when he finally found what he'd been looking for.

He approached the metal paper towel dispenser mounted to the wall right beside the dingy porcelain sink. I didn't get it; it looked like an ordinary dispenser to me, the same kind you saw in crappy restaurants and schools and rest stops all around the country.

Jett hooked both hands inside the lower lip, where the next paper towel was poking through waiting to be pulled free. He yanked the painted metal as hard as he could and the top burst open with a screech, sending a stack of brown paper towels tumbling free.

Inside, Jett retrieved a small, round lens that was obviously some sort of surveillance device.

"Should'a seen this," he grumbled, pocketing the gadget. "They were watching us this whole time." He ran his fingers around the metal cover one more time before letting it slam shut once more. "Too bad it's wireless, I might've been able to use the hardware."

Thom scanned the room, and then his fingers laced through Natty's.

Natty shot me a timid glance, her cheeks flushing.

"We should assume they're listening too," Thom said as he dragged Natty against him, and that was that—the mystery of Thom and Natty was solved. "Don't say anything you don't want them hearing."

CHAPTER TWELVE

BY THE TIME IT WAS MY TURN, BUZZ CUT HAD already come back for everyone else, and I was the last one left. Five hours and thirteen minutes had passed since she'd first come to take Simon away.

Now it was well past eleven in the morning, which meant it was already hot in the Utah desert, and even hotter inside the sweltering closed-up space where we'd been confined. The sun beat down against the one-and-only bolted-closed window, and no matter how much dirt was caked over the outside of it, there wasn't enough to filter out the escalating heat.

Sometime after nine, when Natty was still with me, we'd tried to block the window using one of the thin blankets in the cell. But there'd been nothing to secure it with, and eventually we'd given up.

It was a relief when it was finally my turn, and suddenly the unknown was better than sweating it out—literally—in what had turned from jail cell to sweat lodge. So I was surprised when, instead of being led to some other stuffy room, like some sort of interrogation cell with two-way mirrors, I was led to an enormous shower area.

"Clean up," Buzz Cut ordered, shoving a towel and stack of borrowed clothes at me.

Despite the layers of grime and the rust-colored sand that clung to me, I bristled at the command, and thought about telling her where she could shove it. *I do not want that shower,* I lied to myself.

But she cleared up any misgivings about whether it was an option or not when she said, "Do it or I'll throw you back in the holding cell and you can sweat it out there the rest of the week."

Problem solved. I was definitely showering.

And it was totally worth it. After the morning I'd had, the campground-style, communal showers were like stepping into a luxury spa—a serious indulgence.

I stayed beneath the stream of hot water for a lifetime, which was more than enough time to scrub away not only the dirt, but the residual blood that was dried along my hairline. I rolled my neck and stretched my shoulders, and when my fingers started to prune, I finally turned off the nozzle and toweled off.

Using my fingers, I combed out the tangles from my hair and slipped into the clean clothes she'd loaned me: a loose-fitting pair of sweatpants and a T-shirt that was so threadbare it felt like air against my newly clean skin. I knotted the end of the shirt to keep from being swallowed up by it.

I spent way too long in front of the mirror, looking at the stranger with the russet-colored hair who could no longer pass as Bridget Hollingsworth—the girl on the fake ID Simon had given me. Bridget had looked too much like the old me.

I wondered what kind of name this stranger might have. She could be a different Bridget, I supposed, but she could just as easily be a Maddy or a Mikayla, or maybe even a Kaci with an *i*.

I pressed my hand to the mirror, wondering, too, where Simon and the others were right now. And if they'd been here, in this exact place, before me. Had we really come all this way only to be taken captive?

I jumped, hastily lowering my hand, when the door opened behind me. I expected to see Buzz Cut come marching in. Only this time, there was another girl coming inside, carrying a plate covered with a red-and-white-checked napkin. Buzz Cut was still there, standing vigilantly on the other side of the door, but she stayed where she was. The new girl gave a single nod to Buzz Cut, then pushed the door closed with her hip.

I watched expectantly. This new girl wasn't like Buzz Cut, who looked like she wanted to be one of the boys. Her long hair was dark and shiny, and was pulled away from her bronzed skin, and her brown eyes held me captive as she watched me back. Her skintight jeans showed off her lean legs, and even with her combat boots, she managed to look as if she'd been peeled straight from the pages of *Vogue*.

She kept a considerate distance, as if to say I was calling the shots, rather than the other way around. When she pulled back the corner of the napkin, revealing a plate of neatly arranged apple slices, clusters of green and purple grapes, and wedges of yellow cheeses, she said, "You might not be hungry—we almost never are—but you should still eat." Her smile was almost sad, and suddenly I felt like I wasn't alone in the whole missing-food thing.

I couldn't help questioning the offer of food . . . or the melancholy smile. If the gesture was calculated, it was a pretty good show—I had to give her that much. But it wasn't like I was going anywhere, and she was right, it wouldn't do me any good *not* to eat.

I eased down on the nearest wooden bench. There were rows of them, all with peeling paint, and all bolted to the tile floor. She set the plate down in front of me.

"Where are Simon and the others?" I asked when she straddled the bench, opposite the plate.

She just watched me for several long seconds.

Despite the circumstances, I couldn't help but be fascinated by her. She was more than just pretty. There was something mesmerizing about her, about the purse of her lips and the way her dark eyes felt like they understood you—like she knew you—that made you want to just . . . *look* at her. I found myself searching for the right thing to say, and had to remind myself she wasn't my friend.

"It's safe here," she said instead of answering my question. She glanced around the locker room, but I knew that wasn't what she meant.

She was talking about this place, this camp, and I immediately thought of the way Simon had said that very same thing to me, right before he'd been taken away. That I was safe, and that he'd protect me, and that I had nothing to be afraid of.

So why wasn't I convinced?

"You're not what I was expecting." There was no point pretending I trusted her. I reached for one of the polished green grapes and bit into it.

Food might not exactly be the same anymore, but fruit somehow tasted less *cardboard*-y than most other things. It might not be powdered-doughnut good or anything, but it was the closest to the taste I remembered from before.

She crossed her arms, a small frown pushing her brows together. "What were you expecting?"

I chose another grape, purple this time. I let the juice, sweeter than the green one, roll over my tongue. Shrugging, I answered, "I don't know. I guess I thought I'd be grilled, maybe get the whole good-cop, bad-cop routine, while you guys tried to find out what we're doing here."

I smiled because saying it out loud made it sound kind of absurd. "Maybe a little waterboarding."

She smiled too, and I was bombarded by a sensation of wanting to please her. If she was anything, she was definitely the good cop. "What makes you think I'm not here for information?"

I pulled off a corner of the cheese, forcing myself to remember she was one of them—part of the camp holding us captive. "Just so you know, I don't know anything important." I wasn't lying, at least not yet. The computers were Jett's department, and weapons were Willow's area of expertise. Simon was so damn secretive that even if there was anything to know, he never would have told me anyway.

I glanced at my watch. 12:52. I wished she'd just get to the point. I wanted to be taken to where Simon and Jett and the others had been moved to already.

"Why are we being held like this? We didn't do anything wrong. When can I see my friends?" I met her deep brown eyes and tried to decide if there was anything unusual about them, like Simon's and Natty's, and Buzz Cut's, whose blue was so charged, it practically pulsed. This girl's cocoa-color eyes were deep and rich, but also very ordinary. Outside, I could hear voices yelling—the sounds of drills being called. I itched to look down at my watch again, but I held firm on the girl, determined not to give her any insight on me.

She shifted her weight and I purposely avoided looking at her as she uncrossed her arms. "Let me ask you a question, Kyra." Hearing her say my name shouldn't have surprised me. I'm sure they all knew who we were by now, but there was something about the way she said it. Her voice was low and she leaned forward expectantly. "Who is it you belong to? Simon or Thom?" She examined me closely, and that feeling of wanting her to like me vanished. Now I just wanted her to stop staring.

Her choice of wording made my skin itch.

I might feel a certain amount of loyalty to each of them, for different reasons, but I was my own person. I made my own choices. "I don't *belong* to either of them," I insisted.

"Ooh, a loner. I like that." She got to her feet and stared down at me now. "We could use a girl like you around here."

When she reached down and pushed a piece of my damp hair from my face, I jerked away from her. "Who are you? Where's Griffin? I think there's some confusion—we just came here because we needed a place to hide . . ."

She folded her arms over her chest. "There's no confusion. We know why you're here."

Except I was still confused. "So . . . why hold us prisoner like this? I thought the Returned worked together. . . ."

"There are a lot of things you still don't understand, although I can't say I'm totally surprised. Simon does that, keeps things to himself; he was always that way. And Thom's no better—he's always been a man of few words. Even when they were here, it was hard to know what either of them was thinking."

"So . . . you . . . *you knew them*?" She had my full attention then. It hadn't crossed my mind, that she'd been here when they had. That this girl might know things about them, and their pasts, that I didn't.

She sighed, giving me a conciliatory look. "You really have no clue, do you?"

There was a sharp rap on the door, and then Buzz Cut stepped inside. The brown-eyed girl was halfway across the room before the door had even swished closed again.

I couldn't quite put my finger on it, but I was riveted by the two of them, by the way they interacted. It was *off* somehow. Buzz Cut sat tight, just inside the doorway, until she was invited to join the other girl. And when she did, she kept her voice low and her hands at her sides. I couldn't quite name her demeanor, but she was well-mannered. Quiet.

Not at all the way she'd been with me, and almost the exact opposite of the way she'd been with Simon.

When she was finished, Buzz Cut waited stiffly for a response, which was also whispered. It made me wish I had super-hearing on top of the whole seeing-in-the-dark thing, because I was dying to know what they were saying.

It was okay, though, because I'd figured something out just by watching them, and I felt stupid for not realizing it sooner.

I waited until Buzz Cut had shut the door, leaving us alone again. "Oh my god," I accused. "*You're* Griffin. You're *the guy* we came here to see." No wonder she knew so much about Simon and Thom. *She* was the reason we were here. *She* was the person they thought would help us.

The girl put her hands together once, twice, three times

in a long, slow clap as she appraised me, as if seeing me in a whole new light. "And here I was, starting to think you might be on the slow side. Took you long enough."

I ignored the jab, because it wasn't like she'd given me a lot to work with, what with the whole you-should-eat act, and the *You're safe, trust me* thing. How was I supposed to know she was the one in charge of this operation? "What kind of name is Griffin? For a girl, I mean?" I jabbed back.

Her expression closed off. "My dad wanted a son. I was something of a disappointment."

It was a sad answer, if it was an honest one, and it made me wonder how old she was, or where she'd been born. The idea of being a letdown simply because of your gender was foreign to me, completely antiquated. I could hardly fathom it.

My dad had never made me feel anything but wanted, loved . . . cherished. Suddenly the comment about her name made me feel like I'd sucker-punched her for no good reason. "Sorry," I said, wishing I could take it back. "I didn't mean . . ."

She tried waving it off. "Don't give it a second thought. I don't. Water under the bridge, so to speak. Old news." But the waver in her voice made me think it wasn't *such* old news.

She recovered like a champ, and came back with that same smile she'd been wearing when she'd first walked in, like she was trying for a do-over. "So here's the thing," she said. "I feel like we've gotten off on the wrong foot. What can I do to fix that?" I wondered if she knew how transparent she was.

But I wanted answers, and maybe if I played along, I could get a few before she revealed her true intentions.

What was it Thom had said? There was always an end game with Griffin.

I plucked up a slice of apple and leaned back on the bench. I had to tread carefully. Griffin wasn't stupid. "So if you guys were friends—you and Simon and Thom—then why are we being treated like this? Why ambush us at all?"

She took her spot on the bench again, facing me, and I tried to gauge her reaction. She was definitely suspicious, and regarded me warily. If we'd been predators, it would have been hard to tell just who was circling who. But I knew she was the one who held all the real power here. She might want me to answer some of her questions, but ultimately, we were in *her* custody.

"First," she started, "I never said we were friends. I said *I knew them*. Second, you were wrong when you said you're being held prisoners. You're not. But look at this from my perspective: You guys just show up here, with absolutely no warning at all, saying you're being chased by the Daylighters. For all I know, you've just led those sons-a-bitches right to our doorstep. You can't fault me for wantin' to take some *precautions*." She took a grape from my plate and slid it into her mouth. "We can never be too careful. Surely you've learned that much?"

I nodded. "Fair enough. But I have some questions too." When she gave an unenthusiastic shrug and turned to inspect her cuticles, I took that as my cue to continue. "Why aren't you friends?" Her eyes slid up from her nails, so I elaborated. "You said you knew Thom and Simon, but you said you weren't friends. Why is that?"

"Actually," she corrected smugly, "I didn't say that either. You need to pay better attention. I never said whether we were friends *or not.*" She put extra emphasis on the "or not," and I got the sense she got off on playing mind games, twisting everything around until you weren't sure what your original point even was.

I decided to play my own game—the waiting game—and I refused to give her the slightest hint that she was getting to me. Instead of checking my nails, I tapped my foot to a song only I could hear, settling on "Womanizer" by Britney Spears, not because I loved the song or anything but because it was the first beat that popped into my head.

I felt a huge sense of satisfaction, like I'd just won the lottery or something, when Griffin blinked first, saying: "We *were* once—the three of us. We were close. I thought I could trust them back then, that I could count on them." She made a sour face. "Turns out you can never count on anyone but yourself. They were as undependable as everyone else I've ever trusted."

I tried to attach that word to either of them, Simon or Thom—undependable—but I couldn't make it fit. They were a lot of other things . . . things she'd said. Simon was secretive, plus he was annoying as hell, and Thom was soft-spoken and reserved.

But undependable? Not in my experience.

"What happened to change things between you?" I asked.

"Did you know they used to be the best of friends?" Griffin asked, her brown eyes glittering like she was telling me something off-limits.

I was stunned, but maybe I shouldn't have been. Maybe I should've guessed all along. Only people who really knew each other, and who cared what the other thought, could get under each other's skin so thoroughly.

"They once considered themselves brothers. Better than brothers. They used to say their bond was stronger because it hadn't been forged by the mere circumstance of birth, something as *incidental* as a shared womb." *It's true,* her nod confirmed. "No, they shared something even more important: experiences. They'd *chosen* to be family, to stand side by side and have each other's backs, no matter what." My curiosity was ripe. The idea of Simon and Thom once being brother-like was almost as impossible as the idea of sharing DNA with aliens.

Griffin kept going. "They believed those bonds were the hardest to break. Except that wasn't exactly true. They might not break, but they could certainly be stressed—tested and weathered—and those stresses could cause chinks that ultimately led to fractures." It was almost as if she were repeating a story, the way she spoke. One she'd repeated again and again, like some twisted fairy tale. She reminded me of an elementary school teacher reading during story time, dropping her voice for effect and using exaggerated facial expressions.

Griffin was like that: theatrical.

I asked again, "What happened?"

When she blinked, her composure faltered and her vision drifted back into focus, and she seemed surprised to find me sitting across from her, almost as if she'd forgotten she wasn't alone. "A girl," she answered haltingly. "It all came apart over a girl."

It took her a moment to recover, but when she did, her eyes brightened. "You should've known them before all that. They were different people then. We all were." She shook her head longingly. "We used to have so much fun together as recruiters.

"Our job was to go out and find the new Returned and bring them back here," she explained. "We did that by making them feel safe, special. We were the best at what we did. It wasn't hard. We each had our own techniques, and we were damn good at it. It wasn't necessarily intentional, but the girls were always drawn to Thom and Simon. You wouldn't know it now, but the two of them together were very . . . *charming*, and those poor girls were scared and vulnerable. They needed someone they could lean on. A shoulder . . . or two."

No matter how uncomplicated Griffin tried to make Simon and Thom's relationship sound, it *was* almost impossible to imagine. All I'd witnessed were the two of them avoiding, antagonizing, or barely tolerating each other.

Friends . . . the "best of friends" . . . crazy.

But Griffin just kept talking. "By the time Simon and Thom had explained what had happened to them—where they'd been taken and how they'd been . . . *changed*—those girls were willing to follow Simon and Thom anywhere, to become the newest member of the Blackwater Ranch. *We* had become her new family." She grinned, her shrug less than coy. "Me, I had different assets. I was in charge of recruiting the boys."

I thought of the almost-spell I'd fallen under when I'd first met her, the way I'd wanted her to like me, and I could only imagine how unsuspecting boys might feel around her, wanting to please her, to make her notice them. I felt a little queasy thinking of the three of them using their *charms* to persuade people to join their camp.

"And what if someone didn't want to be part of your *family*?"

Griffin's smile slipped as her eyes narrowed. "The doors were always open. Franco never forced anyone to stay."

Franco? I'd never heard that name before, but it wasn't tough to guess he'd been in charge back then . . . back when Griffin and Simon and Thom had been "recruiters." I wondered if Griffin had used her *assets* to scheme her way to the top.

"If everything was so great here, why did Simon and Thom leave?"

"Weren't you even listening?" Griffin scowled. "Their

friendship, that bond I mentioned, when push came to shove, it all fell apart over a girl."

"What girl? Where is she now?"

Griffin laughed, but not like I'd said something amusing and she was laughing *with* me. It was more like I'd said something stupid and she was laughing *at* me. "I love it. *Love. It.*" She clapped her hands together. "I can't believe no one's told you. All this time, and no one's clued you in." She bit her lip, her eyes bright. She couldn't wait to drop this bomb; it was written all over her face.

"Oh, for Pete's sake, just say it." I sighed heavily.

"Willow." She spat the name quickly, like she didn't want it in her mouth for too long. Then she sat back and waited for my response.

My mouth fell open. "*Our* . . . Willow?" I finally managed, super slowly, because the very idea was so . . . out there. "The one we came here with?" But I already knew it was *that* Willow. How many Willows were there? "I don't understand." I hadn't even realized Thom knew Willow, at least not before Silent Creek.

I could tell Griffin was loving this, having the upper hand. "I figured as much . . . that whole secret-keeping thing Simon does."

"So, what'd she do, exactly? How did she come between them?"

"In case you haven't figured it out for yourself, Willow's toxic. She's dangerous and she's toxic. If it hadn't been for *your Willow*, things might never have changed. We had a good thing going before she came along. I can't believe Simon thought he could bring her back here after all these years."

I frowned. "It's not like we had a lot of options. We needed your help. Besides, I think you have the wrong idea about Willow."

Griffin's jaw tightened and her fists clenched. "And *you* have a lot to learn about who you can and can't trust," she stated, leaving little room for argument.

"Where is she?" I asked, thinking of the way Willow had been separated from us from the start. "Where's Willow now?"

Griffin got up, her brown eyes sending a shiver of warning up my spine. "She's fine. For now." Her boots echoed off the tiles as she strode toward the door. "I could be your ally, Kyra—you should remember that."

CHAPTER THIRTEEN

Day Thirty

Blackwater Ranch

NOT BEING A PRISONER WAS AN AWFUL LOT LIKE being a prisoner, despite what Griffin said.

The only positive side of my captivity was that I hadn't been forced into solitary confinement since Natty and I had been assigned to be *not*-cellmates. While that part was awesome, we hadn't had word from Simon, Thom, Willow, or Jett in two whole days, which felt like an eternity when you hardly slept and were basically under house arrest.

Two new sunrises to endure, both of which felt like they were getting worse. More painful. And two days of letting our imaginations wander. It was a dangerous pastime, especially when the person detaining you was a gun-toting whack job holding a grudge.

Natty and I had been moved, and our new accommodations were less jail-like and more bunk-like, and now I understood what all the tents here were used for: barracks. Our tent was not what I'd call luxurious, but it was the smell that bothered me most, a combination of dank mold and mildew, which seemed odd considering we were surrounded by nothing but sand.

We were pretty easy to guard, though, since there was only a single tent flap leading inside, with no windows or vents to circulate the stale air.

But at least in the two days we'd been here, I'd had a few opportunities to practice my ability.

"You stand guard," I whisper-told Natty, in case Buzz Cut, who refused to tell me her real name, was lingering somewhere on the other side of our tent.

Natty hopped off her bunk and positioned herself in front of the inside of our tent flap. "Maybe this time it'll work," she said, her eyes gleaming expectantly, and I wondered if this was how she'd looked back when she'd waited for *Little House on the Prairie* to come on.

Half grinning, I turned to the pile of discarded clothes I'd left in a heap on the floor. I tried to tap into that frenzied state of frustration Simon had convinced me was responsible for sparking my newfound skill. But it wasn't always easy to summon.

The "getting pissed" approach was tough, mostly because

it was hard to find someone to get mad at. I'd already tried Austin, Tyler's brother and my ex-boyfriend. Austin and I had spent our whole lives falling in love, and when I'd been returned, I'd still loved him. Only that hadn't been enough for Austin. He'd already moved on. With my best friend.

For me, I'd only been gone one night, so it didn't feel like he'd waited *long enough*. But in reality, five years was a crazy long time.

Besides, every time I forced myself to think of him and Cat together, some other random memory would bubble to the surface and ruin all hopes of staying angry. Like the one time when Austin's mom decided he and I should dress like Batman and Catwoman for Halloween, which would've been adorable in the fourth grade, except that I'd decided it would be even better if we switched costumes instead. Austin hadn't even complained, because, back then, he'd done almost everything I asked. And the moment I pictured nine-year-old Austin stuffed into my shiny, skintight black suit with those precious cat ears perched lopsidedly on his head, all of my focus vanished and suddenly I was homesick all over again.

I tried being mad at my mom's new husband, Grant, too. But even that failed, because as much as I wanted to blame him for ruining my family, deep down I knew that was all my fault too. If I hadn't gotten out of the car that night on Chuckanut Drive, I never would've vanished and my parents might still be together.

Agent Truman didn't work either.

Three days had passed since our run-in at the Tacoma facility, which meant the poor schmuck was probably dead by now. And no matter how I tried to look at it, no matter how blameworthy he was for luring us there and trapping Willow, I couldn't choke down my own guilt for what I'd done to free her—that whole Code Red thing.

I bent down and plucked the paperback I'd stolen from the library back in Columbia Valley from the back pocket of my discarded jeans, my mind drifting to Tyler instead. He would never have chosen Cat over me. He would never have given up on me the way Austin had.

Wasn't that what he'd written in chalk on the street in front of my house, what he'd promised?

I'll remember you always . . .

And to repay him, I'd gone and let Simon kiss me back.

It turned out Simon had been right: getting pissed was the key to my telekinesis. Only I didn't have to be mad at someone else. Apparently self-loathing was enough.

I was barely concentrating when it happened: when my T-shirt lifted off the tent floor, hovering in midair for several long, and otherwise impossible seconds.

Natty yelped from her spot near the entrance, and a flush of adrenaline coursed through me.

I did it! I totally did it!

My heart was fighting tooth-and-nail to escape my chest as I reached out and stomped on the T-shirt, suddenly worried that someone—Buzz Cut or Griffin or anyone—might bulldoze their way inside and see it there, floating in the air.

When I turned to Natty, her smile grew. "I knew you could do it," she breathed.

I didn't know if I shared her confidence or if I was convinced I would be able to do it again, but inside, I was positively giddy. It was enough that I'd made that shirt float like that, and I was claiming it as a giant-exceptional-*ginormous* victory. My little telekinetic thing was gaining momentum.

Morning drifted into late afternoon as I sat on my bunk and paged through the book I'd discovered in my jeans pocket. I'd given up trying to read it hours ago. I hadn't expected to have such a hard time getting into it, especially since it was about a guy who believed aliens had abducted him. You'd think it would be right up my alley.

Not to mention Tyler had read it, so surely it should have been worth pushing through.

But instead of reading the *actual* book, I found myself flipping to the back, to the tiny paragraph about the author. To where there was this guy with wild, curly hair who didn't look like such a big deal, even though I knew this book, *Slaughterhouse-Five*, was kind of a huge deal—one of those award-winning books that teachers and librarians loved to shove down your throat and find hidden meaning in.

His bio mentioned his other books, and I skimmed over the list until I got to the part about how during World War II he'd been a German prisoner. That's where I kept getting stuck, like that was the thing we had in common, he and I, not stuff about the alien abductions.

That we'd both been taken against our will. That we'd both lost significant chunks of our lives.

And so it goes . . .

That was a line in his book, something his main character, Billy Pilgrim, says whenever something just was the way it was.

As in, *such is life*, or it was out of his hands and there was nothing he could do about it.

I didn't know if I could have that same attitude, and maybe that's why I couldn't get into the actual book. I wasn't sure I felt like that: *And so it goes.*

Because, to me, you shouldn't just accept whatever came your way. I wasn't willing to have things happen to me, and just shrug and say, "And so it goes." I didn't want to be passive.

For my sake and for Tyler's and my dad's, and anyone else I cared about, I wanted to be willing to do more. To risk more. To stand up and say, "Screw that. It won't go that way. I won't let it."

So rather than reading, all I'd really done for the past several hours was to use the book as a journal of sorts, since I'd left mine back at Silent Creek. I made notes in the margins—thoughts about my time here, and about Griffin, and everything she'd told me about Simon and Thom and Willow. I wrote random things about Tyler and my dad.

And for the first time in days, I had the chance to draw.

I drew pathways and birdcages and feathers, like the ones

Tyler had drawn for me in chalk—although mine looked more like a kindergartner had sketched them.

I drew fireflies. Everywhere, fireflies. On the inside flaps, on the cover, all over the pages of the book . . . even on the palm of my hand.

And so it goes, I guess.

The tent flap wavered and Buzz Cut's voice filtered into our musty space. "Drills."

I shoved the book beneath my pillow and bolted upright. I was more than ready to get outside, and wished they hadn't waited so long to come get us. This part of our day, joining the rigid workout routines of the other campers, even if it meant heading out beneath the blazing hot sun, had quickly become my favorite part. A bright spot amid the dull routine of aimless pacing, scratching out games of tic-tac-toe in the floorboard dust, and our one daily trip to the cafeteria, where we ate even if we weren't hungry because it was more interesting than sitting in our tent.

Plus, I had my book-slash-journal now too, so there was that.

For a camp of not-troubled teens, Griffin kept these kids in tip-top shape. The drills were brutal. On the first day, after only an hour, I thought the combination of exertion and heat would make me puke, and I wanted nothing more than to collapse on the ground, but the athlete in me knew that would only make the cramping worse, so I'd forced myself to take small sips of water and walk it off, until the excruciating stitch in my side had faded to something closer to a dull ache.

Still, when Buzz Cut had called us to drills again yesterday, I'd jumped at the chance.

I'd do it each and every day we were here if it meant not staying cooped inside this musty tent all day. Or if there was even the slightest chance I might get a glimpse of Willow or Simon or any of the others.

So far, though, they'd managed to keep us separated enough that we never ran into one another. And Buzz Cut refused to answer whether it was only Natty and me who were allowed outside.

I was *this close* to changing her name to Buzz Kill.

Slipping on the athletic sneakers we'd been given, Natty shot me an eager look. We'd been doing our best to speak as little as possible, trying to develop our own silent version of communication in order to avoid being eavesdropped on. But Natty wore her emotions all over her face. Her codes weren't all that hard to crack.

"Me too," I told her while I drew my hair back into a ponytail, not bothering to hide my enthusiasm from Buzz Cut.

When we got outside, I leaned my head back, absorbing as much of the sun's radiation as I could until my cheeks were good and smoldering. According to my pink watch, it was nearly six o'clock, and there wasn't a whole lotta sun left for the day.

We were passed off to the drill instructor, the same short guy who'd smacked me with his rifle when they'd ambushed us in the desert. His freakishly developed body made sense now that I knew the workout regimen he put his people through on a daily basis.

He rolled his eyes, making it crystal clear we were a burden he didn't care to be hampered with, but he stepped aside nonetheless, letting us join the rest of his squad, where they were already on the ground doing push-ups.

Training like this made me feel alive. And if I closed my eyes, I could almost imagine I was back in Burlington, on the softball field with my coach calling out the drills and blowing her whistle. The only difference was *this* coach had a squat body and Popeye-sized forearms.

By the time we were running, I had sweat dripping down the center of my back and stinging my eyes. I was buzzing with energy even while I was wilting from the heat. But from day one it had been obvious Natty wasn't exactly built for this kind of conditioning, and it was a challenge for her just to keep up. For her the only benefit of the exercise was being outdoors. Watching her run, the way she clomp-clomped along like her feet were made of iron, was almost painful, and the actual act of sweating repulsed her, something she complained about so much I wouldn't have felt totally guilty to leave her in the dust.

Unfortunately, part of us being prisoners meant we were also bound to the buddy system, and Natty had been assigned as my official "buddy."

"Look," she panted. "Look." The second time she said it, the word came out as an airy wheeze.

It took me a second to follow her rising and falling finger, and eventually see what she was trying to point to.

I almost stopped moving then, which almost surely would have gotten me banned from the daily drills, messing them up like that, but I caught myself in time and found my stride again.

She'd been pointing at Griffin. But not just Griffin—Jett was there too.

I squinted, trying to get a better look from where we were, which was suddenly far too far away from where they were on the opposite side of the field, over near the cafeteria. "What do you think they're doing?" I asked, never taking my eyes away from Jett, who was walking alongside the Blackwater Ranch leader. He was clutching his laptop to his chest, and from where we were, it looked like Griffin was carrying something too. "Is that . . . ?" I lifted my hand to my eyes, trying to shield them from the sun. "It looks like she has Simon's backpack," I told Natty.

Natty saw too, and she nodded. "Yeah," she rasped. "Think . . . so . . ."

"You think Jett's helping her? That they finally cracked the codes to those files?"

I glanced quickly at Natty. She lifted her eyebrows and I realized it was her equivalent of a shrug.

"I wish I knew what the hell was going on here. And why they're keeping us apart."

Griffin and Jett stopped outside one of the few non-tent buildings here, one with a real foundation and wooden walls and crisp white paint that I'd noticed on our way to the cafeteria. I watched as Griffin knocked once before letting herself, and then Jett, inside. It was weird that she'd have to knock at all since *she* was the leader here.

I was about to ask Natty what she made of that when I realized we were no longer alone. Our drill instructor had joined us, keeping pace alongside Natty. Unlike Natty, whose cheeks were flushed so red she looked like an enormous sticky tomato, he'd hardly broken a sweat.

Even though he was several inches shorter, he somehow managed to look down his nose at us. "Since you ladies can't seem to keep up, why don't you hit the showers?"

"What? No, we're fine. Really." I knew I was only speaking for me, but I wasn't ready to go back to our tent for the night.

But Natty was more than willing to take the out, and her plodding stopped and she bent at the waist, gasping for breath. We didn't need a secret language to know she'd had enough "fresh air" for one day.

I guessed my buddy and I were hitting the showers.

I was frustrated with Natty for getting us kicked out of drills, and with the drill instructor, who gave me a cheerful wave as he took off with the rest of his squad, only too happy to be rid of us, and then with Buzz Cut, who swooped in the second we'd been eighty-sixed so she could escort us to the showers. It wasn't that I couldn't use a shower—I totally could, I stunk as bad as Natty, maybe worse after that sweat fest out there. It was just that I wasn't looking forward to another all-night tic-tac-toe marathon.

We took our time, just like we did with everything now that time was all we had, and when I was finished, I wiped the steam from the face of my watch. It had to be dark out by now, I realized, as I tossed my sweaty clothes in the hamper, following Natty on our way out the door.

It was cooler now, too, as I trailed after her, letting her lead the way along the path to the cafeteria, which was our next stop.

Buzz Cut stiff-armed me across my chest. "Not you," she said, her voice low. And then she nodded toward another girl who'd been waiting in the shadows. "Take her." The *her* in question was Natty, and Natty shot me a questioning look, but I didn't have the answers she was looking for.

"Why? What's happening now?" Suddenly tic-tac-toe with *my buddy* didn't sound half-bad.

Buzz Cut just thrust her chin at the other girl once more, and Natty was towed away through the gloom, toward the cafeteria.

I told myself it was fine and tried to channel my inner Billy Pilgrim—the whole *And so it goes* attitude. But telling myself it was fine and convincing myself were two different things, and the acids in my stomach surged with anticipation.

Although I could see fine in the dark, it would be easy to get turned around in a camp like this, where the tents were so packed together, each looking like the next. I stayed close to Buzz Cut as she slipped in and out among them.

The night air was crisp with the smell of scorched clay, and my feet crunched lightly in the sand beneath me. Above us, the night was perforated by thousands of white lights that were somehow brighter out here in the middle of the desert, probably *because* it was so dark.

When Buzz Cut finally stopped, somewhere near the edge of the tents, I examined the stars. From where I stood, I could almost imagine they were far-off fireflies, swarming, and emerging from the sky to warn of a taking.

The last time I'd seen the fireflies, I'd been holding Tyler's hand and assuring him everything would be okay, while wishing with all my heart that was true. I'd give anything—*anything*—to undo what I'd done to him—taking him to Devil's Hole, exposing him to my blood . . . falling in love with him in the first place. If I hadn't done that, then he never would have been hurt at all.

And then, I wouldn't be here right now.

"I thought maybe we were gonna have to send a search party after you." Simon's voice was barely a rustle, stirring the cooling night air around me.

When I spun around, he was there, watching me intently with those copper eyes of his. His arms were crossed casually over his chest as he leaned against the canvas wall behind him. "Simon," I exhaled on a shaky laugh, breathing easier now that I knew he was alive. "You're okay." I still had about a million and one questions for him, but I started with "What about Willow and Jett and Thom? Have you seen them? Are they okay too?"

"I haven't seen them, but they're fine," he assured me before I could ask anything else. He looked to Buzz Cut, who nodded, almost like she was confirming what he'd just told me.

But that couldn't be right, could it?

My gaze shifted, alternating between him and Buzz Cut. "I . . . I don't understand . . ." I faltered.

Simon's eyes crinkled as he pushed away from the wall and sauntered toward me, his eyes appraising me as if he could see as clearly in the dark as I could.

"I told you . . . we have allies here."

No. Uh-uh. No freakin' way.

I'd seen the way Buzz Cut had smacked him with her gun. I mean, she'd shattered his nose. And, honestly, if looks could kill . . . Simon would've been lying in a ditch somewhere, not standing here grinning like he'd pulled one over on me. On everyone.

"Shut. Up." But I was already starting to believe it, because she was just standing there, wearing that same stupid grin on her face. "But I thought . . . ," I stammered. "Don't you *hate* him?"

Simon shrugged. "An act," he said.

"You *broke* his *nose*." Even I had a hard time thinking an ally could do something so brutal.

The corner of her mouth slid up. "Had to make it believable."

Simon frowned at her and rubbed his nose. "Yeah, well, it was believable, all right. Maybe next time you could take it down a notch."

She lifted one shoulder. "We'll see."

And then Simon did that same chin-lift thing at her that she'd done at the girl who'd taken Natty away. "Can we have a minute, Nyla?"

Nyla.

It was weird not to think of her as Buzz Cut. To give her a name—a *real* name.

But it was another thing altogether to see her as an ally.

I guess you never knew about people, and where you'd find someone you could count on.

"Sure. But only a minute. I gotta get her back," Nyla answered, glancing around vigilantly.

"I knew you had a name," I couldn't help mentioning under my breath before she'd sidestepped us.

She just curled her lip at me—a very *Willow-like* response.

Out here, beneath the stars, was about as private as you could get. We were on the edge of their desert camp, where it was dark and isolated and quiet. I breathed deeply, taking stock of the distant landscape of withered trees and rocks and an endless black sky.

"What now?" I asked when Simon came to stand beside me. His relaxed stance wasn't at all what I expected. "Do we make a run for it?"

His voice, when he answered, was gentle. "I could stand here and look at this forever. It's easy to think here."

"And that's a good thing?" I paused to examine him and he wore a bemused expression.

"Depends."

Shrugging, I flashed him a wistful smile. "Sometimes it's *worse* to think. Sometimes I feel like . . ." I stopped myself because I wasn't sure how to finish my own thought. That even though I had nothing but time, I still couldn't sort things out? That being here made me realize how lonely I really was?

Or that even though I missed Cat and Austin, and the way things used to be before I was returned, I'd started to miss *Simon* even more?

No, I definitely couldn't say that last part. I wasn't even sure it was true.

Besides, I still ached for Tyler.

Simon didn't say anything, and he didn't move, so we just stood there, staring into the darkness.

When I finally broke the silence again, my voice came out resigned rather than critical. "She's crazy, Simon. Griffin. I talked to her, and she's out of her mind. What were you thinking bringing us here?"

He sighed, a breathy sound that only added to the calm of the night. "She's not crazy, she's just . . . unhappy."

"Unhappy my ass," I said, glancing sideways at him. "I get the sense she'd like to play target practice with your skull. Besides, I'm unhappy too. You know we've been in lockdown ever since we got here, don't you? How long's this gonna last?" I doubted anyone, not even Nyla, could hear us, but I kept my voice hushed all the same. "And what's all this about Willow and Thom knowing each other? Griffin says Willow's the reason none of you are friends anymore."

I half expected a denial, but he just nodded. "It's true. But probably not for the reasons Griffin said. She has a way of twisting things around."

I guessed that much already. Griffin seemed like the type who enjoyed manipulating words and facts until they suited her. "She didn't say why, just that it was Willow's fault. That everything would've been fine if Willow hadn't come along."

Simon smiled sadly. "Of course that's the way she'd see it. Revisionists have a way of changing history to suit themselves."

The sound of footsteps interrupted us, and Nyla appeared, wearing a *Time's up* expression.

"Please," I begged. "Just a few more minutes?"

She looked from me to Simon and then rolled her eyes. It was her reluctant way of giving in. "Make it fast. You have five minutes."

When she was gone again, I said to Simon, "Okay, so what does Griffin have against Willow?"

Simon caught hold of my hand as he dragged me deeper into the desert. His fingers were strong and warm, and as much as I wanted to uncoil my fingers so I could lace them through his, I stubbornly refused, keeping my fist tightly curled.

He spoke more urgently now that Nyla had put us on a

clock, and at first his story mirrored Griffin's exactly as he explained how he and Thom and Griffin had once worked together. "But it wasn't Willow's fault," he insisted at the point where their versions deviated. "Willow didn't do anything wrong, other than the fact that she was different from the other girls Thom and I were sent after. She wasn't like anyone we'd ever come across before. She didn't have that lost-puppy sense about her that most of the new Returned had. She wasn't freaking out the way most of us do."

I might have taken offense, if he hadn't included himself in that description as well.

"Here she'd been taken and experimented on and then returned, and she just . . . what?" He shrugged more to himself than to me. "She just *accepted* it, the way you would that the sky is blue and a bear shits in the woods." He looked me right in the eye and nodded. "Yeah, that was it. It was that no-nonsense thing about her. Willow's biggest fault, at least in Griffin's eyes, was that Thom and I admired her. That and the fact that Thom and I thought maybe she could work with us, the same way Griff did."

My stomach lurched at the casual way he said *Griff.* I wasn't born yesterday—girls like "Griff," with their push-up bras and badass attitudes, had a way of wiggling their way inside guys' heads, and I couldn't stop from wondering if she was there now—in Simon's head.

But Simon was oblivious to what was going on inside *my* head. "No matter what we said," he continued, "Griffin hated Willow from the get-go. And she went out of her way to undermine her every chance she got.

"At first I thought she'd get over it. I mean, just because we were taking an interest in Willow, that didn't mean we'd replaced Griffin. But Griffin was never like that. She had to be the best at everything. The center of the universe. She didn't like Thom and me having our interests *divided* by the new girl." He was quiet for several long seconds, and then he said, "I just never realized how far Griffin would go to get Willow out of the way." Simon spat in the sand, as if the memory were too sour to swallow.

"What did she do?"

"At the time, Blackwater was having serious problems with the Daylighters. That Agent Truman guy wasn't around back then, at least not that I know of, but there was this other guy, and he was just as relentless. He always seemed to know about our recruiting missions even before we got there. Franco warned us all to be careful every time we left the camp. But no matter how many precautions we took, that agent was always one step ahead of us, and he would snag the new Returned before we could get to them." He shook his head. "We started to suspect someone inside the camp was feeding him information."

"And Griffin thought it was Willow?" I asked, piecing the puzzle together myself.

He shook his head. "That's the thing. I don't think she ever really *believed* it was Willow, but that's what she told Franco. She convinced him that all our trouble started about the time Willow showed up, which was pretty much the truth. She said Willow shouldn't be trusted."

"And he believed Griffin?"

Simon shrugged. "Whether he did or not, I never got the chance to find out. I told Thom we needed to convince Franco that Griffin was wrong, that there was no way Willow was passing information to the No-Suchers' Daylight Division."

"How could you be so sure? What if it really was Willow who was working on the inside?"

"It wasn't. Thom and I already suspected this recruiter named Eddie Ray, who'd been coming up through the ranks. He was power-hungry like Griffin, only he had Franco's ear." He grimaced. "I went to Thom about Willow, but he refused to back me up. He didn't want to go against Griffin. I think that's when I realized she'd gotten to him. That she was willing to do whatever it took to convince Thom, and anyone else who could help her cause, that she was right: that Willow was the traitor."

I wasn't quite sure I understood. "Are you saying they had a thing, Griffin and Thom?"

"I'm saying Thom had a thing for Griff . . . enough so that he'd stopped thinking with his head. I mean, I guess I knew she could do that to a guy; it was what made her such a good recruiter in the first place. I just didn't think Thom would be so . . . *susceptible*."

"And what about you?" I asked, hating the note of

jealousy I heard in my own voice. "Were you susceptible too?"

"Me? Nah. I mean, I didn't blame the guys who fell for her. She had this way of looking at you with those brown eyes of hers like she'd known you forever, even though she'd barely just met you. It was like the two of you had these private secrets that no one else in the world were in on. And, holy shit, when she smiled"—Simon squeezed his eyes closed—"kinda sideways, like it accidentally slipped out, you couldn't help but smile back at her."

I had to wonder if he *had* been a little susceptible, even if he wasn't willing to admit it.

"My grandma had a word for girls like her. She called them wanton." He grinned then. "It was pretty much the worst insult she could give, and that's what she would've said about Griff. She was one of those fast girls you were supposed to watch out for. The kind we were warned about in church on Sundays. Also, why I kinda hated church. I liked girls who weren't buttoned-up and afraid to speak their minds." He looked down at our hands, and his fingers pushed their way between mine, until our fingers wove together. He smiled.

"But I thought Thom and I were . . ." I expected him to say "brothers," just like Griffin had, but instead he finished with "partners," which carried way less punch. "I thought he'd have my back when push came to shove. But he didn't. He backed Griffin, even though we both knew she was lying."

"So what happened?"

"I figured Griffin didn't tell you everything." He shrugged. "Back then I was the council's favorite to take over as leader if anything happened to Franco. So when Franco called a meeting to deliberate over Willow's fate, I was there. When the decision was handed down that Willow was set to be excommunicated, mine was the sole vote against it." In the dark, Simon's eyes met mine and he let out a slow breath. "It doesn't sound so bad, except it was practically a death sentence for Willow. We still had a very real information leak in our camp and the Daylighters were sure to find out where Willow was being sent. I couldn't let Willow be captured by those bastards just because Griffin didn't like her." His fingers tightened around mine and my stomach flipped. "So that night, we left. Willow and I snuck out of camp. I didn't tell anyone what I planned to do, not even Thom."

I thought Simon's grandmother was wrong about girls like Griffin—wanton was the wrong word after all. Simon might have been off the mark when he said she wasn't crazy.

Griffin's brain was scrambled like those eggs in that don't-do-drugs commercial:

This is your brain.

This is your brain after being transported 200 million light-years and having your DNA messed with by aliens.

I would probably use the words *stone-cold crazy* for someone like her.

"Where's Franco now?"

His eyebrows bunched together. "That's the thing. A few

months later, Franco was ambushed during a recruiting mission, same way the other recruiting teams had been. He was never heard from again. About that same time, Eddie Ray just . . . *disappeared.* I mean, if he wasn't guilty, then where'd he go?" His lips tightened as he shook his head. "Griffin had managed to worm her way into the camp's council, and it wasn't long before *she* was voted in as leader of the camp."

"And Thom? How come he left?"

His gaze clouded over. "I don't know the whole story. We never talked again after Willow and I took off, at least not until that morning when we showed up at Silent Creek. But most of the camps stay in contact through a convoluted communication system. Gossip manages to get around. Indirectly, I heard he couldn't stomach the new leadership, and if I had to guess, I'd say he finally figured out Griff had been using him all along."

"Time's up." When Nyla interrupted us again, I peeled my hand away from Simon's. It was the second time Nyla had caught us like that, and I was sure she was starting to get the wrong impression.

I meant to ask Simon if he'd ever regretted leaving with Willow, or questioned her loyalty. But I already knew his answer, because Willow was as trustworthy as they came.

It was Griffin whose loyalty I suspected now.

Was it possible she'd been the one responsible for betraying the Blackwater recruiters all those years ago as a means to get to the top of the pecking order? Was anyone really that narcissistic and power-hungry?

Cold dread settled heavily in my stomach at the very thought.

I prayed I was wrong.

CHAPTER FOURTEEN

IN A PLACE LIKE BLACKWATER, WHERE NO ONE really slept, there was always activity. So by the time we'd reached the heart of the camp, the darkness that stretched far into the desert had been replaced by strategically placed floodlights that made it almost as bright as daytime.

It was as if night never even existed.

When we reached the cafeteria, Nyla dragged me to a halt. "When Dakota brings your friend out, you'll join them and she'll take you back to your tent." I assumed Dakota was the girl who'd shuttled Natty away after our showers.

"Don't worry, I'll work this out." Simon was quiet when

he spoke. "You won't have to stay under guard much longer. I promise."

I was just about to tell him I wasn't ready for him to go, not quite yet, when Griffin's voice pierced my newfound calm seeing Simon again had given me. "You shouldn't make promises you can't keep."

"Are you kidding me?" I exhaled dramatically before facing Griffin. I felt like a kid caught with my hand in the cookie jar. I hoped this didn't mean I'd lose the small freedoms I'd been allowed so far.

Griffin emerged from the tent maze, her attention not directed on me or Simon, but on Nyla. She looked thoroughly hacked. "I knew when I couldn't find her"—she indicated me when she said that—"that *he'd* be involved." This time she gave just the slightest nod of her head toward Simon. "But I never suspected you," she reprimanded Nyla, her eyes narrowing, and she looked dangerous when she said it. The kind of dangerous that made my skin pebble all over with stiff goose bumps.

"Griffin, don't blame her. This was all my idea." Simon stepped in front of Nyla to explain, and I was thinking it wouldn't matter what he said because Nyla had betrayed Griffin—a real betrayal, not the made-up kind she'd accused Willow of, either. There was no way she was letting Nyla off the hook for this.

But then something happened, and suddenly none of those things mattered.

Suddenly everything changed, at least for me they did.

It was the laugh that did it.

I had to reach for Simon in order to stay on my feet, because all at once my legs were unreliable, like I was standing on stilts I had yet to master. The sensation of guilt over getting caught with Nyla and Simon turned to something else entirely as it spread, prickling my skin everywhere and making every tiny hair on my body stand at full alert.

My heart stopped—like *stop-stopped*—and I waited for it to start again, the same way I waited to hear that sound, the laugh, for what seemed like forever and a day. And when I finally did, when I heard it, my heart not only started to beat once more, it pounded.

Thud-thud, thud-thud, thud-thud . . . beating so freaking hard I almost gasped.

Simon looked down at me, and I wasn't sure if I saw sadness in his copper eyes, or if he was asking for an explanation I couldn't offer, while inside hope was struggling to the surface.

All around us, people like us, other Returned, were doing the things they did—training for whatever Griffin told them they were training for, running in their symmetrical clusters, talking to one another, eating, and some of them, somewhere, were probably even managing to sleep.

Yet I was here, living in my own world. Trapped in a bubble. Caught between states of disbelief and hope so overpowering they threatened to smother me.

So far, all I had was that laugh, but it wasn't enough to prove anything.

I took a step forward because I needed to know if it was him or if I'd only imagined it.

I turned toward the sound, but one of the floodlights was shining right in my face, and it was blinding me. All I could make out were several hazy outlines. It was enough to know that there was more than one person, and that they were almost to us now.

But I no longer cared about anyone else, because when the shadowy figures became clear, my grip on Simon's arm tightened.

I saw him then. Undeniably.

I saw the way his green eyes squinted and his dimple creased his cheek as his eyes fell on Griffin.

"Tyler." I croaked the word, and it barely made it past my lips, but it was the sweetest, most magnificent word I'd ever uttered, and suddenly the past twenty-three days melted away.

The last time I'd seen him, he'd been covered head-to-toe in pustules that had made it too painful to even touch him. He'd been blind and taking his very last breath.

This Tyler, though, the one standing before me now, was so incredibly-breathtakingly-*irrefutably* beautiful all I could do was stare. I took him in, and I felt myself come alive. It was as if *I* had just been returned all over again, seeing him standing there, alive. Whole.

Safe.

He stopped where he was, his feet planted on a patch of dry grass. There were so many expressions that passed over his face in those split seconds that there was no way I could catch them all. I totally understood how he felt. It was exactly what I was feeling too, finding him here of all places—confusion, shock, doubt, curiosity, relief.

"Tyler," I said again, only this time it was louder as I let go of Simon, and I knew I was for sure going to cry in front of everyone.

"Kyra?" The hairs that had already been standing on end vibrated as his voice, a voice I'd been waiting to hear for three and a half weeks, a voice I'd willed myself to dream about, brushed over them.

I was running then, closing those last steps that separated us. I didn't stop to ask why he was here, or to worry about whether Griffin or anyone else was watching, or what they thought about me or Tyler or the fact that we knew each other. I launched myself at him, and he caught me, wrapping his arms around me, and it was amazing to feel him.

To smell him. To know his heart was beating just inches beneath my own . . . that it was beating at all after everything he'd been through, after everything *I'd* put him through.

It had been a risk to take him to Devil's Hole, and it had paid off. Tyler had been Returned.

"Tyler. Oh my god, Tyler . . ." I couldn't bear to let go. *I might never let go,* I thought as I got lost in his embrace. He felt leaner than I remembered, which wasn't at all impossible, and possibly more muscular, like maybe he'd been following the same workout regimen as the rest of Griffin's camp.

But his T-shirt had that same Tyler smell I remembered,

which made me think of home, and the thought came to me that I *was* home as long as I was with Tyler. I wanted to tell him so many things, including that, but for now, this—right here—was more than enough. More than I could have dared to hope for.

"Kyra," he repeated, and I wondered how many times he'd said my name at the same time I'd said his. "I . . . I can't believe you're here."

"I know," I said back, while he pulled away and gazed down at me with this wonderstruck look in those incredible-amazing-*brilliant* green eyes of his, and I tried to decide if they were more brilliant than they'd been before or if they'd always been this dazzling. "I was thinking the same thing. How did you get here? How long have you been back?" My face crumpled as the tears finally broke to the surface. "I . . . I wasn't sure I'd ever see you again."

Tyler crushed me to him, his chin bumping against the top of my head. It was all so familiar—the hug, and being consoled by Tyler, who was like that, *familiar*—that I almost didn't hear what he said next. I mean, I heard it, it just didn't make sense to me. "I was gonna say the same thing to you. I don't think anyone thought they'd ever see you again." His arms tightened and his voice rose, an elated kind of sound. "I can't even imagine what Austin would think if he was here."

My heart stopped again, but this time in a bad way.

And then he pulled back, and that hopeful look on his face fell away. "We can't tell him," he explained, saying it like this was new information to me, his voice dropping super low as he tried to make me understand. "Austin, your parents, they can't know you're back."

I blinked. What the hell was he even talking about? They couldn't know what . . . that I was back? I turned to Simon, whose face gave nothing away, and then to Griffin, who had her eyes trained solely on Tyler, and wasn't paying any attention to me at all.

"You two know each other?" she asked Tyler, and there was something slippery about the way she looked at me, like she totally already *knew* all this. Like I'd been played.

Tyler glanced back at her and put his arm around my shoulder in a very pal-like way. *Pals*, he told her with that gesture, and my stomach sank achingly. "This is the neighbor I was telling you about. Kyra Agnew." He shrugged, and his pal-hug tightened. "I've known her since . . . forever. No one's seen her in . . ." He did the math and blinked at me, and even before he said how long it'd been, I wanted to vanish again because I knew where he was going with this. "Five years," he finished, grinning down at me and letting out a low whistle. "Five long years."

"You've known all this time," I accused Griffin, wishing she hadn't sent Tyler away, but seriously glad to be alone with her so I could have the chance to give her a piece of my mind. "I heard him—he *told you* my name. He *told you* I'd been taken. All this time we were in the same camp and *you knew* we knew each other. *You knew* he'd want to see me, and you didn't bother telling either of us. Why would you keep us apart like that? *What's wrong with you?*"

But Griffin, or "Griff" as Simon so adorably referred to her, didn't seem the slightest bit fazed by my allegations, not in the way I wanted her to be. I wanted her to be ashamed the way a normal person would have been.

Instead she stared at me expressionlessly, like the dictator I suspected she was. "I did it for Tyler. He's only been here a short time, and I wanted to ease him into camp life. Keep his old life separate from his new one. You showing up here, that was . . . *inconvenient.* I would've told him eventually."

"Bull." My hands were shaking at my sides and blood pounded past my ears as I challenged her.

Griffin just snorted. "Really none of your concern what I do, or do not, tell my people."

"Tyler's not one of your people."

"He is now. Ask him." She smirked, and I knew she had me. I'd seen him. I'd seen the way he looked to her as his leader. And I'd heard the way he'd described me—like I was his brother's girl and the two of us were pals, the way we'd been *before* I'd come back.

"How did that even happen?" I asked, trying to stay angry with her but losing steam. "How did you . . . *find him?*" It was supposed to be me, I wanted to shout at her. Or maybe I wanted to shout it at myself for failing yet again. *I* was supposed to find him.

Griffin gave me a tight-lipped look and said, "I have people who give me information." Then she turned to Simon and explained, "Tyler's a good kid. He's fitting in here—"

But I cut her off as I spun on Simon now, unsure who I was more upset with: Griffin for laying one of those Finders-Keepers claims on Tyler—*my* Tyler—or Simon for not helping me get to him first. "Did you know?"

Simon threw his hands up, hostage-style. "Leave me out of this. I had no idea what she was up to." Simon looked at Griffin instead of me, and I couldn't help thinking of our conversation about Tyler that day in the library, when Simon told me I couldn't wait for Tyler forever.

"Okay, yes, Simon told me you were looking for a boy. Someone who was important to you," she said in a pacifying voice as she tried to smooth things over. "But how was I supposed to know you were the same Kyra Tyler had been talking about?"

"How many *Kyra*s do you know?" I asked, but there was no point arguing. Griffin held all the cards. She was in charge of whether I would see Tyler again, or not. The best thing I could do was keep my mouth shut.

She gave me a condescending smile. "Look. Tyler didn't know much when he got here. He didn't remember how he'd been taken, and he certainly didn't say anything about having a girlfriend back home." I hated the way she was determined to remind me of that. She seemed to enjoy making it clear that his memories didn't include me, at least not the important parts.

He didn't remember the day I'd stumbled into his kitchen and fallen into his arms, mistaking him for Austin. Or the beautiful chalk drawings he'd done for me. Or taking me to his favorite bookstore and leaving me gifts outside my window and sending me messages at all hours of the night.

He also didn't remember any of the things that had gone wrong after I'd cut myself on that box knife right in front of him, contaminating him . . . and the way he'd gotten sicker and sicker until I'd been left with no choice but to drag him up to Devil's Hole to be taken.

As far as he was concerned, I'd vanished five years ago and had never come back.

And now Griffin acted like her claim on Tyler trumped our history together, as if none of those things ever existed at all.

Simon surprised me then, when he said to me, "This must be hard on you," because it had to be hard on him too. He rubbed his hand across the back of his neck, watching me anxiously. I tried to tell myself he didn't seem worried that Tyler was here, and that worried wasn't the same as threatened.

But I knew better. I could see it written all over his face: Simon wanted more, and I couldn't help wondering if he'd hoped we'd never find Tyler at all.

I couldn't worry about Simon's feelings, or the fact that Tyler couldn't remember me. All that mattered was that we'd found him, and I was determined to make him remember me if it was the last thing I ever did.

"When can I see him again?" I begged Griffin, still frustrated she'd sent Tyler away with Nyla. "Please. I'll do anything." I refused to acknowledge that hurt-puppy look in

Simon's eyes, and ignored his words altogether.

"I'll have Nyla bring him to us, but first . . . there was a reason I was looking for you," Griffin said slowly, her voice sticky. "Jett needs to show you something."

Jett. I'd waited days to see Jett again, face-to-face.

I followed clumsily, eager to reach Jett, to hear what he had to tell me, and just as twisted up about when I'd get to see Tyler again. Griffin led Simon and me to the same white building where I'd spied her and Jett earlier while I'd been doing drills with Natty. She knocked again, the same way she had then, only once, and then we, too, slipped inside.

It wasn't only Jett I was reunited with inside—Willow was there too, safe and sound. When she saw me, she winked at me.

Winked, as if to say: *Hey pal, long time no see.* It was completely surreal.

If Griffin hadn't been there, watching our every move, I might have hugged Willow because it was so damn good to see her again. But the last thing I wanted was to give Griffin even the slightest insight into my state of mind. She already had enough ammunition to use against me, having her hooks in Tyler and all.

So instead of hugging, or even winking, at her, I lifted my chin, which had to make me seem totally stuck up, but it also kept my feelings where they needed to be: under lock and key.

"What is this place?" I asked, my eyes landing on Jett as I gave him that same aloof nod I'd given Willow.

He looked unsure for a minute, and I wondered if it was because of my greeting or the question. But then he scratched his cheek and said, "It's the computer lab. Pretty fancy digs, right?"

He wasn't wrong. The first thing I noticed, besides how much warmer it was in here, probably from all the electrical equipment—the computers and monitors crammed into such close quarters, making it downright stuffy—was that it was a lot like the place Jett had kept back at his old camp. Back at the abandoned Hanford site when I'd first met him. I was impressed.

"How long have you been here?" I asked.

"Since the first day we got here." He grinned at Griffin and I had to stop myself from rolling my eyes. "Been workin' ever since."

Not you too, Jett? I wanted to shake some sense into him, but I could hardly blame him for falling under her spell. Talk about finding the key to Jett's heart.

I doubted Griffin had batted a single lash this time; all she'd had to do was give him access to a bunch of computers and hook him up to a satellite feed. He'd have been eating out of her hand in ten seconds flat.

Damn her!

Jett indicated his trusty laptop, which was linked to their network. "I don't know if anyone told you, but we may have something."

I was all ears. "Something like what?"

Jett plopped down in the rolling chair and cast me

an expectant look. "I don't want to get your hopes up or anything, but we may have gotten another message from someone claiming to be your father." His brow lowered as he rubbed his palms over the tops of his knees. "Don't get too excited, but . . . I think it might be legit."

My eyes widened, and for just a second, just a teeny, tiny second, I was able to forget all about Tyler and Griffin, and whatever reasons she had for keeping us apart while we were here. "My dad? You think it might be him . . . *for real* . . . ?" I didn't know if I could allow myself to believe it might be true.

Jett stopped me before hope could take root. "We can't be sure yet. I'm just saying we can't rule it out either. We've done IP traces and we've definitely ruled out the Tacoma facility. But if it is him, he's being extra careful. Whoever it is, he's taking as many precautions as we are."

"Then let *me* talk to him," I gushed, knowing I could figure it out if they gave me the chance. "I'll ask him things only he'd know."

I stepped toward Jett, but Griffin's fingers dug into my shoulder. "We can't do that. Not just yet," she said. "Not until we make sure whoever he is, he isn't running a trace. We can't be too careful. When mistakes are made, people die."

I wrenched out of her grip, not caring that she had a point. "So, how long will that be?" I asked, directing my question to Jett instead of Griffin because I was so over her.

He just shrugged. "Could be a coupla hours, could be

a coupla days. Could turn out to be a hoax altogether. I just thought you should know." When he met my gaze, he silently told me he didn't think it was the latter, and I nodded back, thanking him for that.

"What about the files?" Willow finally spoke up. "Tell them where you are with those."

"We're definitely in," Jett explained, eager now, and Simon stepped closer to peer over Jett's shoulder.

"Find anything interesting so far?"

"Not yet," Jett answered, glancing back at him. "Even with the encryption codes, all of their internal files are password protected, so every time we break one code, we have to break another. It's slow going, but we're piecing it all together a little at a time. Soon, though."

Soon. That sounded a heckuva lot faster than when I'd know about my dad.

There was a thump at the door, and when it opened, Nyla materialized, and right on her heels was Tyler. Butterflies swarmed my stomach.

I became *that girl*, the one who was worried about how she looked and whether her breath was bad, and I had this sudden urge to check to see if I had a booger hanging out of my nose and I so totally hoped I didn't because I was sure I would absolutely die of sheer embarrassment if I did. If *that* was his second first impression of me after we'd just re-met each other.

I glanced at Griffin, who looked downright stunning. How in the heck had she found the time to apply lip gloss when she had an entire camp to run?

I smoothed my hand over my hair, wishing I at least had some other style besides finger comb and rubber band. I had to remind myself that even if he didn't remember it, this was the boy who'd given up everything to help me, and we'd seen each other in far worse circumstances.

"Hey," Tyler said, and when he smiled, I forgot all about my hair and boogers, and almost even about my dad.

"Hey," I said back.

And then I almost died anyway when I realized he wasn't talking to me at all, but to Griffin, and all of a sudden I was back in junior high all over again as I had one of those awkward moments in the hallway when someone waves to you and you wave back, only you realize a second too late that they were never waving at you at all, but at the person standing behind you all along.

So. Embarrassing.

My cheeks blazed like someone had thrown a gallon of lighter fluid on them, and I lowered my gaze, unable to look at anyone. Humiliation brimmed in my eyes and I had to blink several times to keep them from spilling over, certain my charcoal cheeks would cause the tears to sizzle.

On the other side of me, I felt Simon's fingertips brush over the back of my hand, but I curled my fingers until all that was left were white-boned knuckles. I didn't want his pity. I never had.

But Tyler rescued me when he nudged me with his shoulder. "You guys almost done here?" And this time he was most definitely talking to me.

My breath caught as I glanced up again. He grinned at me with his way-too-alluring lips, and the butterflies beat rather than fluttered like a flock of spastic birds in the pit of my stomach. "I am."

"You wanna get out of here? Maybe go someplace we can catch up?" He looked to Griffin for approval and the butterflies died a horrific death. I didn't want him to seek her approval. I wanted it to be just us, him and me, so we didn't have to do any of this in front of the rest of them—not her or Simon or Willow, who was giving me the eyebrow version of a thumbs-up. "Do you mind?"

Griffin took it all in, from Tyler's far-too-eager-to-please expression to my less-than-thrilled, arms-crossed-over-my-chest stance. She was in her element, being in control like this. Having the final-ultimate-*absolute* say in whether we would be alone or not.

All I could do was wait, telling her with my own eyebrows to give it a rest. But all the while my lungs were paralyzed as I waited for that single, almost imperceptible nod. And when she gave it, I tried not to be too obvious. The last thing I wanted was to give her the satisfaction of knowing she had me all twisted up inside . . . even though she totally did.

I'd have done anything for her in that moment. Traded anything.

Given up everything.

"Have her back in her quarters by dawn," Griffin told

Tyler as he passed her. "She's staying in Paradise. Sector nine."

Tyler paused and shot her a puzzled look. "Paradise?"

She lifted a brow, letting him know the conversation was over, and Tyler just shook his head.

"Come on," he said, reaching for my hand. When his fingers closed over mine, I didn't shy away from him the way I had from Simon. I let our hands melt together, our fingers interlocking as if they'd been made for this—two halves of one whole that fit together, like jigsaws in a puzzle.

He dragged me enthusiastically, and I followed, just as eagerly, impatient to make him remember he loved me.

CHAPTER FIFTEEN

MEMORY WAS A TRICKY THING.

As much as I wanted to fix the gap in Tyler's mind, the place where I should've been—where we'd spent our time together—it wasn't that simple. I couldn't just hand the missing chunk back to him.

I understood, of course; I'd lost time too. Five entire years. I mean, it wasn't exactly the same since I'd really been gone that whole time and his was more of a glitch in his memory, but that didn't mean I didn't get how weird it would be if I were to just spring it on him, the news that we'd been a thing, he and I, something he had absolutely no clue about.

Instead, it was like a do-over, like I was meeting seventeen-year-old Tyler that first time. He was looking at me and thinking about me the same way he had been that first day I'd come back.

Except this time we had something new in common: *we were both Returned.*

We walked in silence past the training field, and for several long, almost too long, seconds I thought maybe we'd have nothing to say to each other. It was strange, seeing him and trying to put myself in his shoes. He'd been here at Blackwater ever since he'd been sent back, which, if everything I'd been told about the whole forty-eight-hour thing was right, must have been several weeks already.

That was a long time to be indoctrinated into Griffin's way of thinking. To be training with her so-called army.

I understood how Tyler could end up in a place like this. I even understood why he'd want to stay.

It was terrifying being one of the Returned, finding out you'd been taken and experimented on, and you could never go back to your old life. It made it easier to know there was someplace you could go, someplace safe, with others who'd been through the same thing you had.

I wouldn't want to go through it alone.

Heck, if Griffin had found me first, I couldn't say I wouldn't be one of her soldiers now too. Instead, I'd ended up with Simon.

But who's to say that had been the right choice, that there weren't other camps, with other leaders, and other causes that might have been better, safer . . . *righter.*

It seemed like a crapshoot if you asked me, and my dice had just so happened to land on Simon. Tyler, well, he'd gotten Griffin. And Natty, she'd rolled Thom.

"I like your new hair," Tyler finally said, glancing down at me once we'd cleared the fields and were in almost the exact same place Simon and I had just been when Nyla had snuck me away from the showers so we could meet in private. He grinned, and that dimple of his, the one I'd spent so much time thinking about, obsessing over just a few short weeks ago, made a welcome appearance.

I smiled up at him, and he scratched behind his ear. "Weird, right?" he asked. "This. Running into you here, of all places." And then his dimple vanished. "And both of us being, you know, *Returned* . . ." It was almost comical the way he said "Returned," like he hadn't quite gotten used to the idea yet, and I wondered when I *had,* because it hadn't been all that long ago that I'd said it the same way he did.

There was a large flat boulder, low to the ground in front of me, and I kicked it once. I wasn't sure how to respond, because everything I wanted to say was unsayable. I couldn't tell him I loved him or that I'd missed him, because as far as he was concerned, five years had passed, and the last time I'd seen him he'd been a kid. I propped one foot against the rock, struggling for the right words.

"Is this Simon guy your leader? Have you been with him

all this time?" Tyler asked, searching my face through the darkness.

"No . . . I, uh . . ." How could I even start? "I only just came back a few weeks ago. Right before you were taken." I wondered if now was the best time to tell him the rest.

His eyes widened like he hadn't even considered that. "So this is all new to you too?"

"Pretty much," I admitted. And then, because I was dying to know more about him, I asked, "So what happened? Where did you wake up?"

He moved closer, and I had to stifle a shiver that had nothing to do with the night air. He sat on the boulder and tilted his head back so he could look at me. "Somewhere not far from here, I guess. I honestly don't know exactly where I was or what I'd have done if Griff hadn't've come along when she did." Somehow I managed to keep the cringe off my face when he mentioned Griffin, saying her name the way Simon did, but I felt it deep in my gut. I didn't want him to be grateful to her. I didn't want him to be anything to her, which made me feel petty on top of everything else, considering she'd saved him and all.

But I wanted to be the only important girl in his life.

There, I'd said it. So shoot me.

Tyler kept talking. "Would it make you think less of me if I admitted I was scared shitless when I woke up?" He grinned and regarded me sheepishly, the same look I remembered from before. "I had no idea where I was or how I'd gotten there," he explained.

I laughed. "It totally wouldn't," I confessed. "I know exactly how that feels. One minute I was arguing with my dad over college, and the next I was waking up behind the Gas 'n' Sip. At least that's what I thought."

"Dude. You woke up behind the Gas 'n' Sip?"

I smirked. "Talk about weird, right?"

His grin grew. "Talk about *gross*."

The butterflies were back . . . every time he smiled at me. I couldn't help it. I remembered exactly the way those lips felt on mine. "So how much do you remember?" I asked, changing the subject before my entire body burst into flames.

Shrugging, he told me, "Just that. Me waking up surrounded by sand, and then Griffin and some of the other Blackwater Ranchers showing up with this crazy story." He patted the spot next to him on the rock, and I didn't hesitate to take it. Somehow the rock was still warm, but his arm, where our skin made contact, was even warmer. "I'm sure I don't have to tell you I thought she was smoking crack when she first tried to tell me what happened. I mean, it's pretty nuts, the whole alien thing." I had to laugh, because we'd had this conversation before, only it had been me trying to figure out a way to explain it to him without sounding like *I* was on crack. It was funny to hear him being so *whatever* about it. "I guess it's hard to argue with the healing thing, though," he said as he nudged me again. "You know, I do it faster than anyone else."

"Wait. What?" I bumped against him when I sat up

straighter. "The healing? What do you mean faster?"

He gave me a you-should-be-impressed kind of look. "You heard me. Like, if you cut me, I heal faster than anyone ever has before. That's what Griffin says, anyway."

My knee-jerk reaction was to argue, because there was no way he could heal as fast as I could, right? But I couldn't be sure whether my reaction stemmed from my competitive streak, or whether I was just in shock. Was it really possible there were two of us who could heal faster than the rest? And could it really be a coincidence that that person had turned out to be Tyler?

It took me forever to even come up with, "So, who all knows?"

"I haven't told anyone, if that's what you mean. Griffin told me not to. But I figured it's okay to tell you . . . since we're friends and all."

Friends. The word felt like a knife through my heart. I didn't want to be Tyler's friend. I mean, I did . . . of course I did. It's just that's *not all* I wanted to be.

I hoped we could be so, so, *so* much more than just friends.

I nodded, either a *Yes, we're friends* or *Yes, you can trust me,* I wasn't sure which or whether it made a difference.

"Did she say why?"

Tyler's mouth turned down when he shrugged. "Nah. She just says I shouldn't let it get around. Not yet, anyway."

"No. That's probably a good idea." I thought of the way Simon had kept the way I could move things from the others. I wondered if they hadn't already known I could heal faster, if he'd have kept that from them too.

"So, I guess if you haven't been back that long, you probably don't know, then," he said, his voice growing apologetic and kinda drifty. "About your parents . . ."

I shrugged, since I was still in that gray area—not sure how much I should admit—but I didn't want to lie either. "No. I do. I . . . *know*," I finally admitted.

He nodded. "I couldn't go back to see mine." This time his expression was downright pathetic, and I was reminded that at least I'd known I was saying good-bye to my parents. The last time Tyler's parents saw him, Agent Truman had told them I was contagious and if he stayed with me, I would contaminate him. I wondered where they thought he was now. Tyler didn't remember any of that. "Griffin says since we're not safe to be around, it's better for them to just think I . . . ran away."

"What do you think?"

He cocked his head to the side, his eyes overbright. "She's probably right. It just sucks, is all. I miss 'em." Then he bumped into me again, this time not so much a nudge as it was a brush, like he wanted to connect with someone. He glanced down at me.

"I know what you mean. I miss my dad."

"Who'd'a thought he was right all this time." His eyes sparkled just a little. "I mean, after everything that happened, and everything everyone thought of him, turns out he was the sane one in all this."

I lifted my eyes to his. "Well, I don't know about sane, but yeah."

There was a prolonged silence as I tried to decide if this whole thing was awkward or not, when Tyler reached over and picked up my hand. My heart tripped over itself as I watched him study it, almost like he was seeing something new . . . something he'd never seen before. Curiously he flipped it over and uncurled my fingers, flattening them until my fingers were splayed, and then he pressed his own against mine so our palms were aligned. His fingers dwarfed my own like I was only a child by comparison. "Do I look different?" he asked, his voice rough and low.

A lump rose in my throat as I struggled for the right answer. Different how, I wondered? Different from the Tyler he thought I remembered—the one from five years ago? Or different from the Tyler I'd fallen in love with, the one I'd seen just a few short weeks ago? The one I'd been desperately-hopelessly-achingly searching for?

"No," I whispered, my eyes locking on his. I could've stayed like that forever, even if he had absolutely zero memory of me. "You look the same as I remember," I finally said, because I couldn't lie.

I could never, ever lie to him.

His fingers closed over mine and he squeezed once, an apology squeeze, before he let go. "I'm sorry. I don't know what got into me. I think I'm just homesick, is all. I . . ." He didn't finish.

"It's okay." I didn't want him to stop or to be sorry

or . . . to stop. Ever. "I totally get it. I miss everyone and everything. It's nice to *know* someone. From home." I took his hand again, wishing I could convey all my true feelings. "It's *nice*," I ended lamely because it was all I could say.

Tyler accepted my "nice" speech. Our fingers intertwined, and even though it wasn't like *before*, when sparks flew and fireworks exploded, it was comforting. And right now comforting was a million times better than nothing at all.

Maybe comforting was better than fireworks anyway. Comforting fit like a sweater, and kept you warm, and made you feel protected.

Comforting could kick fireworks' ass any day of the week.

He gave me a sidelong glance before talking again. "I don't know if it's weird for me to bring this up, but I miss Austin."

"It's not weird, Tyler. You're allowed to miss your brother. It would be weird if you didn't." I let out a sigh and leaned my head against his shoulder.

"I just wasn't sure . . . if . . ." He did this shrug thing, and it was completely filled with all the words he didn't want to say, and I knew exactly how he felt because I had just as many words I was holding inside.

I let him off the hook. "I know about them too—Austin and Cat."

"I didn't realize."

I know, I wanted to tell him, and then I wanted to bury

my fingers in his hair and drag him down and kiss him, full on the lips. If only I could taste him, just one time. And press myself to him.

Instead I smiled a small, sad little smile.

"They didn't do it to hurt you," he said, exactly the way he'd said it a month ago, when he'd explained it to me the first time, and my eyes burned because he was so the same Tyler I remembered that I wanted him to remember too.

I nodded again, and then one more time, my eyes still stinging, to let him know I'd heard enough. Enough about Austin and Cat, and enough about our old lives with our old families. This was our new life, and even if he never remembered, if this was where we were starting from, we'd get through it, and everything would be okay, I told myself, because here we were, Tyler and me, together again.

We stayed like that for hours, huddled side by side. Sometimes he'd talk and sometimes I would, and sometimes we'd just stay silent. But for the first time in weeks I anticipated the morning, because this time, when the sun rose, there wouldn't be the familiar stab. Tyler was back at long, long, *long* last.

Except, the moment the first streaks of dawn finally appeared, gilding the desert with its warm blush, I knew I'd been wrong.

Tyler wasn't the cure.

I nearly doubled over as the sun ascended, crippling me as it claimed its place in the sky.

"Are you okay?" Tyler worried. "Should I get you back?"

But I shook him off, biting my lip until the pain had passed. "It's nothing," I lied. "I'm just so glad we have each other."

He reached over then and squeezed my hand in that sweater-hug safe and comforting way that blew the fireworks and sparks out of the water, and I leaned my head against his shoulder to tell him a silent thank-you while I finally let the tears fall.

Natty pounced on me the second Tyler had delivered me back to our tent, just the way he'd promised Griffin. "*Ohmygosh*, Thom told me all about it. How you found Tyler . . . right here, *in Blackwater*," she gushed as if it had been accidental that we hadn't run into each other sooner. Like Griffin hadn't had a hand in keeping us apart.

It would take a while to break Tyler of whatever hero worship thing he had for Griffin, but I had every intention of dethroning her and reclaiming my place in his heart.

I knew it sounded like I wanted to control Tyler, like this was some sort of catfight where Griffin and I were fighting over a boy. But it wasn't like that. I wasn't about to fight Griffin, and I certainly wasn't fighting *for Tyler*. I knew you couldn't control a person and you couldn't force someone to love you—you should never have to. What I was fighting for was a chance. *Our* chance.

I just wanted him to remember who I was. Who *we* were . . . together.

And if, in the end, he remembered all that, and he still

chose Griffin, then so be it.

The thing was, I didn't think that would happen. I believed, to the very core of me, that if his memories returned, he'd still want me.

And if they didn't . . . well, if he didn't, then he'd fall in love with me all over again, because it wasn't circumstance that had made us the couple we'd been, it was us. It was ingrained in us. It was who we were.

In the same way Griffin had immediately disliked Willow—the way some magnets repelled each other. Tyler and I were the ones that attracted. The ones that, no matter how far apart, would forever be drawn together.

Meant to be.

I didn't always believe in such things, but now, finding Tyler in this Utah compound with Griffin and her fanatical militia . . . now I couldn't believe otherwise.

"It was perfect," I told her.

"So he remembered you?" she asked nervously.

It didn't matter that she'd asked it nervously or that she hadn't guessed right. "No. But he will." I sat on my bunk. "What about you? Have you been here the whole night?"

Natty perked up. "Thom was here. They're letting us see each other. He just left." It was the most animated I'd ever seen her.

I wasn't sure what to say, what I *should* say. If it were Cat, I'd ask what they did . . . like exactly *what they did*. But that definitely felt like prying. "Did you . . . have fun?"

So. Awkward.

Natty didn't notice. She beamed as she nodded, her eyes gleaming. "We talked all night." She lowered her voice, letting me know she was sharing a secret. "He told me more about Blackwater, and he said they call this part of it—where they're keeping us—*Paradise*."

I leaned closer. "Did he say why?"

"It's like what Willow said about not trusting the government names that sound the most innocent. That if you hear something called Operation Rainbow, it's gonna be majorly bad. Paradise is where they keep the people they don't trust." She shrugged with her face, her eyebrows rising and her mouth drooping. "Like us."

I wondered if letting Thom spend the night with Natty might be a step in the right direction toward letting us off house arrest, if we might be earning our way out of Paradise.

But then I remembered the look on Griffin's face when she'd busted Nyla for sneaking me away to meet Simon, and I sincerely doubted it. Thom and Natty might earn their freedom back, but Simon and I would likely be trapped in Paradise forever.

Just then there was a knock, or as much of a knock as there could be on a tent door, kind of a flapping sound against the canvas. I jumped up and pushed the opening aside.

I felt a surge of triumph when I saw Tyler standing there, back so soon. "Couldn't stay away?" I beamed, unable to contain myself.

He held his hands behind his back. "I brought you something." He said it like it was no big deal, but he was self-conscious, and he bit his lip. It was completely adorable. "It can get kinda boring here." And even though I understood what he was saying, I couldn't disagree more. At this moment there was no place in the world I'd rather be than right here. This camp was the most exhilarating place I'd ever been.

He clumsily withdrew his hands and presented me with a book, his hands shaking. "It's my favorite," he told me, holding it gingerly, and my face nearly crumpled as I reached for it, pressing my hand over its paperback cover. The edges were worn, tattered.

I lifted my eyes to his and swallowed hard. I didn't tell him that I'd already read this book—*his favorite*. That he'd given a copy to me before and that I'd memorized line after line and that he was the one who'd taught me the beauty of reading. "Thank you," I managed while he let me take it from him.

Our fingers brushed, more than brushed, as the book exchanged hands and my cheeks ignited all over again.

"I can't stay," he whispered. "I just wanted to give you this. I gotta go." He glanced back at me once more after he ducked his head, leaving Natty and me in our tent as he left to meet Griffin, or do whatever it is her trainees were supposed to be doing all day.

I clutched the book to my heart.

"I see what you mean," Natty joked when I finally spun around and saw her watching me. "A book. That's pretty serious."

"It's *Fahrenheit 451,*" I breathed, ignoring her mocking tone as I held the book even tighter. "It was the first gift he ever gave me."

The bantering look melted from her face. "He doesn't remember?"

"It doesn't matter. He gave it to me again. It means something."

Natty didn't argue, and I went to my cot and sat down with my treasure, looking at a cover I'd looked at a hundred times before, and ran my fingers over it. This wasn't just about the book.

But as I peeled the cover back and began thumbing through the pages, my heart throbbed savagely, achingly.

Tyler might not readily recall the other things from our old life together the way I did, but they were still there, buried somewhere in his subconscious. I knew for sure because I was looking right at them with my very own eyes.

The best things in life are worth the risk.

The phrase was scribbled in Tyler's familiar handwriting across the top of one of the pages, and had been traced over again and again, as if he'd considered them. Chewed on them. Come back to them time and time again.

I wondered if he even knew who he'd written them for . . . if he knew he'd meant them for me. Or if that was what haunted him. If the memory was right there, elusive and insubstantial and just out of his reach.

I could picture them clearly, though, even if he couldn't. Vibrant and crisp and artfully chalk-drawn on the road between our houses: *The best things in life are worth the risk.*

That's what he'd written. About me. About us.

The birdcage was there on the page too, with the small bird escaping from it.

And as I flipped through the book, there were others. Tyler had copied the chalk pathway he'd drawn for me—the one that had extended from his side of the road to mine, joining my house to his. Him to me. And the words he'd drawn over the top of it:

I'll remember you always.

It was still true, I told myself.

Those memories might not be right at the surface, but they were absolutely-totally-*undeniably* there, waiting to be called back. The book, and what he'd scribbled inside of it, was proof of that.

I thumbed through the pages, and for the first time in forever I hardly wondered what time it was, as instead I let myself get lost in the drawings and words, and in the passages I'd read before. I let all of it dredge up the past and tried to hold on to the feelings they elicited . . . the emotions, the sensations, the memories.

I got lost in Tyler.

I barely noticed when Simon sat down beside me.

"I didn't mean to scare you," he said, even though we both knew he hadn't.

I shoved the book beneath my pillow, right next to my

stolen copy of *Slaughterhouse-Five*, not wanting to share it with him—the book itself or the meaning behind it. When I glanced at my watch, I was stunned to realize that hours had passed. Glancing around, I was even more surprised that Natty was gone. How had I lost track for so long? "What's happening?" Simon wore a serious expression, and my stomach dropped. "Did something happen to Tyler?"

Hurt flashed behind Simon's copper eyes, and immediately I regretted letting Tyler's name slip past my lips. I might not understand what had happened between Simon and me, which pretty much amounted to a whole lot of nothing, at least from my vantage point, but that didn't mean I needed to rub this whole Tyler-coming-back thing in his face. Simon had never seen things the way I had. That I wasn't available the way he'd wanted me to be, no matter how much I'd protested. He'd made it pretty clear he wanted something between us.

"No. He's fine." His voice was flat. "I came to check on you."

"Sorry," I said. And then again, my whole body relaxing: "Really. I'm sorry. I don't know what's gotten into me. I just . . ." I sighed because it wasn't really a mystery what had gotten into me. It was everything. Being here at Blackwater, finding Tyler the way we had, which should have been the best thing ever except that he didn't remember anything about us, and then learning about Simon's history with Griffin and Thom and Willow. It was . . . *a lot* to take in.

Simon's shoulders fell. "No, I'm the one who's sorry." His expression was pensive. "I shouldn't have put so much pressure on you."

We were silent for a long time after that, not in a weird way, but in a comfortable way. The way I wished things could have been between us all along. This was the Simon I felt like I could confide in. Count on.

Outside, the constant shout of someone calling drills filtered into the tent.

"So, what's with that, anyway? All the training?" I finally asked.

Simon didn't miss a beat. "Preparation," he said, like the answer was obvious.

But it wasn't obvious to me. "Preparation for what?"

"For a war."

There was no way I'd just heard him right. "Are you kidding? Griffin's preparing for *war*? Who could she possibly be going to war with?"

Simon shrugged like this was no big deal, but it so completely *was* a big deal. "The NSA?" he said. "Maybe the world. Pretty much anyone who messes with her."

I wasn't even sure what to say to that. "I mean, I get the idea of *preparation*." I didn't actually use air quotes on the last word, but there was no missing my skepticism. "I'd like to stay in one piece as much as the next girl, but really? From what you've said, the other camps lay low, like Thom and the Silent Creek camp. Why can't she just do that? Seems like she's got a pretty good thing going here . . . you know, in the desert. Does she really think a bunch of buffed-up teens stand a snowball's chance in hell against *the government*?"

Simon leaned closer when he asked, "You wanna know why Griffin has such a grudge against the government?" He didn't wait for me to answer. "I guess it helps to know where she's coming from . . . what she thinks of us. It's pretty messed up, what happened to her."

"Of us?" I asked hesitantly, because wasn't that a strange way to phrase it? Griffin was *like* us.

Swallowing hard, Simon pushed on. "Remember when you asked me if I ever felt like a monster, knowing I had alien DNA?"

I winced. "I didn't mean it. I was just . . . having a hard time accepting . . ." I shrugged. "You know . . . it's weird."

"I hear ya," Simon said. "Weird doesn't even begin to explain it. But the thing is, Griff never got to that point: acceptance. She doesn't even call us hybrids, the way we do. She uses a different word: chimera. It *literally* means monster."

"Monster," I repeated numbly, feeling sick that I'd ever said that word myself.

The truth was, I felt exactly-wholly-*completely* identical to the same person I'd always been. If it weren't for the fact that I knew, logically, that my body had been changed at a genetic level, I probably wouldn't even believe it.

"But she's one of us. Why would she say that?"

"Griffin's case is different from ours," Simon explained. "Not different in the sense that she's not a hybrid, because she is. But different in the *reason* she's a hybrid."

I raised my eyebrow, prompting him to go on.

"Her dad worked at this place called the Los Alamos National Laboratory, back in the '50s. It was the same place they did the first atomic bomb tests back in '45." Simon chewed his lower lip before continuing. "Her dad was kind of a big deal—some super scientist who knew a whole helluva lot about biochemistry. This was right after Watson and Crick had discovered the double helical structure of DNA, so there was still a lot to learn in the field."

"Apparently, there still is," I interjected. "Otherwise, why would the Daylighters be so desperate to get their hands on us?"

"I think even without the alien intervention there's still a lot to learn. But yeah, I think we're somewhat *exceptional*," Simon added. "There was also a lot of fringe activity in the government around these covert alien meetings, supposedly involving President Eisenhower."

I remembered this. "Jett told me about those. I think he called them the First Contact meetings. He said there were all kinds of scientists and high-up officials and even that President Eisenhower had these meetings with aliens. It sounds crazy."

"Crazy, maybe, but hard to dispute when you know the truth," Simon said. "Griffin's father was one of the scientists invited to the meetings. Only he didn't just get invited . . ." Simon stopped and inhaled, because apparently what he had to say next required a deep-breath kind of delivery. "He offered Griffin as some sort of . . . *goodwill contribution* to the efforts."

"Shut up," I scoffed, but I seriously doubted Simon was making this stuff up, so what I was really thinking was: How messed up is that? "And they took her?" I asked, but the answer was obvious: of course they'd taken her, or we wouldn't be having this conversation now.

Cat had always referred to scenarios like these as train-wreck moments.

Of course, Cat had always meant something along the lines of the kind of nasty breakup where one person cheats on the other, or juicy scandals, like when Mr. Jasper got caught breaking into the girls' locker room and trying on our stinky gym uniforms. That sort of thing.

In this case, we were talking about a girl's life forever altered by someone she should've been able to count on. All things considered, no wonder she had trust issues.

"They did. And when she came back—the way so many of us do—she was never the same." He shuddered. "But you have to remember, it's not like she was the first to be taken. Thom was taken before she was," he told me, and I thought about that. Natty had mentioned that Thom had barely been a teen when he'd been taken, sometime before the 1950s. But that made him, what, at least in his seventies, didn't it?

I pictured him the way he was now, aged so much slower, the way all of us would age. He looked older than the rest of us, sure, but not by much . . . twenty, maybe twenty-one years old, but definitely *not* an old man.

I'd vaguely considered the way I'd had to leave my friends and my parents so I couldn't hurt them, but I'd never really thought about what they would mean down the road. Like what my life would be like in twenty . . . thirty . . . fifty years.

As far as I could tell, from the way the other Returned were living, it would be exactly the same as it was now. I'd be living the same way, with the same people . . . trying not to be caught by those who hunted us.

The idea was depressing.

No wonder Griffin was angry.

But Simon was still talking. "To hear her tell it, when she tells it at all, she might as well have been the first."

"How so?" I asked.

"Dear Old Dad wasn't quite done with her after she was returned. He wasn't satisfied with making her a sacrifice. He was a scientist, and he wanted to know just what they'd done to her, and how—if at all—she'd changed. She became like his very own home science kit."

"That's sick."

"You're telling me," Simon agreed.

"No wonder she hates the government so much. Her dad must'a done a number on her head."

"Her dad and everyone else at the lab. She became property of the US military after that."

"For how long?" I asked, feeling a stab of guilt for judging her so quickly and so harshly.

Simon's voice bled into the shadows. "Until she killed him."

"Her own dad?" I asked, rubbing my arms absently. "What happened?"

"He never realized how much she hated him for what he'd done. One day, he came to take a blood sample from her, and when he wasn't looking, she cut his safety suit with a scalpel she'd stolen. She'd been waiting for an opportunity like that . . . for her chance to get even.

"She could've used the knife to cut through her straps and escape—she'd had the time. But instead she'd hidden it and plotted her revenge. The thing was, he didn't even realize what she'd done right away; it wasn't until the symptoms started setting in that they even thought to check his suit for damage. He never suspected she was planning a thing, and he didn't take enough precautions against her. His own fault, really. He was a goner the second the exposed air reached his lungs. Poor guy never had a chance," Simon finished.

But I didn't share Simon's sympathy for Griffin's dad. It was hard to feel bad for a man who'd sentenced his very own daughter to a lifetime of being less than human. He'd taken away her chance at an ordinary-everyday-normal life. Of growing up and growing old. Of going to school and graduating and having a family. "That *poor guy* was responsible for changing her in the first place. She never asked for what he did. For the rest of us, it happened by chance. What he did was on purpose," I argued.

Then something struck me.

"Kind of like what I did to Tyler?" I asked, but I asked it flatly, and Simon just shook his head, wearing an expression that said he saw right through me: I didn't mean it. Which was true, because I didn't.

"That's not even kinda the same."

I'd known Tyler would never be able to see his friends or his family again when I'd decided to let him be taken, but I *hadn't* known a thing about the *not*-human part. Besides, even if I had, he would have died if I hadn't done anything at all.

Not much of a decision, if you asked me.

But understanding more about Griffin, suddenly I wasn't so sure I *didn't* want to stay with her at Blackwater. To train with her army.

Except I knew that wasn't true either, not really. I was angry—for her and for myself and for all of us—but I'd never be *that* angry. I'd never been a rage-against-the-machine kind of girl.

Cat had been the one who had causes. She'd been the one to boycott big businesses and start petitions and join groups to raise social awareness. I'd always been along for the ride. Even if I did stay at Blackwater Ranch, that's what I'd be doing, going along for the ride.

I didn't have that kind of fire in my heart, no matter how much I hated the way the Daylight Division was relentless in their pursuit to capture us. I would still rather steer clear of them than try to take them down, because to me, you might as well be Jack trying to slay the giant. Even if we managed to take one down, they always had more giants.

They had more resources than we ever would.

Besides, I still couldn't wrap my brain around this whole us-versus-them thing.

In my mind, I was still one of them. Maybe not Agent Truman and his Daylight Division, but regular people, like my parents and my little brother, Logan. Like Cat and Austin and all the kids I'd gone to school with, who even though they were older than I was now, were still the same ones I'd grown up with my whole life. It didn't matter that I could see in the dark or needed less sleep. None of those things changed the fact that when it came down to it, I was the same dorky girl I'd always been. I still liked to watch *The Little Mermaid* over and over again and to sing at the top of my lungs in the shower, and I wanted to play softball and be kissed like I was the only girl in the world.

I mean, weren't those the things that made me who I was, not the fact that if I concentrated super hard, I could levitate a book with my mind, which when you really thought about it, so could a lot of guys in Vegas who wore sparkly suits and did magic tricks.

It seemed to me, those of us who'd been returned should be on the same side as everyone else, even if we were *different* now.

"You don't have to agree with Griffin," Simon said, getting up and standing in front of me. "But it helps to understand where she's coming from," which was probably true of everyone if you stopped to think about it.

His hand moved then, and his thumb skimmed the underneath of my chin, slipping beneath my jaw. “I’m glad you’re okay,” he said. “And no matter what happens, now that Tyler’s back, I’ll still be here for you, Kyra. Always.”

Then he bent forward and his lips pressed a soft kiss on my forehead. And before I could tell him no, or stop, or this so wasn’t a good idea, he’d already turned around and left me all alone.

PART THREE

Nothing happens until something moves.

—Albert Einstein

CHAPTER SIXTEEN

Day Thirty-One

IT DIDN'T TAKE LONG FOR NATTY AND I TO FIGure we were stuck in this weird kind of limbo—not really being detained, but still . . . kind of being *watched*. Nyla was no longer stationed outside our tent, and she hadn't been replaced by another guard or anything. But we also weren't completely free to roam the camp.

Natty was the one who figured that part out, when she'd gone out exploring. It was at the same time Simon had stopped by to check on me.

She told me about her strange experience as we hunched over a plate of fresh berries and sliced cheeses that evening in the cafeteria, pretending not to be aware of the sharp-eyed glances directed our way.

Natty thought she was only being paranoid at first. But when the same blond girl kept popping up wherever she went, no matter how hard she tried to ditch her, she realized she was being tailed.

Eventually the girl approached her, suggesting Natty should go back to our tent, using some lame excuse about Natty having had enough sun for the day. *Seriously?* I'm sure that was what she was worried about—Natty being overheated or burning or whatever.

But according to Natty, it wasn't an order or anything. It was more like a vigorously reinforced recommendation. A recommendation that came with a new blond shadow. Natty thought she could have objected, but rather than try to dodge her new stalker for the rest of the day, she'd just given in.

The girl had escorted Natty the entire way back to Paradise . . . you know, to ensure Natty didn't "get lost" along the way.

But at least we knew where we stood now. We weren't prisoners, but we weren't *not* prisoners either.

Clear as mud.

Natty tried to find the blond girl again so she could point her out to me—on our way to the cafeteria, while we ate, and during our walk back—but whoever she was, she was clearly off-duty.

Too bad. I wanted to know who our non-guards were.

Tyler was waiting at our tent when we got back, and the anxious look he gave me, along with the way he rubbed his hands over the sides of his khakis, made it clear he wasn't the spy assigned to keep an eye on us.

"Hey," he offered, his deep dimple gouging a path through his cheek.

Suddenly I felt like I needed to wipe my palms, too, as I bit my bottom lip and grinned back at him. It was silly, knowing all this about who we'd been and having to start from scratch. Silly and awesome all at the same time, because maybe it wasn't so bad, having all these firsts all over again.

"Hey," Natty said, and Tyler blinked, all surprised-like, as if she'd just . . . *poof!* . . . materialized from out of nowhere.

But Natty didn't wait for a hint, she did this roll-her-eyes-and-shake-her-head-sighing thing that made it clear she knew she wasn't invited to this little party. "I'll just . . ." She pointed to our tent. "I'll be in here. See you later." She slipped inside and left the two of us alone outside.

Tyler's grin grew as he rocked back on his heels. "She seems nice," he said, and I wondered when he'd possibly come to that conclusion. During the two seconds he'd glimpsed her waiting for me inside our tent when he'd first dropped me off, after we'd first been reunited? Or just now, during their awkward, barely-two-seconds-longer run-in?

Still grinning, he shoved his hands in his pockets and lifted his shoulders. I swear, his smile could literally melt the sun, which was the lamest compliment ever, but was so totally true it didn't even matter. He was that hot. "I . . ."

He nodded his head in the direction we'd just come from. "I was supposed to . . ." What I initially thought was nervous, and somewhat cute, stammering was getting uncomfortable.

I frowned. "What? You were supposed to what?"

"Griffin," he finally blurted out. "She wanted me to come get you."

If I could have buried my head, like an ostrich, I would have. I was part embarrassed that I thought he'd been looking all awkward because of me, which I still sort of hoped was the case, and part mad because Griffin was the real reason he was here.

"Griffin?" I parroted numbly.

He nodded, stuffing his hands deeper into his pockets. "Yeah. She's waiting for us. *For you.*"

Not exactly the way I imagined my evening unfolding after finding Tyler on my front step, but . . .

I tried not to sound too disappointed when I exhaled. "Fine. Lead the way."

Tyler bumped my shoulder as he fell into step beside me, seemingly relieved that I understood. I kept telling myself this was what I'd been waiting for—to spend time, even just a few seconds at a time, with him . . . regardless of the reason.

He took me to Griffin, who was waiting for us in a place where there were none of the giant spotlights and it was dark all around. Simon was there too, as was Nyla.

"What's going on?" I asked Simon.

But it was Griffin who answered. "I have a job for you. All of you."

I looked to Simon, and then Tyler, before asking, "Job? What kind of job? And why us?"

"Not Tyler," Griffin answered. "He stays here. With me. But I need the three of you to go on a recruiting mission."

"Seriously? You want us to *recruit* for you?" I shot Simon a skeptical look, then shrugged at Griffin. "Why would we do that? You've held us hostage for days and now you want us to *run errands* for you?"

Then she exhaled. "I'm giving you a chance to prove you can be useful. Earn yourself some freedoms around camp." When I started to argue, to tell her I didn't need to prove anything, she just lifted her hand to stop me. "I've already explained this to Simon and Nyla, but we believe the No-Suchers know about this kid too. I don't want to send one of my teams, but I will if I have to. The last thing we want is for the Daylight Division to get to this kid before we do. You have no idea what they do to those like us."

But she was wrong; I knew exactly what they'd do. And the very mention of the No-Suchers, and their Daylight Division, made my blood run cold. The thought of saving this kid from their clutches made me feel like some sort of hero.

And if I could get Griffin to loosen the leash she had me on in the process, then all the better.

"You don't have to do it," Tyler said, easing up alongside me as he gripped my arm. "She's right, there are other teams who can do this. It's dangerous." His breath tickled my cheek, and even though it was dark, I had no trouble seeing the earnestness in his green eyes as they searched mine.

Griffin cleared her throat. "But I'd be grateful if you did. And I'd go out of my way to make things easier on you here at camp if you did."

"Natty too?" I asked, thinking of the way she'd been followed just hours earlier.

Griffin held my gaze. After several long seconds, she nodded. "All of you."

I looked to Simon, and then to Nyla. "What do you think?"

"I think I'd rather have you stay here, at camp." Simon answered me but glared at Griffin. "But it's been made clear that's not an option. From what we've heard, we have a big enough head start that I think we can get there and back by dawn, no problem." I wondered what I'd missed, and whether Tyler knew what had transpired between Griffin and Simon before we got here.

I chewed the inside of my lip, turning to Griffin once more. "And we'll have more freedom?" I just wanted her confirmation one more time. When she nodded, I took a deep breath. "Fine, then. I'm in too."

"How much farther?" I had to yell to be heard from the backseat. The bandanna Nyla had given me to tie my hair back barely contained it, and the wind whipped stray pieces around my cheeks as we flew along the road in the open-air Jeep.

With her smooth head, Nyla didn't have to worry about pesky hair flying around, stinging her face. She hollered over her shoulder while she drove, "Little town called Delta, about two hours from here."

I checked my watch; that would put us there sometime around 2:30 in the morning, plenty of time to get back to camp before sunup, just as Simon had predicted.

"What makes Griffin think this kid we're going after is one of us? How exactly does she get her intel?" I was fascinated by the process. By the way they did things in this Returned world I lived in now.

I assumed there was some kind of shared superhighway of information, like all those crazy files my dad had kept on everyone who'd disappeared, including where they'd lived, where they'd last been seen, their favorite music, and if they'd ever returned at all.

Pretty much everything there was to know about them.

I sat forward to hear better, but also hoping the seat might block some of the wind assaulting me.

Simon faced me from the passenger seat. "Depends. This time she got a call from an inside source saying they had the boy in town," he called back to me, "under medical observation. I guess when they found him, he told the sheriff the last thing he remembered was being with a friend back home . . . which apparently was *nowhere near* Utah."

My palms got sweaty and I rubbed them on my jeans. I

remembered that not-knowing sensation, of being one place and then waking up in another. It was . . . disturbing, to say the least.

Like a really, *really* bad case of déjà vu.

"So, where was he from, then?"

I watched the scenery zip past. The only lights out here were from our headlights and the stars overhead. It might have been beautiful, if only I hadn't known that we were on our way to change someone's life forever.

Simon interrupted my thoughts when he handed me a piece of paper.

Unfolding it, I assumed Griffin's "inside source" had gotten her this police report as well. It listed all the pertinent details about the boy and his disappearance:

Alex Walker, fifteen years old. From Florida.

According to this, his grandmother had reported him missing from their home in Tallahassee just two days earlier. Since he had a history of running away, she'd told local police he'd probably run off again.

Yet late this evening, Alex Walker had walked into a truck stop near the edge of Delta, Utah, and asked the waitress, and I quote: "What circle of hell is this place supposed to be?" When questioned further, he claimed to have absolutely zero memory of how he'd gotten all the way from Tallahassee to Delta, or where he'd been for the past forty-eight hours.

Forty-eight hours . . . the exact amount of time most Returned were missing.

The report said he was being held for observation at the Delta Medical Clinic, and his grandmother had been contacted.

He was at the hospital.

My stomach knotted painfully.

I'd been taken to the hospital, too, back when I'd first been returned, and it hadn't ended so well for the lab tech who'd drawn my blood. My body had tried to heal around the needle, and because I hadn't known better, he'd been exposed to what I realized now was my poisonous blood.

I seriously hoped history didn't repeat itself in this case.

"Griffin mentioned that the Daylighters already know about him. How can she be so sure? Did her inside source tell her that too?"

Simon looked to Nyla for the answer.

"Griffin said the message came from a camp in Texas, who heard it from another one in southern New Mexico," she called back to me. "That's the way it works—we get these bulletins that bounce from camp to camp. It's not a bad system, and most of the time the information's pretty accurate."

I wanted to be cool, and make it seem like my stomach hadn't just clenched painfully, but I had to ask, "Most of the time? And what if they're wrong this time? About our head start?"

"Kyra . . ." The way Simon said it was supposed to mean I shouldn't worry, but I couldn't help it. I worried plenty.

Nyla didn't seem half as concerned. She leaned back and

shouted, "Relax! If Griffin really thought there'd be trouble, she wouldn't have risked sending a team at all."

Or, I thought as my stomach clenched tighter and tighter, until it was just a shriveled little knot, *she'd send a crew she considered expendable.*

My eyes wandered to my watch to count down the minutes. But for once, time couldn't ease the crush of anxiety that built inside me, reaching a crescendo as each second passed, growing leaden and filling all my insides. I had to tug at my shirt so the air could reach down in front.

Damn, I couldn't remember the last time I'd sweated so much.

Eighty-six minutes . . .

Sixty-three . . .

Forty-four . . .

When we finally saw Delta, the city's lights were like distant stars. Something about knowing we were so close to reaching our destination made me restless, and even though I'd considered the unrelenting wind that battered me cold just a few miles back, I leaned into it now to dry the perspiration that prickled my skin.

I was nervous. What if we were too late, and the Daylighters had beaten us and had already whisked the kid back to the Tacoma facility?

What if this was another trap?

We passed a sign that read: You Are Now Entering Delta, Utah. Population 3,457.

I never once saw Nyla consult a map or a GPS, or ask directions. She didn't say if she'd been here before, but if she hadn't, then she was just one of those people who had an innate sense of direction. Their own built-in compass.

I was super jealous of people like that. I'd always been fast on the mound, and now I could add super strong to my list of talents, but even as a kid I'd always been directionally challenged. To the point that Pin-the-Tail-on-the-Donkey had been less like a game and more like a hand-eye coordination test.

One I almost never passed.

When we got there, the Emergency entrance was brightly illuminated against the dark backdrop of the rest of what I assumed was supposed to pass for a hospital. Even if it hadn't been dark, the place we pulled up in front of was really more clinic-sized than hospital-sized, but Delta was a small town, so clearly they made do with what they had.

Out front of the blazing ER doors there were two parked cars, which would have made my heart race and set my suspicions into overdrive, except that one was a beat-up station wagon, circa 1960-something. And the other was a bright yellow convertible Volkswagen Beetle.

Neither screamed Daylight Division.

Off to the side, and closer to the sidewalk, was a man smoking a cigarette and murmuring into his cell phone. Again, since he was pushing seventy and wearing a hospital gown, I deemed him at least relatively harmless.

Rather than parking, Nyla decided to wait for us, which was probably a good idea, since no matter how I tried to spin it, I couldn't come up with a reasonable story for the three of us to be skulking around the hospital at three in the morning.

Also, with her shaved head, I didn't imagine Nyla went unnoticed all that often.

There was only a small check-in counter inside, and the girl working it looked barely older than we did. When Simon and I stopped to ask where we could find Alex Walker, she chomped obnoxiously on her wad of gum and pulled out a spiral notebook, which didn't seem very hospital-y at all. She had us sign one of the lined pieces of paper after asking us to confirm that we didn't have any cough or flu symptoms, and then she just blurted out his room number.

Not, "Are either of you family members?" or concerns for privacy laws or anything. Just a raised eyebrow that asked, *Are we done here?* and we were on our way, wandering the halls of the hospital in the middle of the night, without so much as a glance at our (fake) IDs.

Apparently security wasn't much of an issue in Delta, Utah.

We only had to go up one floor, which shouldn't have been a big deal, except that, because the building was so old, the place was put together like a ransom note. The building looked small from the outside, but it seemed bigger inside, and it was as if every hallway had been added on as a second, and then third, thought.

I was beginning to feel like a rat in one of those science mazes, and that we should get some sort of reward for figuring our way through.

After several turns and dead ends and some backtracking, Simon and I finally found an elevator. When we got off on the second floor, I breathed a sigh of relief that there was an actual sign pointing toward room numbers 2024–2050, since Gum-Chewing Girl told us Alex was in room 2046.

I pulled Simon to a stop outside the closed door. "What did you mean when you said Griffin didn't give you a choice about bringing me here?" I stalled, suddenly nervous. I mean, how do you even start to explain that everything this kid knew, his entire life, was a lie? That his whole world had just changed, all because he'd gone missing for less than forty-eight hours.

Simon leaned his head out of the small alcove and glanced down the hallway, making sure we were still all alone. It was end-of-the-world quiet out there. The flickering overhead fluorescents were dimmed, and it was super weird that we hadn't even passed a nurse's station on this floor, considering it was a hospital and all. "She didn't say it in so many words, but I think she wants to keep you away from Tyler," he explained. "If I didn't know better, I think she feels threatened by you."

I pursed my lips. "And that doesn't worry you? Look at what she was willing to do to Willow when she was threatened by her." Now it was my turn to look down the hallway, my heart picking up speed.

Simon put his hands over mine. "Relax, Kyr. Her beef with Willow had to do with power. I don't think that's her issue with you. I think she's worried Tyler might be a little too interested in you." He took a step closer, too close, and suddenly my heart beat like a sledgehammer. "Frankly, I'm worried about that too."

He leaned toward me, closing the gap that had already grown too small. There was a shift in the air, something tangible and sharp that I felt all the way to my toes. I could smell him—his skin, clean and crisp, but with the hint of the dust-blown air clinging to him. His eyes, so rich and coppery, landed on mine, begging me to tell him this was okay, what he was about to do.

I yanked back at the last possible second, just as his lips were about to brush mine, and my head thumped against the wall behind me.

His eyes sparkled then, like he'd been about to get away with something he'd known he shouldn't have.

"You never give up, do you?" I accused, shoving him, and giving myself the space I needed to breathe again. And then, because it was easier to change the subject than to deal with the lingering tension, I eyeballed the door to room 2046. "Should we knock or just go in?"

Simon was still chuckling beneath his breath, and had his hand on the door, when we heard the elevator down the hallway sliding open once more. I couldn't explain why exactly, since this was a hospital and people came and went at all hours in places like this, but something made me stop him from opening it.

I had the strangest feeling we should wait, for just a split second . . . for just the barest-tiniest-briefest of moments.

I craned my neck from the recess we were standing in to watch as two men stepped out of the elevator, and I flinched, dragging Simon back until we were out of sight.

The men were wearing suits—starched suits with crisply starched shirts. Even their ties looked stiff and starched. In any other place, at any other time, I'd say there was nothing special about them, these two men. Their suits weren't matching, they weren't dressed all in black, and they weren't wearing sunglasses indoors or anything.

Except we already knew we were only a step or two ahead of the Daylighters, and these two were just . . . off somehow. In the same way Agent Truman had seemed off when I'd met him that first day, when he'd come to my front door.

The hairs on my arms went on high alert, and Simon dragged me back as we took one step, and then another and another, until we'd disappeared through the open door beside room 2046 and were hidden in the darkness of room 2048. Behind us, over my shoulder, I heard a machine pulse, beeping on even intervals that felt like it was keeping time with my heart.

My eyes were wide as we stood there, listening for the men's footsteps in the hallway outside, and as they neared, their heavy soles falling against the tiles, my heart rate overtook the beating of the machine.

I squeezed Simon's arm when I heard one of the men mumble, "Two-oh-four-six. This is it."

2046. It was them. They were here for Alex too.

I had Simon in a death grip, afraid to let him go. He gave a curt shake of his head, letting me know to keep my mouth shut, as if I hadn't already thought of that. My entire body was shaking and had broken out in a cold sweat, making me shiver like an insane person.

We were trapped in here.

"Who are you?" a voice, so small and so frail, asked from behind us.

I practically jumped out of my skin, spinning to see who was there, and even though I could see in the dark, the person was nearly invisible in the shadows, making it impossible to tell whether it was a man or a woman asking.

"What do you want?" came the whisper of a voice again.

I gripped Simon even tighter. What if those guys out there had heard? What if they came in here to find out what was going on? We had to shut whoever it was up before they got us caught.

I let go of Simon and crept over to the center of the room.

I nearly hesitated when I reached the bed, but then leaned down and pressed my lips together. "Shhh," I said almost inaudibly to the tiniest, most fragile-looking woman I'd ever laid eyes on. She had an oxygen tube tucked beneath her nose, and her skin was mottled with brown spots, skin so thin it was nearly transparent—Simon might not have known this, not in the dark, but I could see it clearly. Her eyes were pale, milky even, and it was a wonder she'd seen us at all. "We're only staying for a minute," I crooned softly, hoping she could even hear me above the still-beeping equipment surrounding her.

She frowned, and I worried she was going to argue or call for help, or maybe try to find enough voice to scream. She had that look, like she wanted nothing to do with a couple of kids, strangers, in her room at this hour. I bit back the knot of fear, the sheer and utter panic, as I cast quick glances over my shoulder, while Simon continued to watch the door.

"I'm sorry. We can't stay long," I said, taking her hand and hoping I could convince her not to rat us out . . . at least not just yet. Her hand was delicate like a bird, her bones hollow and light, her skin papery and warm.

Her face lit up when she smiled up at me as her gnarled fingers closed over mine in a grip I wouldn't have imagined possible from her. "It's okay, dear," she said back to me. "I know you try. You do what you can. I know that." And then she let go and her head collapsed back to her pillow, and all at once her eyes closed.

I waited for a minute, listening to the machines and hoping she hadn't just up and died on me. But the beeping noises continued, and so did her almost imperceptible shallow breaths.

She'd only fallen asleep, that was all.

I let out a sigh of relief as I released her hand, patting it once to let her know I was sorry I wasn't whoever she'd thought I was. I felt bad for this woman, wondering if there really was a girl—maybe my age and maybe not—who didn't come by often enough to visit.

Simon was behind me then and when I turned to face him, his fingers bit into my arm as he made a screwed-up face. But it was the way he was looking at me that told me something else was wrong. "Aw, hell . . . Kyra, we gotta get outta here."

Frowning, I asked, "Why? What's wrong with me?"

He was still cringing when he shook his head. "It's your eyes," he said, like it was a bad thing . . . a really frickin' bad thing. "They're . . . I swear to Christ they're glowing."

I flinched, and my hands automatically flew up to touch them. I turned to the sink, which had a mirror above it—the metal kind that, even in the light, would have made me look distorted. But Simon was right; there was a too-vivid quality to my eyes that made them almost luminescent.

Like phantom fireflies.

Simon's grip on my wrist drew me back to the situation at hand. "We need to get you the hell outta here before these guys come out of that room and find us. I have a feeling they'd way rather have you than that kid in there."

"What about Alex? Shouldn't we try to figure out a way to get him too?"

"It's too late for him," Simon whispered insistently. "Even if they didn't come all the way from Tacoma, I doubt they're planning to leave 'til they know for sure if he's one of us. Agent Truman made that mistake with you—I doubt these guys plan to repeat it."

He eased the door open and when he gave me the

all-clear signal, I followed him. As we passed room 2046, I could hear them in there, talking to the boy, to Alex Walker, and my step faltered, knowing what he was in for. I couldn't believe we were about to leave him behind.

Simon must have sensed my reservation because he reached for me, pulling me faster as we hurried, running now, down the hall, this time passing up the elevator for the stairwell beyond.

We took the steps two at a time, almost tripping in our effort to get down them, and away from the two starched-suit men, who Simon believed would just as willingly, maybe more so, take me rather than Alex back to the Daylight Division.

So they could flay me open to see what makes me tick.

CHAPTER SEVENTEEN

NYLA HADN'T WASTED A SECOND WHEN WE'D raced out the ER doors; she was there with the engine already revving. She'd seen them too—the Daylighters—when they'd strutted right past her.

She'd spared me only the briefest of glances when I'd jumped in the backseat, right before saying, "Well, that's new," and I knew she meant the whole glowy-eye thing since that's where she was looking, directly at my eyes. But then she'd jammed the Jeep in gear and peeled out of there, not bothering to look back—either at Delta, which faded in the distance, or at me.

Simon might have checked on me, but I wouldn't have known since the second we were on the road, I'd leaned my head back and shut those eyes of mine, trying to block out the guilt about leaving Alex Walker behind.

I felt sick most of the ride back to Blackwater Ranch.

I mean, I guess we'd had to do it. I doubt we'd have been able to get him away from there, from those guys, unnoticed. And then what? They would have followed us? They would have known exactly *where* we were, where Blackwater was?

What kind of option was that?

As it was, I was so freaked out that they were only a few hours away, back in Delta, that when the sun had finally crested over the horizon, stabbing me with its presence, it felt more like penance for my failure to save the boy. Like I deserved each spasm that rippled through me.

This time when we got back to camp, the only ambush awaiting us was Griffin, which was almost worse than what facing her entire army had been when I saw the tightening of her lips as she gave the Jeep a once-over, doing a mental head count even before we'd come to a complete stop.

"What happened?" Her voice was filled with accusation as she turned to Simon, and then me, pointedly letting us know we'd let her down on our first recovery mission.

Nyla answered before either of us had a chance to explain. "Daylighters got there ahead of us. Nothing we could do."

"Daylighters," Griffin echoed. "They didn't see you, did they?"

Before that moment, when I'd seen the look of abject

horror cross Griffin's face, I'd had my doubts about her, like that maybe this whole sending-us-on-a-mission thing had been a setup. That she'd tipped the Daylighters off herself in order to get rid of Simon, Nyla, and me.

Mostly me, I'd suspected.

But now . . . now I didn't think so. I doubted she'd sacrifice her own camp like that. Not on purpose anyway.

Nyla gave a decisive shake of her head as she jumped down from the Jeep. "'Course not. You think I'da come back here if they had? Nah, they got to the kid before Simon and Kyra could, and then we cleared outta there."

"Damn," she muttered. "So they got him? Too bad you couldn't've gotten there sooner." Griffin lifted her chin defiantly at Simon. "What happened? You used to be the best."

There was a pause—the kind of extra-long one that makes you aware that there's so much more than just a pause happening. That subtle communication of locked gazes and eyebrow raises and signals no one else was probably even aware of.

"That was a long time ago," he said, finally backing down. "I didn't ask to do this, Griffin. This was your idea. Kyra and I should never have been there at all." He moved closer to me, creating a united front. "I'm not a recruiter anymore."

Griffin scowled at me, giving me a this-has-nothing-to-do-with-you look that made me feel like an outsider all over again, and I had to remind myself what Simon had told me about her . . . about her father and everything he'd done to her. It kept me from wanting to slug her for being such a *major B* about everything.

No wonder she doesn't trust anyone, I reminded myself. *It's not entirely her fault.*

Then she looked Simon up and down as one of her tapered brows ticked up visibly. "Mmm . . . so I see." And when she was finished giving him an unspoken slap on the wrist, she shrugged as if it had never mattered in the first place. Like what's-done-is-done.

And so it goes, Billy Pilgrim would have said.

Except this was a real-life person we were talking about, and I wasn't sure I could flip the switch that easily.

"Well," Griffin announced, "good news is Jett made amazing progress while you were off playing Rescue Rangers. Now that you're back, he wants us to join him in the computer lab . . . so he can show us what he's found so far. We can have him track Daylighter communications too. We wanna make sure they have no idea where we are, or that we ever even knew about the kid in Delta."

My chest tightened at the mention of the boy, and the proximity of the agents. I choked back a healthy dose of guilt, trying not to imagine him strapped to a gurney, the same way Willow had been back in their central lab. I couldn't help wishing we'd done more. Tried harder.

I had a moment of panic, though, as I reached nervously for Simon. "My eyes . . . how are they?"

His mouth turned downward as he leaned close, reassuring me with a whispered, "Can't even tell in the light." He nodded toward Griffin. "*She* didn't notice."

True. There was no way she'd have let something that significant slide.

By the time we'd reached the computer lab, I was disappointed Tyler hadn't come out to meet me. That would have been the one consolation to this whole mess, to find him there . . . preferably all alone.

And, in a perfect world, without his shirt.

The alone part wasn't so far off, however. In fact, when we got to the lab it was practically deserted. Last time I'd been in here, the place had been bustling, with about a half dozen or so of Griffin's soldiers assigned to monitor radio frequencies, internet traffic, and online activity.

Now it was just Jett and Thom waiting for the four of us.

Apparently Griffin was just as baffled as I was by the absence of activity. "Where is everyone?"

"I cleared the place. What I'm about to show you needs to stay between us." Jett turned to Nyla. "I think she should go too. We can't risk it."

Nyla looked like she might argue, but Griffin nodded toward the door—an unspoken order. Nyla stalled, her shoulders, face, and arms tense while her eyebrows drew together in an uncertain line, like she was pained by the decision. Ultimately, though, her need to obey Griffin won out.

When the door closed behind her, Jett took a seat, this time not at his laptop but at one of Griffin's computers, and went to work. "Here . . . ," he said.

I watched as the large monitor in front of him came to

life, filled with the same NSA logo I'd seen that first day when Agent Truman forced his business card on me, the one with the golden firefly on it that signified his super secret-y Daylight Division. Jett entered a series of commands, line after line of code, as fluently as if he had full NSA security clearance.

I chewed the inside of my cheek while my eyes drifted to my watch, slowing my mind.

When the last of the files unlocked, and the screen in front of Jett, and all of the screens around us, began to fill with information, I took a step back, my eyes wide. There were files that looked like printouts and scanned documents—some official and some not so official. Pictures, old and new.

All about me.

It definitely wasn't what I'd expected to see. All those images. All those memories. Like a blast from the past. My face, my name, my information. My birthdate, the address of our house in Burlington, my school and medical and Social Security records. My birth certificate with my teeny, tiny newborn footprints. Snapshots of me standing alone and posing for the camera on my first day of school, and then again with Austin on our way to Homecoming in the tenth grade. Portraits of me with my softball teams throughout the years.

And one photograph I didn't remember being taken—of me on the day I'd returned—in the hospital in Burlington, with those orange and black ribbons I'd been wearing for our championship game still tangled through my hair while

I'd been wearing the ugly blue hospital gown.

They all filled the screens. Filled up every last square inch of pixelated space in front of, and all around, us.

"What . . . is this?" It was like staring at an online homage to me. A *This Is Your Life*, my dad would have said, which was some old-fashioned TV show he always brought up whenever we busted out our family albums.

This was what the NSA—what Agent Truman and the Daylighters—had been hiding inside all those encrypted files? But . . . why? What was so interesting about me?

"Is there one of these on each of us?" It was the only thing that made sense: they were tracking all the Returned this closely.

Thom just closed his eyes, letting me know with a look that I was off the mark with my guess.

"So, what, then? What else was in the files?" I asked.

Griffin was apparently as clueless as I was. "Yeah. What are we missing? What's so special about *her*?" I kind of liked the way she said "her," like I was a bad taste in her mouth. She didn't even bother looking my way.

Jett did, though. He glanced over his shoulder at me, and there was something in his eyes, those unusual, kaleidoscope eyes that clicked then. I recognized that look—it was the same one Natty had given me just after we'd raced out of the bowling alley, after . . .

He knew. I wasn't sure how, whether it had been Natty or Simon who'd told him, but Jett for sure knew my secret.

I frowned back at him and shook my head. "It's not . . .

it . . . *no* . . ." I leaned over his shoulder, scanning the screens and the files for mention of it.

"*No*, what?" Griffin insisted, turning to scan the monitors. "Does someone want to tell me what's going on? What was so important that you cleared the room . . . ?" But as she finished her sentence, her attention was caught by one of the screens. It was clearly an NSA document, with a red "CLASSIFIED" stamp across it.

I didn't have to guess who'd told Jett my secret after that; it was right there in black, white, and bright-classified-red. Agent Truman had written up a report all about me. But what I focused on first—and most—was the section on what I'd done to him:

Subject displays an uncanny ability to move objects without making obvious physical contact with them. Subject appears capable of some form of high-velocity telekinesis.

Subject. My very identity had been whittled down to a designation rather than a name.

Agent Truman had put what I could do in writing, in a secret government file.

That I could move things. Without touching them.

"What else?" Griffin demanded. "What else can she do?" Again, she said "she" like it was a dirty word, only this time she was staring right at me.

I wanted to answer her, really I did. I just couldn't come up with a single response because everything, all of it, being exposed like this, in front of them, felt . . . *too personal*. Especially with Griffin, who couldn't even say my name.

"She can see in the dark," Jett finally blurted out. "And she doesn't need to breathe as often as the rest of us."

I hated being set apart like that. Being different.

"So you knew about this?" Griffin asked him.

Jett shook his head. "Not about the telekinesis thing." He flashed me a hurt look, and suddenly I felt like a jerk for not confiding in him. "You could've told me."

"It doesn't matter," I told Jett. I told all of them.

But Jett just frowned. "Kyra, they have your blood work too. From when your parents took you to the hospital, after you came back."

I shrugged. "So what. You already told me our DNA's different. I assumed they knew that much too." But there was still that feeling in the air and I knew I was still missing something . . . something crucial.

"Yours was different," he said. "Different from any of the rest of ours. From anyone's. *You're different.*"

Griffin took a step toward me, her expression shifting as she examined me. "Different," she repeated, and I couldn't tell if she was saying it in a bad way, like I was one of those chimera-monster things Simon had said she considered us, or whether she was just saying it, like it was a fact—the sky is blue, the earth is round, water is wet—that kind of thing. But she was looking at me differently.

"Like . . . *how*?" I asked, giving a cockeyed shrug and trying to laugh it off like it was nothing. A mistake.

But inside, where my heart was going a million miles a minute, I understood it wasn't nothing. I understood it was a huge-giant-enormous something. I could tell by the way they were all looking at me, watching to see if I was ready to hear what they had to say.

Like they were about to unload a pile of *Can she handle this?* on me.

Unconsciously, I reached up to rub the back of my neck, suddenly thinking it had gotten at least ten degrees hotter in here in the last five minutes.

Griffin didn't seem to notice. She was impervious to the heat and the constant hum of the computers that was starting to make my head ache, and to the fact that her bra must be at least a size too small to be pushing her boobs halfway up to her neck the way it was, something I'd only just noticed, but now couldn't stop thinking about. I told myself to look away because it was weird that I was staring at her chest, but it was easier to look there than at the interest I saw spark in her eyes. "Oh my god," she breathed. "You're the one they've been searching for. Your blood work proves it. And until they find you, they'll never stop searching."

"Who . . . the Daylighters?" But yes, that was exactly who she meant. "Why me?" I went on, not needing her to answer my first question. "What's so special about *my* blood work?" And what I meant was, what made mine different from theirs, because I already knew mine was different from any normal person's.

"It's the DNA," Jett finally said, pointing at the place on

the monitor that had some sort of sophisticated, science-y looking chart on it. "The Daylighters ran an analysis of your DNA, your genetic makeup. I've seen some similar blood tests, from some of the other Returned, and the rest of us . . . well, we still have most of our human DNA, mingled with some foreign—or what we suspect is the alien—DNA we told you about. Yours . . . ," Jett started, but then he hesitated.

"Mine . . . ? Mine, what?"

Jett grimaced. "Yours is missing that."

I wanted to say something along the lines of, it seemed like they were making a big deal out of nothing, I mean, wasn't that a good thing, me not having any of that alien DNA mixed in?

Simon jumped in then. "He doesn't mean yours is missing the alien kind. He means yours is missing the human kind."

And like Cat used to say: *Boom goes the dynamite!*

Just like that, the world slanted beneath my feet. I thought I'd heard everything. Or maybe I'd finally just cracked and this was me slipping deliciously-deliriously-*painlessly* into sweet insanity, because holy hell, who can even handle hearing something like that?

Not I, said the Fly, another of my dad's stupid expressions that popped into my head, and for the first time in forever I wished I *couldn't* hear his voice.

Not human? Not at all?

So, what, then . . . ?

"Nope. No way." I shook my head, unwilling to even engage their level of crazy. "It's not even possible."

Griffin spoke up, playing the voice of reason. "Possible? Kyra, look around you. Think about who we are. Are any of us really in any position to question what is, and isn't, possible anymore? And clearly you already knew there was something different about you." She said it kinder, and even used my name, and almost made me believe she was trying to be nice.

"Different?" I shot back. "Different is having a weird eye color or needing to wear braces for an extra year. What you're talking about doesn't make me *different*, it makes me . . ." I threw my hands in the air. "I don't even know what it makes me." I wanted to pull my hair out because what they were saying was just . . . too much.

But.

Griffin wasn't so far off with the whole who-are-we-to-question-what's-possible thing.

And then there was that one thing, with the NSA guy at the Tacoma facility, that one down in the ducts, where he'd shone his flashlight on me and said, "*It's you*," all serious-like. And again, with Agent Truman, when he'd told those guys in the alley, "*She's the one we want.*"

I'd figured it meant something, even while I'd tried to convince myself it was nothing.

"So, what does this all mean?" I finally said. "I mean, how and why and . . . *how*?" I felt broken as I held out my hands, palms up as if to say, how was I even standing there if

I wasn't me? "If I'm not human, then what the heck am I? It doesn't make sense." I just kept shaking my head, like some damaged bobble-head doll.

Simon reached for my hand, and even though my heart fully and completely belonged to Tyler, just like it had all along, I let Simon give me this—his comfort, and his strength—because I needed it. I needed it so damn much. "You're more human than anyone I've ever known," he whispered, and I almost smiled, because usually when people called each other human, they were explaining away making mistakes, so it should have been an insult, him calling me human like that. Except I knew he meant it in the best possible way, so I gave him a quick squeeze in return.

"My father used to tell me about how he first met them," Griffin said, turning her gaze toward the ceiling, the sky. "Some called them the First Contact meetings, but my father, he just called it 'the Meeting' and we all knew what he meant. People think the president was there." She shrugged. "Maybe he was at some point, but not for the first one."

The room went silent while she talked; even the computers seemed to hum less noisily, as if her words had suddenly become a physical presence demanding to be noticed, something you could feel and see and taste.

"He said they struck a deal at *the Meeting*—those scientists, the ones like my dad, and whatever those things were, from wherever they came from. A deal?" She gaped, leveling her gaze on us. "Can you believe that? To trade people for technology." She gave a peevish shake of her head. "It's not like we had a choice in the matter, about whether to agree or not. People had already been taken and experimented on, even before then. The agreement only ensured that the government would be *compensated*—paid in the form of cutting-edge technology—for turning a blind eye to these abductions. They would benefit from this *obviously* advanced culture." She stressed the word *obviously*, making her less-than-generous feelings known.

I felt like I was gonna be sick as I tried to process where I fit in all this. Whether I was supposed to consider myself part of this "advanced culture" now, or if I was still just plain old me.

I thought about how thickheaded I'd been when we'd gone through my dad's things and I'd seen all those stories about government cover-ups, all the accounts of secret files and covert government agencies, and how I'd scoffed at the very idea. I almost felt stupid for being so close-minded.

"Sounds like your dad got exactly what he deserved." I didn't pretend not to know what Griffin had done to him. As far as I was concerned, anyone who was willing to let his own daughter be used as an alien-lab-rat in exchange for some cool gadgets had punched his own one-way ticket to hell.

Griffin didn't comment one way or the other about her father. "In the end, the deal never worked out the way my dad, or the other scientists and politicians, wanted it to. The 'technology' our side was promised wasn't delivered in the form of ray guns or X-ray glasses or anything like that. The scientists were promised alien DNA that they could experiment on, that they'd planned to learn from. Potentially even harness." She grinned a wicked grin. "There was only one problem with their plan: we were harder to catch than they thought we'd be."

I gasped, finally clueing in. "*We* are the alien technology?" No wonder we were constantly being sought after. Hunted.

She shrugged. "Think about it. Our metabolisms are slower. We need less food and sleep than normal humans, we age ridiculously slowly, and we heal spontaneously. Why wouldn't we be valuable? What pharmaceutical company wouldn't pay millions, even billions, to get their hands on a few strands of our DNA? Or even better, what government wouldn't kill for an army of soldiers with lethal blood?"

The way she said it, like we could be used as a weapon, made my skin crawl.

"And what do they get out of it, this trade? The aliens?"

Simon jumped in. "We've asked ourselves the same thing a million different ways. Thing is, we're not even sure who they are exactly. Maybe our DNA has something they need. Or maybe, the way we use lab animals, *we're* just guinea pigs to them. Maybe they're doing all this weird shit to us, and then releasing us back into the wild."

"And me?" I asked. "What does that make me? If I'm not . . . still me?" I looked at my hands again, my fingers, the lines running across my palms, because they looked so . . . so ordinary. Same as they always had.

Griffin sighed. "My dad liked to talk. He was one of those guys who liked the sound of his own voice, and when I was"—she exhaled again—"when I was one of his *subjects*, a captive audience, he told me one of the things both sides wanted all along was to create a replicate—an exact human copy. Not a hybrid, but more like an alien clone that looked entirely human. It was what they referred to as a *Replacement*. Made from the genetic material of the aliens but still containing all the memories and life experiences of the human they were replicating.

"My dad called it the ultimate scientific achievement. He said it would decide what truly defines life: heredity or history."

I recoiled from her words. Her explanation. Especially since I was "the human" in question. "Life?" I had to ask. "What does that even mean? My heart is beating, my blood—even though it's not the same human blood it was before—is still pumping. I'm breathing. Aren't those the things that make me alive?"

"Are they?" Simon cut in. "Is it your genetics that make you the person you are? Or is it about *who* you are? The other things—the stuff your parents taught you about being a good person or that you throw a killer rise ball and win championships—all the things that have nothing to do with DNA or blood . . ." He reached out and tugged at my new fake brunette hair. ". . . or hair color?"

I thought about something Tyler had said to me, back

when I'd first explained to him about the whole healing and aging thing, and he'd tried to convince me that neither of these things changed who *I* was: "It's your memories and life experiences, your hopes and fears and dreams and passions that make you who you are, and none of those things have changed, have they?" and I wondered if that applied here too. If he'd still feel the same way now.

I wasn't so sure.

"Who else knows?" I asked, suddenly wishing no one knew, not even me. I wanted to go away. To start over and never think about this, about how different I was again.

"Natty was here when we opened the file," Thom explained, and he'd been so quiet I'd almost forgotten he was here at all. "She didn't see the DNA report, but she already saw how fast you heal when we were rescuing Willow."

I heard Griffin suck in a sharp breath. "Heal?" she repeated dazedly. "No one mentioned that."

"Yeah," Simon said. "She heals like"—he snapped his fingers—"*that.* You've never seen anything like it."

Except, I remembered what Tyler said: that Griffin had told him he could heal faster than anyone else at camp. I wondered, then, was it a leap to read more into that? If we shared more than just being Returned?

I opened my mouth to ask Griffin what she thought, when she caught my eye and shook her head at me. The action was discreet and curt, but the message was loud and clear: I needed to keep my mouth shut.

Hadn't she said the same thing to Tyler? Told him not to tell anyone?

I glanced around—at Jett and Simon and Thom—and tried to imagine who, in here, she didn't trust. But I did as she instructed, swallowing back my questions.

Inwardly, however, they buzzed through my brain.

Did Tyler have any new and unique abilities too? Was there anything he could do the other Returned couldn't?

And what about that other part—that thing where I'd been gone for five whole years? Was that because I was a Replaced and not just a regular Returned?

If that was the case, then where did that leave Tyler? I didn't know how long he'd been gone, but it couldn't have been too long. It certainly hadn't been five years. Days at most. Yet when I'd come back, my memory had been whole, complete. His was a mess. Sure, he remembered things from before, but there was a definite gap, a missing chunk from right before he'd been taken . . .

. . . the entire part where we'd fallen in love.

It was the best part, if you asked me.

"Let me ask you a question." Griffin's eyes narrowed as her brief flash of concern over Tyler was safely tucked away. "How much control do you have over this *telekinetic thing* you have? Can you . . ." Her brows fell in a silent ultimatum. ". . . can you show it to me, so I can see how it works?"

I shook my head. "I wish. I have to be *focused*."

Focused was putting it nicely. Angry, panicked, completely freaked out, all those probably made more sense.

Griffin nodded then, and I thought the gesture was for me, a kind of *Okay, I get it.*

But then the door opened and six of her soldiers stormed in all at once. They were armed to the teeth, their black rifles held at the ready, and suddenly the room that had been empty seconds earlier was busting at the seams.

I'd been wrong. Everything wasn't okay, and Griffin didn't *get it.* The nod had been a signal, all right, but not for me.

Simon was bulldozed out of the way by two of Griffin's giants, who moved to stand on either side of me, while two others flanked Griffin. The two remaining soldiers stayed on their toes, eyeballing Thom and Simon vigilantly.

Jett, apparently, was not a threat.

Simon didn't seem concerned that he was outmanned or outclassed. He jumped to his feet, his face red. "What the hell is this?" He shot daggers at Griffin, and then to Thom, who stared at him blankly.

"I'm sorry to have to do this," Griffin said as one of the guys—a hulk of a dude—snatched me by the arm. I saw Simon lunge for him, but one of the other giants turned and pointed his gun, the nose of it aimed directly at Simon's chest, causing him to crash against it.

It wasn't aimed at his shoulder or his leg, places that could heal, but at his heart, and I doubted the gun would be firing beanbags.

"Simon, don't!" I cried, just as Jett got to his feet too. Thom stayed where he was, his hands in the air.

I had no idea what was happening, but whatever Griffin was up to, it wasn't worth letting any of them get hurt, or worse, killed. I turned back to Griffin. "Leave them out of this."

Her brows pulled together. "They were *never* in it. No one was. This is about you, and only you." She turned her back on me as she told the guys who were on each side of me now, squeezing my arms and dragging me toward the door, "Take her to the holding cell. And don't take your eyes off her."

Simon was still yelling, screaming, at Griffin when his voice finally faded to oblivion.

CHAPTER EIGHTEEN

REPLACED.

The word made me feel *not real*. Like a thing—a mannequin or one of those wax statues you can barely tell apart from the real celebrities they're fashioned after. Like Wax Elvis or Wax Marilyn Monroe or Wax Lady Gaga.

Maybe I was Wax Kyra.

Except that I could eat and breathe and think. And feel. I knew because no matter how hard I tried, I just couldn't buy into this crazy theory about my memories being transplanted—the memories that kept running through my head, the ones I couldn't let go of even now. The ones of my dad and Tyler and my mom and Cat, and even Austin. I couldn't make myself believe they didn't belong to this body, a body that wasn't really my own.

They felt real. They felt real all the way to my bones. Like they were ingrained in every molecule, every cell, every breath I took.

They were as much a part of me, of this body and who I was, as the skin that surrounded me.

I even tried pinching myself, because maybe this whole thing, being told I was no longer human, had all been a dream—one long, whacked-out, surreal dream. But the pain receptors, *my* pain receptors, convinced me otherwise. This was happening, all right.

Replaced, I silently repeated the word again. Replicated. Copied. Made from an amalgamation of alien DNA and human memories. It didn't matter how I tried to reframe it—I had a hard time making it fit. But only because it was so damn freaky.

Yet I couldn't deny it either. There were too many things that pointed to the fact that it might be true. Things that separated me from the other Returned.

So the question was: Could I live with that, if it turned out Griffin was right? If I really was a Replaced?

I guess the answer was simple: What choice did I have? I wasn't exactly a woe-is-me, I-can't-go-on-another-day kind of person.

Person. Another word that no longer seemed to fit.

But what if Simon was right? What if I could allow

myself to believe what he'd said about what made me human? What if all these memories and thoughts and feelings really were enough?

I had to cling to that, because deep down, I knew who I was. I was still Kyra Agnew, regardless of what my blood tests showed. No one could take my past, *my* history, the narration of *my life* away from me. Although, evidently, they could take away my freedom. Exhibit A, the claustrophobic cell I was now confined within.

I forced myself not to think too long about how dark and narrow this space really was. It made the first place we'd been contained in seem glamorous and roomy by comparison. If I stared for too long at the walls, or considered how far one of them was from another, I got that tight-chested feeling that was almost claustrophobia. Yet another reminder that I was more than just a bunch of chromosomes strung together, because that squeezing in my chest was part of what made me the same as I'd always been.

Instead I looked out, past the narrow bars—because yes, there were bars just like in a real jail—to where two of those thugs were guarding me like there was some chance I might somehow rip off the bars in a fit of rage and try to escape. I wondered what they'd been told about me. I wondered, too, what they thought I was actually capable of, because there was no way these bars were budging. Trust me, I'd tried.

If only I could bend iron with my cool telekinesis thing—that was what kept looping through my mind.

And, of course, Tyler. I thought about Tyler a lot.

But also the bending-bars thing, because how cool would that be, if I could just King Kong my way out of here with my mind?

And then maybe I could find something to knock those two goons out with . . . again with my mind since, hello, they were giants.

But as far as I could see, there was nothing I could use against them. Nothing I could levitate with my new "alien ability."

So I paced—not far, and mostly in tight circles in front of the bunk that was bolted to the wall, doing my best to steer clear of the stainless steel toilet, not because it was dirty or anything—in fact it sparkled so much it was practically mirror-like—but because it was a toilet, and well, gross. I paced and I checked the time. Mostly I checked the time, giving myself permission to just . . . stare. To watch the second hand. To track it as it moved around and around and around.

Hours had passed, and I'd spent most of those doing nothing and thinking everything.

I was surprised, then, when Griffin stepped beneath the dull lights of the hallway. I hadn't even realized there'd been a change of shift until she nodded to the two new guards, indicating for them to give us some privacy.

Like good little minions, they did as they were told.

"What do you want?" I didn't bother getting up, just stayed where I was with my hands lying on my stomach.

"We need to talk," she said, her voice even. "We have a problem."

"Oh we do, do we?" I asked, lacing my voice with as much sarcasm as I could round up. "Seems to me you got everything under control."

She waited a second before adding, "It's Tyler."

She had me. I couldn't pretend not to care, and I sat up.

"That's what I thought." I wanted to wipe the smug look off her face, but this was about Tyler, and I bit back the *Bitch* hovering on the tip of my tongue. "I think we both know why I'm here," she continued, her voice way, way lower now, like she didn't want even her own guards to hear what she'd come here to say. "I think he's . . . *like you*."

I went to the bars, to where she was clutching them, and I leaned close so we were nose to nose. "How long was he gone?" I asked, trying to piece it together.

Her dark eyes searched mine. "When we found him, he wasn't sure, so we had to figure it out for him. Daylight Division chatter put his disappearance somewhere around twenty-five days ago." I did the math in my head. That was right. That was when he and my dad and Agent Truman had vanished from Devil's Hole. "We picked him up some five days later—the day he said he was returned."

Five days, not five years.

Still, that was three days past the forty-eight-hour mark.

She must've read my thoughts, because she said, "I knew it was too long, and at first I assumed he was confused. It happens. People—those of us who've gone through it—tend to lose track of time. It's disorienting. But even when I figured out he was right, I didn't tell him how *unusual* that was." She didn't say *unheard of*, because we both knew that wasn't true; I was proof of that. "And then . . . when he could heal the way he could, I assumed they'd done something more to him. More than they'd done to the rest of us. It just never occurred to me . . ."

I nodded because I knew what she meant—even with everything her father had told her it would be a stretch to assume Tyler had been successfully Replaced.

I could hardly believe it myself.

"His memory," I whispered. "Do you think that's a side effect? Maybe they sent him back too soon . . . ?"

"Maybe." She looked over her shoulder. Ever since we'd been here at Blackwater, I hadn't known her to be anything but confident and in command. It was strange to see her so spooked.

"Do you think he'll get it back? The part he's missing."

Griffin gave me a look. "That's the least of my concerns." Then she smoothed her hand over her hair. It was a nervous gesture. "Who knows. Look, I get that you want this to be like some kind of happily-ever-after fairy-tale sort of thing, but that's not the way the world works. I'm just trying to keep him alive. I can't worry about your little crush."

My heart crashed. "Alive? Why? What happened?"

"Kyra," she said, saying not just my name, but saying it

so sincerely and looking me in the eye that I couldn't help the jolt of alarm that boomeranged in my chest. "I need you to get Tyler out of here."

I didn't understand why Griffin was being so secretive, or why she was all of a sudden confiding in me, especially considering she'd been the one to order my detainment in the first place.

"Where are Simon and the others?" I demanded, wondering if they were being held the same way I was.

"Simon's safe. He's making plans as we speak."

"Plans? He was there when you had me arrested. I seriously doubt he's helping you make any plans."

"I explained everything to him; he gets why I had to do that now."

"Mind explaining it to me?" I gave her my best this-better-be-good look while I waited.

Griffin pinched the bridge of her nose, releasing her breath on a hiss. "I know you don't trust me, but you need to believe me when I tell you we have a traitor in our midst."

Traitor. The word hit me like a thousand tons of lead.

I thought of Simon's *complicated* history with Griffin.

"It's not Simon," I defended, my voice raising and echoing off the concrete walls. "And it's not Willow either."

"Shh!" she shushed, flapping her hands and warning me to keep it down. And then she met my gaze directly, her expression weary. "I know that, Kyra. It never was."

I lost some steam with her admission. "So who, then?"

Pulling out a key, she unlocked the door and opened it. I

didn't know if she was coming in or if I was coming out, so we both just stayed where we were. "I wasn't sure until I had you locked up. I had to make it look believable, so everyone would think I was keeping you prisoner."

"Well, bravo. You were convincing." I cocked my head to the side, crossing my arms. "But for what purpose?"

"I needed whoever the traitor was to think I was willing to trade you myself. That I planned to turn you in to the Daylighters. And then I waited."

"For what?" I asked.

"For someone to try to get a message out."

"I take it they did." It wasn't a question. Of course they had or Griffin wouldn't be here now, telling me what her plan had been, and asking me to get Tyler away from this camp. "So . . ." I was almost afraid to ask. "Who was the traitor?"

Griffin came inside and dropped to the bunk. She put her face in her hands. It was a strange reaction, not at all what I'd expected.

I ran through the list of possibilities. I'd already ruled out Simon and Willow, and I mentally ticked off Jett, and Natty since she'd been with me almost every minute of every day since Simon and I had landed in Silent Creek.

"Thom," I breathed, almost at the same time Griffin said it. But even hearing her voice echoing mine, I shook my head. "No . . ."

"It had to have been him back then too." The accusation was pitiful, as if it was painful for her to say. "He must've been working with them, colluding all these years. I've always wondered how they could know so much." Her face lifted so we were eye to eye. "Has Simon ever wondered how the Hanford camp was found out?"

"Thom?" I asked with almost as much disbelief as her. "But . . . why? And if they knew where the camps were, why didn't the Daylighters just round you all up years ago?"

"Because we're not the ones they really wanted. They've been looking for a Replaced. The Returned are child's play." Even her shrug was unenthusiastic. A whisper. "I mean, sure, they're willing to do their experiments on us if we're all they can get. They extract our DNA and dissect us and . . . who knows what else they do in that lab of theirs." I hugged myself tighter, her words making my skin tighten. "But it's always been about finding a Replaced. Thom's no good to them, none of us are, not if they can't get their hands on one of you."

"One of us. You mean, me and Tyler?"

She nodded wearily. Tiredly.

But we couldn't afford to be tired. "What about that Alex kid? What if he was a Replaced? What if *they . . . the aliens* are honing their skills and there are more of us out there? What if they no longer need five years, or even five days? What if we're coming back in forty-eight hours?"

"That's not our concern. At least not yet. For now, I need to get you two out of here."

"And go where?" Just yesterday, the idea of leaving here

with Tyler was exactly what I'd wanted. Now it just made me feel sick.

"Simon's working on that. He's setting up a rendezvous for you, a way to get you safely away from here."

"What about the rest of you? What happens to you now? Is the Daylight Division on their way?"

"We're doing what we always planned to do: fight."

"I'll help you," I told her, "if you tell me the truth. Why Tyler? Why do you care so much what happens to him?"

She didn't hesitate. "I think you already know the answer. He's special."

"So you care about him?" I asked, not sure why I was putting myself through this. I'd seen the way he looked at her. Hadn't I already wondered if his feelings were more than just innocent when it came to her?

"Don't we both?" she said, getting up and reaching for my arm. "Now, come on, we don't have time to waste. We need to get you out of here, before it's too late."

CHAPTER NINETEEN

WE WERE AT THE EDGE OF THE OBSTACLE COURSE when the helicopters appeared overhead. But even before we heard them—or smelled and tasted the dust being stirred in the air, signaling their approach—there were shouts, calls to action all around us.

Griffin's camp came to life.

It was no longer a group of teens being drilled in make-believe war maneuvers. Her Returned were fine-tuned soldiers under attack. There were far more of them than I'd ever imagined as they swarmed the field and the perimeter, looking like an endless stream of ants as they poured forth, coming from everywhere all at once. They manned their stations, and moved with the fluid quality of those who'd spent years on the battlefield.

They were prepared, and Griffin was their general.

The sounds of gunfire split the air, and even without knowing which direction it was coming from, instinctively I ducked my head, lifting my arm to shield myself. It sounded close, and seemed to ricochet inside my head.

"Keep moving!" Griffin shouted. "Simon's getting Tyler!"

"What about Thom? Did you catch him?"

"No! After we intercepted his message, I sent a patrol after him, but he was already gone. His girl was gone too."

His girl . . . "Natty?" I shouted back as I tailed Griffin through the tents, staying as close as possible. "No. That's a coincidence. She wouldn't betray me."

"I can't say if she did or didn't. But no one could find her. Makes her look guilty, if you ask me."

We were almost to the cafeteria, near the computer lab, when a voice—a voice so familiar and chilling, and so out of place in Blackwater that I actually stumbled over my own feet—reached out to us from the shadows. "Don't make any sudden moves, neither of you. Nothing fancy, just turn around slowly."

That dark, grating sound that reached into my core and made me cringe.

My nemesis.

Alive, despite the Code Red.

I tried to imagine how that was possible, when I noticed the way Griffin's face had gone all gray, like the color of old ash, and it dawned on me: I wasn't the only one who'd recognized Agent Truman's voice.

When we turned to face him, I wanted to fall to my knees and cry. We'd gotten so close to escaping, Tyler and me. To running away, no matter where we were headed, and maybe being able to start a new life. Away from this place. Away from Agent Truman and the Daylight Division that was hunting us.

But it was Griffin's whispered plea that made me choke on a mouthful of bile.

"Dad?" she practically wheezed while everywhere the sounds of weapons firing pealed through the air. "But . . . *how*?"

Dad?

"Are you . . . Griffin . . . *Truman*?" I could hardly get my voice out, pairing her name with his, because surely he couldn't—no way, no how—be *her* dad. "Is that your name?"

But Agent Truman wasn't half as shocked to see Griffin as she was to see him, when he revealed himself, stepping out from where the tent had kept him hidden. His face was pinched in a weasel-like expression that couldn't mean anything good. Not for us anyway. "Of course it's not. You didn't think Truman was my real name, did you? And Griffin here, she didn't keep hers either." He bit back a cruel smile.

I searched the both of them for some sign of resemblance,

something that said they were father and daughter, but I couldn't find it. No matter my opinion of her, Griffin had flawless skin and hair that gleamed and bee-stung lips. Agent Truman's skin was rawhide tough, his eyes dead and ice cold. He was a cowboy in a suit.

"Bennett," Truman explained, taking in Griffin. "That was our last name. Dr. Arlo Bennett and my daughter, Griffin. Funny how little names matter when you become a pariah. Isn't that right, sweetheart?" He watched—we both did—while she scrubbed her hands over her face as his voice took on a sweet-talking quality. "Do you need a minute? You seem surprised to see me. Don't tell me you thought you were the only one of us who'd get to live forever?" He sneered at her. "I have to admit, I wasn't sure they'd take me. Back at the Meeting, when we struck our little deal with those alien buggers, they made it clear they did not want us adults. We were too risky. Our bodies were too old and damaged.

"But when I went to them . . . told them I was sick and had no other option on account of what *you'd* done to me, they gave me a chance anyway."

My eyes lowered to his hand—his cast-free right hand, which was holding his gun perfectly. Precisely. "You weren't hurt," I accused. "Up at Devil's Hole." But it felt so lame to add lying to his list of offenses when there were so many more horrible things he'd done.

He shook his head. "No, I was hurt," he corrected. "Just not as bad as you thought. I was mostly good as new by then, but I had to put on a good show." He grinned, a shark-toothed grin. "One of my finer acts, if I do say so myself. Plus, it hurt like a . . ." His gaze narrowed on me as his words trailed off. "I don't forgive you, by the way." He grimaced. "Like I said, my body is older. One of the side effects is that I heal slower. And more painfully, so it seems."

Suddenly so many things made sense. The way Natty and Jett and the others had told me he hadn't fled when everyone else had, after I'd shot myself.

Why would he? He wasn't afraid of the dreaded Code Red because he was one of us. His blood was just as lethal as ours. And what about that other thing, the way he'd disappeared that night at Devil's Hole? Had he been taken at all, or had they let him get away, the way they had Simon and me?

"But you . . ." His dark expression grew even darker as he leveled his gaze on Griffin. I wondered if he could really go through with it, killing his own daughter. "You thought you got the best of me with that stunt of yours, but look who's laughing now, daughter dearest?"

He didn't wait for an answer, and I had mine the instant he pulled the trigger.

Pulled it for real, and a bullet, the actual kind and not the beanbag kind—the ones that could most definitely kill us if fired into exactly the right place—ripped through Griffin's right shoulder.

The sound blended into the backdrop of all the other shots being fired, and I gasped because I seriously hadn't believed he'd go through with it.

I still couldn't.

Griffin must have felt that same disbelief, because her eyes flew wide. She fell against the canvas wall behind her and then she slid to the ground, leaving a smear of blood on the dusty field of army green. He raised his weapon again, only this time, instead of pointing it at Griffin, he aimed it at me, training it right at the center of my forehead, and all I could think was that if he'd shot his daughter, he would definitely-absolutely-*unequivocally* shoot me.

I shook my head. I couldn't help myself. Even as I stood there facing the barrel of his gun, I heard myself asking, "If you're one of us, how can you work with them?"

He looked at me like the answer was obvious. "What else was I supposed to do? Go with Griffin? Be part of her army?" He pointed the gun at her again, to where she was struggling to get up. And then he fired, this time at her left shoulder, sending her flying against the tent all over again. He ignored her yelp as if it made no difference to him—and maybe it didn't—as he continued, "I hardly think so. The Division gave me a chance to continue with my experiments. Most of those guys don't even know who—or what—I am. That information's on a need-to-know basis. Classified shit." The gun shifted, so it was pointing at my head again. "You wanna know what else is classified?" His finger stroked the trigger.

I took a step back, trying to put some distance between him and me, my heart picking up by several beats.

"What's that?" I asked, keeping his attention trained on me as I took still another step away from him, hoping he'd stay right where he was.

From where she was on the ground, Griffin muttered something about *son-of-a-bitch*, but both of us were ignoring her now as Agent Truman or Dr. Bennett or whatever the heck his name was concentrated on me, and I concentrated solely on creating distance between me and that gun in his hand.

"The information in those files you stole."

It was his one big mistake, reminding me how different I was from the rest of them. In all the chaos, I'd nearly forgotten my worth, even if it was only as a science experiment.

I stopped backing away and lifted my chin. "You won't do it," I challenged. "I'm the one you're after. I'm the one you've been after all this time."

He flashed his teeth, and just like that he was the polar bear and I was a three-year-old girl. "Makes no difference to me." His words hung there for a minute before he pushed on, "We have another one, just like you. Picked him up a couple hours from here." His brows rose challengingly, his forehead bunching up. "Funny thing is, after running some tests, you know the ones, kid healed just as fast as you . . . maybe faster. Bet he can do all kindsa crazy shit, that one."

Hearing him talk about Alex Walker that way turned my stomach.

I nodded then. Not at Agent Truman, but at the person

waiting behind him. The one I'd really been backing away from this entire time.

When Willow swung the bat she'd been holding, I heard it whistle through the air. And when it struck the side of Agent Truman's head, there was a moment when I thought I might actually lose my lunch. I had to keep reminding myself he could heal . . . even if, like he said, it was slower than the rest of us.

I hoped he hadn't lied about that other part, though, and that it hurt him like a mother.

I kind of envied Willow's power. I'd always been more of a line drive hitter.

She only struck him once, but it was more than enough. The bat made this disgusting sound as a fine spray of blood filled the air, and a look of sheer horror passed over Agent Truman's face. He blinked once, and only once, and then his eyes rolled all the way back in his head before he dropped forward, falling heavily on his knees and then landing face-first in the sand.

"It was my turn to save you." Willow beamed, shouldering the bat.

Griffin was already scrambling to her feet, gasping and cringing because the wounds on each of her shoulders were beginning to pucker around the edges. It had to sting like you-know-what.

She tugged my arm. "Simon and Tyler are waiting for you at the Jeep, out in front of the camp." She turned to

Willow then as she sucked in a breath through her clenched teeth. "You take her. I'll stay here and handle . . . *this*." Her gaze moved to her father—Agent Truman—who was still lying blacked out in the dirt. She reached out and nudged him with her boot. "Go!" she hissed at us. "I mean it. *Go*, before the old man wakes up."

I didn't wait to be told again, and I didn't look back. Griffin could handle her father, the agent-slash-doctor, I had no doubt about that.

Then Willow and I were literally dodging bullets as we made our way through the tent maze. Willow knew exactly when to zig and when to zag, and she got us through the chaos not only unscathed but also unnoticed, and suddenly I was even more impressed by her, glad she was on our side.

When I saw Tyler, though, I nearly gave up on that whole not-crying-in-front-of-others thing. I thought I'd be the only one feeling panicked, but the strain across his forehead told me he was at least as worried about me.

His brow crumpled when he saw me, and before I could run to meet him, Willow grabbed my arm. She used her own body to shield me as she dragged me across the last stretch of open ground to where Tyler was waiting to meet us.

When I felt his arms go around me, and his lips against my forehead, I had a hard time stopping the words *I love you* from bubbling up my throat.

"I need to get you two out of here without anyone seeing us," Simon insisted, jumping into the Jeep and firing up the engine.

I didn't get the chance to thank Willow for saving my butt, because when I turned around again, she was gone.

"Where are we going?" I asked Simon as Tyler and I climbed into the Jeep behind him.

"Buckle up, keep your head low, and try not to distract me. I'll do my best not to get you killed," Simon told us as he pushed the vehicle into gear and spewed a cloud of dust in our wake. "We only have an hour to get to the designated meeting point. If we're late, we miss our chance. And if we get caught, we're dead."

And with that, I felt Tyler reach for me from the backseat. I let him take my hand, gripping his in return as the wind battered us while we raced across the desert.

CHAPTER TWENTY

SWEAT TRICKLED DOWN THE BACK OF MY NECK as we hurtled along the two-lane highway.

Every now and then, even from the distance we'd put between us and Blackwater, we'd hear, and feel, an explosion so loud it rocked the ground beneath us, making the Jeep shudder as it coursed along the plane of the asphalt. Acid burned in the back of my throat as I worried about everyone who was still there, back at the camp—Jett and Willow, who'd stuck with me even though I'd never really declared myself one of them, and Griffin and her people, who were now fighting our fight.

And then there was Natty.

I had no idea where Natty was now. No idea if she was on our side . . . or on Thom's.

But regardless, I couldn't help the way my stomach knotted when I thought about her. Until I heard otherwise, I couldn't force myself not to care about her, just because, as Griffin pointed out, her actions made her "look guilty."

Friendships were never that simple. I knew because of Cat.

Cat, who was five years older than me now and had moved on with her life while I'd been gone.

Cat, who was Austin's girlfriend now.

Cat, who would forever be my best friend, no matter how hard I tried to deny it.

I checked my watch. And I checked it again, and afterward, I craned my neck to check on Tyler, but he was already checking me checking him. I smiled because even if he couldn't remember us—the us that curled my toes and made my cheeks burn every time he grinned his crooked grin and feathered his finger along my lower lip, he was looking at me like that now. With that same crooked smile.

There was something about being trapped like this with Simon and Tyler that had me feeling twitchy and tingly, and I couldn't decide if it was the good kind of twitchy and tingly, or the super weird kind.

Simon had managed to get us away from Blackwater Ranch undetected, yet even away from the onslaught of the Daylighters, alarm bells were still going off inside me.

As the road, and my heart rate, leveled out, I finally asked Simon the question that'd been driving me crazy. "Did you know it was Thom—that he was the traitor? I mean, did you ever suspect?"

Simon's jaw tensed, and I could see it was eating him up inside. "Not until Griffin . . . until she came to me and told me about the message they intercepted." He seethed. "Griffin asked Jett to look into it, and it was Jett who discovered it. Jett helped lay the trap. He was the one who traced it to Thom."

I sighed, shooting a furtive look to Tyler, and wondering how much he already knew. About who he was and what had happened to cause all this. I imagined since he was here, running away with me, Griffin had told him pretty much everything by now, and his nod, and the sympathetic look in his eyes, pretty much confirmed my suspicion. "Sorry about your friend."

I shrugged. "I guess he wasn't really our friend."

Above us, a strange sound rippled the air. It wasn't loud at first, but it was coming at us fast—a sheer, tearing noise that seemed to be shredding the sky. I unbuckled so I could turn around and get a better view, straining to see what it was.

Whatever it was, it was still far off, but getting closer and closer. It sort of looked like a plane, but I couldn't be sure because it was almost . . . too fast. Plus, it was heading right toward us.

Simon was watching it, too, from his rearview mirror.

"Damn," he cursed. "How the hell did they find us so fast?"

"That's . . . *them*?" I asked incredulously, gripping the seat back as I watched its steady approach. "What is that thing?"

"Military drone," Simon stated matter-of-factly.

"Drone? What's it doing?" I asked.

"Tracking us!" Simon shouted from the driver's seat. "And if it can get within range, they won't let us escape. Not alive, anyway."

But Tyler shook his head as he leaned forward. He looked from me to Simon. "I don't think so. Griffin said they need us."

"Something must've changed," Simon said. "Or someone didn't get the memo you two are worth more alive than dead."

Pins and needles prickled my skin as I thought about what Agent Truman had told me back at Blackwater, about Alex Walker . . . about how quickly he'd healed. "Not anymore they don't. They have Alex Walker," I breathed. "They have another Replaced." We were expendable, Tyler and me.

Tyler turned to Simon. "Can we lose this thing?"

"Hang on tight!" And with that, Simon forced the steering wheel hard to the left, veering us off the highway and onto the rocky terrain of the desert. We bounced awkwardly, and I dropped back onto my seat. I felt Tyler's hand reach out to my shoulder, giving me a reassuring squeeze, and if I hadn't been hanging on to the sides of my seat for dear life, I probably would've reached back to return the favor. As it was, all I could think was, *Please don't throw up . . . please don't throw up . . . please, dear God, do . . . not . . . throw . . . up . . .*

Each time the Jeep hit a rock, it felt like my brain was being rattled against my skull as my head smacked against the headrest and my heart felt like it might rip a hole through my chest, and the entire time I wondered, *Why are they doing this to us? And how the holy hell are we going to outrun a military aircraft?*

"What if we can't lose them?" I called out to Simon, my voice hoarse as I glanced over my shoulder and saw how much closer the drone was getting.

My throat nearly clamped shut as I saw a grim look darken his face. And then I looked at Tyler, who I'd already sentenced to death once when I'd cut myself in his presence. Could I really let him die again just when I'd gotten him back? Was it fair that these two suffer just because I had to go and be some sort of freak that Agent Truman had to get his hands on?

I released the buckle on my seat belt again and glanced down at the dirt and rocks that blurred past. I'd jumped out of a moving vehicle once before, on Chuckanut Drive the night my dad and I had fought after my championship game. It hadn't worked out so well for me then. I'd lost five years of my life because of that move.

I certainly wasn't about to jump again.

Instead, I shot to my knees as I faced the approaching drone.

I stopped trying to stuff that I-might-puke feeling down,

and embraced it, along with the shaky, sweaty dizziness that threatened to engulf me. Everything that came with the wave of sheer dread consuming me. I tapped into it. I used it.

I wasn't even sure this would work, but it wasn't like we had a lot of options at this point. That aircraft up there was closing in on us. We were running out of time. When I narrowed my eyes and felt the zip of tension burst along my spine, stars erupted in my periphery.

"Down!" Simon yelled, reaching over and yanking at me.

I'd already seen why, though. Something was coming straight at us . . . besides that drone thing, I mean. I had to assume it was some sort of missile, which meant we must be within range, as Simon had pointed out.

But Simon hadn't seen what I had right before he'd grabbed for me. The part where that drone had wobbled, its course slightly altered. And even though I couldn't say for sure that I'd been the one responsible, I couldn't say I hadn't been either.

Regardless of the reason, that slight alteration must have been enough, and the missile had been off course also. Just enough.

It was close, though.

There was a bright flash when the missile struck the rocky ground, followed immediately by a shock-wave explosion. Black smoke billowed around orange flames that expanded in every direction. It was so close I could taste bits of sand, dirt, and fuel. It took several seconds for me to blink away fragments of debris from my lashes, but when I did, I flipped back around and saw that the aircraft had regained its trajectory.

I concentrated again and wondered if I even had it in me to do what needed to be done. That thing up there was a gazillion times bigger than any library book or T-shirt. But this wasn't just fear I was channeling. I was learning the feel of this ability. I knew the way it moved through me and how to draw it out.

Biting my lip, I dug deep, tracking the drone for one . . . two . . . three seconds, less than one full breath.

It wasn't kinda like being on the mound; it was exactly like that. That same level of intensity. What coach and my dad called single-mindedness. Until there was only me and the drone. Nothing else.

Then I unleashed everything I could muster. I let it pour through me, out of me, and I released it—whatever *it* was—at that thing that threatened us, the same way I had when Agent Truman had threatened my dad, the same way I had when Simon had made me mad in the library.

I meant to send it swerving, to divert it so far off its flight path, it couldn't find us again.

And at first I thought I'd done just that, as it wavered.

But I'd misjudged my own strength, just like when I'd tossed that softball to Tyler, and it didn't just shift off course. My stomach plummeted as it went hurtling, rotating, spinning out of control. My hand covered my mouth as I shot all the way to my knees, trying to track its trajectory.

"What the . . . ?" I tried to say, but nothing came out of

my mouth, not even a breath.

Everything slowed as I watched the drone's nosedive descent. Behind me, Simon slammed on the brakes just as the aircraft slammed into the earth.

The blast was more massive than the missile's had been—the flames wider and hotter, the black smoke greasier as it choked me, and the caustic odor singed my nose hairs.

"I take it that was a mistake," Simon said blandly.

I tried to nod, but I could hardly swallow. I felt paralyzed.

"I'd like to see what you can do on purpose," Tyler threw in.

A tightness spread across my chest, and then I turned to Simon. "We have to go back. We have to see if the pilot . . . if anyone . . ." I knew it was useless, but I couldn't stop myself from needing to know. ". . . survived."

Simon half smiled, a small, wry smile. "Kyra, that was a drone. An unmanned drone. There was no one flying it."

If I'd been standing, my legs surely would have buckled. As it was, I let my forehead drop against the back of the seat as a shaky laugh escaped my lips. "Are you kidding me? Oh my god, I thought . . . I thought I *killed* someone."

But it was Tyler who interrupted my internal cheers. "The question is, how did it know where to find us?"

I looked to Simon. "They must've known where we were going. Did you tell Thom?"

"No, only Griffin and Jett."

I thought about Griffin, and the way I'd once suspected

her. But there was no way. She hated the Daylighters, and her father even more, for what they'd done to her.

That left . . . "You don't think . . . ?" My mouth went dry just thinking it. "Could it have been Jett?"

"No way. Not Jett," Simon insisted. "You don't know him. Not like I do."

I frowned. "How do you know him? I mean, I know he wasn't at Blackwater with you and Willow, so where did you meet him?"

Simon ran his hand over his head. "When me and Willow found him, Jett was in Nevada." Simon grinned. "He was all alone. The three of us started our camp together. I'd trust him with my life."

I glanced to Tyler. "Who, then? How?" I chewed the inside of my cheek as my eyes nervously drifted downward, to check the time.

And my stomach dropped.

Thom.

Thom was the traitor. Thom had been feeding Agent Truman and the NSA's Daylight Division information all along. It was probably the reason he hadn't let Natty go with us to the Tacoma facility without him—he didn't want us getting her captured.

But it was also the reason he'd taken an interest in me after we'd arrived at Silent Creek, once he'd learned I might be different from the other Returned—that I had night vision, and could go longer without oxygen and could heal faster. The telekinesis just confirmed what he already suspected, that I was a Replaced.

"Thom gave me this." I unstrapped the watch I'd treasured from the moment he'd given it to me, and threw it at Simon. "Soon after we left Tacoma. He said it was a present. It's this. This is how he's tracking us."

"That son of a bitch," Simon fumed.

Simon picked it up by the pink band and inspected it, probably thinking the same thing I had: How could something so harmless-looking be so deadly?

He gave it one last hard look before hurtling it into the desert. "We got less than half an hour to get to our rendezvous point," he said, putting the Jeep in gear and leaving the still-flaming crash, and the tracking device Thom had planted on me, in our wake.

We drove toward a completely unknown future, leaving everything—our friends, allies, pasts, and even our identities—behind to start over again.

We had to hope Thom didn't have any other tricks up his sleeve.

I had to hope Simon knew what the hell he was doing.

And most of all, I prayed Agent Truman, or Dr. Bennett, or whoever he was now, never, *ever* found us again.

There was a left-for-dead pickup truck with giant rusted-out patches that was half-in and half-out of a storm ditch when Simon pulled off the road.

"You think we missed 'em?" I asked, looking for signs of another—street-legal—vehicle.

So far, Simon hadn't given me a single straight answer about who we were meeting. All I'd managed to get out of him was I could trust this person, whoever he was.

I was about to push again when Tyler, who had already hopped out, reached up to help me down. When his green eyes locked on mine, the breath caught in the back of my throat.

I didn't bother telling him it was only a Jeep, not a tank or anything, and that I doubted I *needed* his help getting down. Instead I almost died inside when his hands found their way to my hips, and I let him *catch* me when I leaped the maybe two feet to the ground.

I stood in front of him, wishing this moment, our bodies touching this way, meant half as much to him as it did to me. *Eventually*, I told myself. *Soon.*

When I finally ducked my head, too embarrassed to stand there gawking at him a second longer, I eased past him and found myself face-to-face with Simon. He was leaning against the side of the Jeep, watching me—and probably the whole Tyler-helping-me-down thing—with an exasperated look in his eye.

"What?" I complained, wishing he'd quit looking at me like that. And then I stopped dead in my tracks. "Did you hear that?" I lifted my head, desperately trying to see around him. But all I could see was his face—his big, fat smiling face.

"You're welcome," he said, his voice all rumbly.

Tears were already welling in my eyes, even before I

knew for sure what I was hearing, and then I was shoving past Simon, no longer caring that Tyler was there at all. I heard her before I saw either of them.

When she appeared from behind a rocky outcropping, as enormous and beautiful as I remembered, I nearly stumbled. She continued her incessant wails, loudly letting everyone within earshot know we'd arrived. She would make the world's worst secret agent.

Thankfully, there were no spy plans in her foreseeable future.

"Nancy!" I shrieked, my feet tearing through the sand as I raced away from the shoulder of the highway where we'd parked.

She jumped up on me, her feet hitting my shoulders, and her disgusting dog breath assaulting my face. It was the best smell ever.

"You're so filthy!" I accused, but I threw my arms around her mangy fur, refusing to let her go even when she wriggled and whimpered to break free.

"Supernova?" That was the voice that nearly shattered me. The rough edges, like he was reluctant to hope this was real, that he could possibly find me twice, almost doing me in.

I finally released poor Nancy, who let out a relieved yelp as she loped away through the sand to greet her next guests. I stood there for several long seconds, facing the one man we truly could trust. Simon had been right about that much for certain. I could always-constantly-*forever* count on my dad.

I exhaled, letting everything melt away all at once, the fears and worries and reservations. "I thought I'd never see you again."

Saying good-bye to Simon was weird. Weird and hard.

We didn't have much in the way of belongings, me and Tyler, but what we had was moved from the Jeep to my dad's beater pickup, the one I was sure had been abandoned. Nancy was already waiting in the narrow space behind the worn bench seat, and my dad and Tyler were inside, pretending Simon and I were invisible, even though it was only glass that separated us.

We walked back to the Jeep, to do this whole awkward good-bye thing.

"I don't know why you can't come with us," I told him. "I'd feel better if you did." It was true, but only partly. I'd feel safer, and better knowing he was safe, but having him and Tyler so close together was just plain *uncomfortable.* And somehow it was worse because Simon and I were the only ones who knew it.

"I have to go back. I have to make sure Willow and Jett, and Griffin," he added almost as an afterthought, "are all okay. I need to find out what happened back there."

I nodded, rubbing my palms over the front of my pants. I wanted that, too, to know how everyone was. "Can you contact us? Let us know?"

"Not yet, but eventually. Your dad knows how, and when the time's right, we'll see each other again." He grinned, his lids lowering heavily, and there was something devilish about the look, and it made my knees feel all quivery. "And by then, I have a feeling you'll be dying to see me."

I started to complain, to tell him he was full of it because I had Tyler back now, and Tyler was all I'd ever wanted. But Simon being Simon, he never gave me the chance.

He reached for me, and the second his mouth was on mine, whatever protest I'd been formulating turned to gibberish. I rationalized it by telling myself this was good-bye, and I had no idea when I would see him again, if ever, so maybe that made it okay, the fact that he was kissing me. And also that I was sure, from where the Jeep was parked, that neither Tyler nor my dad could see us.

But even if they had . . . I might not have stopped him. In fact, I may have slid my arm up, and around his neck. And I may have kissed him back, more than once. And I'm pretty sure that, when his lips left mine, I heard a sigh and it probably wasn't Simon's. I'd almost bet on that one.

"Jerk." But even as I said it, I was trying not to smile, and not to cry at the same time.

"Remember what I told you, Kyr. You're as human as anyone. You have to believe that." He leaned down, giving me one final kiss—a soft one, supersoft, right on the tip of my nose. And then his copper eyes, those eyes I'd noticed the very first time I'd seen him, looked into mine. "I do."

EPILOGUE

I WOKE WITH A START, MORE BECAUSE I'D ACTUally been sleeping than from any dream or because I wasn't sure about where I was or anything.

I'd been sleeping.

That by itself was disorienting.

I glanced around. The embers of the fire my dad had made before "hitting the sack" were still smoldering, but the last thing I could remember was poking at the flames with a stick, while Tyler and I had been swapping childhood stories. Mostly embarrassing ones. And mostly embarrassing ones involving Austin. It was good to laugh again. And especially good to laugh where it concerned Austin.

I felt better about the way things had ended up, even between Austin and Cat. Tyler said they were good together. That they made each other happy, and they'd gotten each other through the rough parts of me disappearing. How could I possibly fault them for that all these years later?

Then Tyler had leaned in and confessed—again—how, even as a kid, he'd always had a crush on me.

I'd loved watching him admit it, even for the second time. The way he got all flustered and his cheeks flushed and his dimple carved into his cheek. It was sweet, and it had been almost the exact same way he'd acted that first night he'd said those words when we'd been on the swings, the night I'd returned.

The night he told me he'd never forget me.

The only thing we didn't talk about was my dad's story, about what happened to him that night up at Devil's Hole . . . after the fireflies had come. But my dad had told me about it.

Like Tyler, he'd claimed he didn't remember vanishing, even though he was sure that was what happened since he'd woken up in his van the following morning, just north of San Francisco in a Walmart parking lot. Nancy had been there, too, licking his face, like it was any other morning.

Except for the part where he didn't know how he'd gotten there.

I knew exactly how he felt.

Basically, Tyler and I had talked about everything in front of that fire except what was really important—our relationship before he'd been taken.

Tyler still didn't know how close the two of us had gotten, or that I was the one responsible for poisoning him and forcing this new and far-too-isolated life upon him.

Every time I meant to tell him . . . every time I opened my mouth to even try, the words just . . . evaporated. Like steam in a kettle that was boiled too long.

Or a boy taken in the night.

Poof!

Gone.

But we had gotten closer these past days, being on the run together—me and Tyler. I guess it was like that when you shared harrowing experiences; they drew you together. Bonded you.

I tried not to think about what Simon had said back in the library . . . right before we'd kissed . . . the thing about feelings being intensified due to guilt. That was different.

Besides, Simon had been wrong about the guilt thing. My feelings for Tyler were real. They always had been.

I got up and dusted myself off, wondering how I'd managed to fall asleep on the ground. I brushed sand from my hands, hair, and face, from where my cheek had been smooshed into the dirt.

I wondered where Tyler was, and thought maybe he'd gone into the tent with my dad after I'd fallen asleep, but somehow I doubted it. There was barely enough room in the two-man tent for the one grown man and his giant mutt of a dog, and I knew for sure Nancy hadn't left my dad's side because I could hear her in there, sleep-whimpering.

At times like this my super night vision came in handy. I followed a pair of tracks that led through the sand from our campsite out into the desert.

Tyler was there, standing before an enormous rock wall that stretched high overhead. In the light of the chalklike moon, I hardly needed to see in the dark to recognize his ghostly outline.

I couldn't tell what he was doing, but his actions were crisp and short and choppy, and as I approached, I could hear him muttering beneath his breath.

"Tyler?" I called when I was close enough, and I thought he'd hear me.

Not so much as a flinch.

He was completely engrossed in whatever he was doing, and as I approached, more slowly now, I studied him . . . taking it in.

He was drawing.

He was using the sharp edge of some sort of stone to draw on the sheer face of the cliff wall. I watched, stunned. Completely and absolutely speechless.

I had no idea what it was, but it was a masterpiece.

Lines intersected curves that crisscrossed over clearly marked points and more lines. There were circles, and shapes, none of which made any sense but surely had a purpose . . . at least to Tyler.

And the entire time he kept saying, "*Ochmeel abayal dai . . . ochmeel abayal dai . . . ochmeel abayal dai . . .*"

I put my hand on his shoulder, and he jerked to a stop.

I nodded toward the wall again. "It's beautiful," I whispered. "What is it?"

He looked back at it. "*Ochmeel abayal dai,*" he said again, and it was weird, so weird, because it almost didn't sound like him. The voice—*his voice*, I had to remind myself because it *was* his—had a strange wheezing quality, like he needed to clear his throat.

But his response totally threw me off.

I gripped his arm. "What does that mean?"

Tyler cocked his head before opening his mouth again. He looked confused, and then he reached up and rubbed his brow. He blinked at me then, the faraway look in his eyes coming into focus, as if he only just realized I was standing right beside him.

"The Returned must die," he said at last.

ACKNOWLEDGMENTS

THERE ARE A ZILLION PEOPLE TO THANK FOR every book, and *The Replaced* was no exception. A lot of the folks remain the same, and as always, I have to start with my agent, Laura Rennert, who's still killing it after all these years, along with the rest of the Andrea Brown agency—thanks for giving me my start!

To my amazing team at HarperTeen: Jen Klonsky, Alice Jerman, Booki Vivat, the *entire* cover design team (I adore you!), and my brilliant publicist, Olivia Russo (who's even sweeter in real life!). And to Sarah Landis and Kari Sutherland, who are no longer with Harper but had such a huge hand in making this series what it is. You guys are the best!

Thanks to Deb Shapiro and Kate Lied for your *tireless* efforts in promoting *The Taking.*

Thanks to my fancy Hollywood agents at WME, Alicia Gordon, Erin Conroy, and Ashley Fox—you ladies have introduced me to a strange and wonderful world. And a special thanks to a certain "B.S." (who will remain nameless at this time), you might not realize it, but your comments about Kyra changed the way I wrote *The Replaced* . . . so thank you.

There are also many people behind the scenes who are just as deserving of shout-outs as those on the front lines, and at the very top of that list is my critique partner (and friend) S.R. Johannes . . . or as I like to call her: Shelli. Thanks so much for helping me develop pitches, reading pages when I'm in a pinch, and taking my desperate (early morning) phone calls.

To Melissa de la Cruz, Kami Garcia, Melissa Marr, Richelle Mead, and Alyson Noël for saying such thoughtful-wonderful-*amazing* things about *The Taking.* You ladies truly are the best!

Thanks, too, to Saundra Mitchell, who gave me a little insight into military operations (and the way they're named), as well as being a badass graphic designer! To my niece, Nyla, for having such an awesome name . . . and for letting me "borrow" it for *The Replaced.* To Emily Ellsworth from Em's Reading Room for schooling me on Utah colloquialisms. And to my daughter Abby for reading over my shoulder and reminding me that I'd *already used* the name "Logan" in the first book and I would need to rename a character in *The Replaced* (not an easy task because it was a pretty major character). But thank you, Abby—without you, apparently *all* my characters would be named "Logan."

I also have to thank the best group of friends a person could ask for. You come out to cheer me on, drink with me when I need a glass of wine because I'm having an off day, and give me space when I'm under a deadline . . . and hardly ever complain when I don't text back right away. I don't know what I'd do without you. Thank you times a million!!!

And lastly to my family. To my mom for being the world's greatest cheerleader. To Amanda, Connor, Abby, and now Hudson for just being. And to Josh for putting up with me for over twenty years. You're the most supportive partner, best friend, and husband a woman could ever dream of. Everyone should be so lucky.